strong like wildflowers

Eric Thompson

This is a work of fiction. Though some characters and events have been inspired by my life, many details have been altered, or created entirely from imagination.

Copyright © 2023 by Eric Thompson

All rights reserved. No part of this book may be reproduced or used in any manner without written permission of the copyright owner except for the use of quotations in a book review.

Licensed images via Shutterstock
by Roxana Bashyrova and Koji Hirano

Cover design by Lisa Vega
Typesetting by Arjan van Woensel

First edition: 2023

https://www.erictauthor.com/

Step aside a moment please and let me talk to younger you. The you who played with cars or sticks or dolls or imaginary friends or at playgrounds. I have just three things to say to you, so eyes and ears on me for a moment please.

You are seen.
You are worthy.
You can go ahead and be silly.

PROLOGUE

The storm, the wolves, the forest, and life have brought us to the end of the world and of ourselves.

My wet, pruned hand rests on a massive evergreen, which is transferring the stress of violent winds directly to my bones as I crouch beside it. It may snap and fall on me at any moment. I keep my hand on the retching beast. I need to catch my breath and gain strength from this giant, however tenuous its roots' hold on the earth.

Please, let him be alive and—

Blinding light retreats from the darkness as quickly as it appears, immediately followed by a crackling noise that momentarily drowns out the sounds of rain and winds. My hand jerks back from the tree to cover my head. I duck nearly into a ball, squinting my eyes.

I hold hope with clenched, aching fingers. Fingers longing to be held in return. The sound and light have retreated. My fears and the storm rage on.

Please let him be alive and not alone.

I raise just slightly out of my crouch, opening up to risk one more crack of lightning. My face relaxes as much as it can with unusually large drops of rain attacking me from branches heaving in the winds.

Please protect the little boy.

I remember the first time I met Rafael.

CHAPTER ONE

My eyelids were closed and my legs crossed in a child's pose. I drew in a deep breath. My cheeks curled up in a slight smile and my shoulders dropped.

The air smelled fresh.

My brow wrinkled and head tilted. *Where am I?*

Eyes still closed, I set my hands out to lean my weight on them. *I'm on rock?*

I opened my eyes and saw the sun shining on everything around me. I sat on a boulder the size of a truck. My face felt more relaxed than it had in months. The back of my neck let go of tension I'd forgotten it held.

A hundred feet in front of me was a lake with glassy, calm water.

What was this place, why did it feel like magic was there, and why did I feel nervous?

My neck was regaining some of that tension, and I felt it when I twisted to see what was around me. Stiffness reminded me I'd reached my forties. Curiosity overcame my aging vertebrae and muscles, and I twisted further to see a ridge rising up starkly behind me. To my left and right, lush, tall grasses spread out. Before me, the grasses led to the lake's edge, where the water was deep blue, absorbing the color of the sky. The rays on my skin didn't seem hot, though I was sure it was midsummer.

Why does this place seem familiar?

Déjà vu surged, and I remembered stories I'd heard of the expanses of Alaska.

A screech tore through the air. My head snapped upward just in time to see an eagle fold its wings tightly to its body and fall like a rock. Just before crashing, the eagle spread its wings, opened its talons, and, amid a wall of splashing water, emerged with a fish in its grasp. Wings whooshed and talons clung to a fish with scales that flashed gold, pink, and silver in the sunlight.

My forehead hurt from squinting tightly against the brightness, and I dropped my gaze back to the lake. There, at the far end, stood a little boy.

A tremor ran through my veins. My bones shook. All the skin on my body prickled, and the hairs on my neck tingled

The grasses and the lake rustled.

Not rustling. Shivering. They feel it too. It was an odd thought, but one I accepted.

My breath caught in my chest, and my heart beat in my throat.

The little boy stood on the opposite shore, staring at me with unwavering eyes.

Tears pooled in my eyes. Who was he? Why was he alone?

I shifted to my right arm and unfurled my legs, preparing to jump from the rock down to the grass. My heart's pace quickened, pumping blood so I could run to the boy, shield him, and protect him forever. No time could be spared.

The boy continued staring at me. The lake shivered again. A breeze blew across my face, and my breath caught once more. I fell back slightly, replacing my left hand on the rock. A tear ran down my face, chilled by the wind. My unblinking eyes dried.

The boy's face seemed to mirror mine. Eyes wide, mouth open, arms down. We both waited, vulnerable and unguarded

Whatever it is, he feels it too.

I stood up, spreading my arms slightly from my sides. *I wonder if I could fly on this breeze. Fly like the eagle. Away from hurt and heaviness.*

It didn't make sense, and I dropped my arms to my side again. Maybe it was a dream. The air stilled, and I nearly closed my eyes

Then, a little to the boy's right, a man entered my view. The breeze arrived with him, now stronger than before. The lake and the grasses shivered again.

Did this place know him? I shook my head. That was preposterous. "Who is this man?" I asked the lake, the boulder, and the grass.

The man and the boy spoke to each other. I strained forward to hear them, but they were too far away. I couldn't hear a word. The man's mouth moved, and a gust ruffled my shirt before it whispered imperceptible words in my ear. That knocked me back, and I barely caught my balance.

I couldn't make out the whispered words. I only knew they made me want to speak with the man. I craved answers.

Who was he? Could he help me? Could he or the magic of this place help the boy? And who was the boy?

I took a step toward the edge of the rock again. I needed to hurry across the grass and around the lake to reach them. Once again I stopped. More tears threatened.

Stop it! Stop crying!

My lips pursed, my nostrils flared, and my eyes steeled.

Then I awoke and saw the darkness of my bedroom on a cold, rainy February morning in Oregon.

CHAPTER TWO

An old hinge cried from a door across the hallway from the little boy's bedroom, followed by the creak of floorboards and the sound of his door opening.

Rafael scrunched his face and pulled the covers over his head. From behind his eyelids he was sure it was too dark to be time to wake up. He brought his knees nearly to his chest under the blankets. The sound of rain drops on a cracked-paint windowsill meant another gray day in the sleepy town of Corvallis, Oregon.

He hadn't heard any footsteps walking back away and knew it meant the figure in the doorway was about to rouse him from his warm bed. No matter how much he knew she cared for him, the wake-up calls always came.

Most mornings Mama would wake him up despite protests, so she could make it to work on time. He'd wake, and wander to the bathroom squinting his eyes nearly shut, complaining, "It's not fair," to the walls.

On her way to work, she would drop him off with a family whose children attended the same school. He would cozy up to a heater vent in their home until it was time to go. Sometimes he got to eat pancakes with cinnamon and sugar their mother made for him and her children.

Yesterday had been a sun-filled Saturday break in the midst of a run of gray days. He'd done what he did so often on days Mama didn't need to go to work. When the sun peered through the curtains, he crawled out from the covers, slipped across the hall, and cracked her door open without hesitating to ask permission.

Mama worked at the university and took care of him at home. He noticed how often she was tired, but he knew she would never turn him away, though all she wanted in these early morning moments was a little more sleep. If there was one thing she made him feel, it was welcomed by her arms.

So yesterday he'd crawled up onto her bed, gently pulled her arm open, and rested his head on it like a pillow. They'd repeated the pattern many weekend mornings. Finally, when her arm began to fall asleep, she hugged him, rose, and began the day.

Now, in the darkness of this Sunday morning, Rafael felt her looking at him. He lay willing her to close the door and let him sleep a few more minutes. He shielded his face from her view with the covers, peeking out from under them to confirm it looked too dark out to get up yet. Droplets streaked the glass of his old, single-paned window.

"Wake up, little *liebchen*," she said, speaking the German word for "sweetheart." Her warm voice belied the cold gray outside.

"Unnnhh," he groaned. "It's too early!" He remained facing away from her, shielded by his bedding. He scowled and pulled the covers tighter to him.

"It's time to get up, Raf," she persisted. "Today is the day! We have to go so you can get on the plane to Alaska."

Having shared this home with only his mother, Rafael had become an expert on her cues. She sounded like she was forcing enthusiasm she didn't feel.

His enthusiasm, on the other hand, couldn't be contained. In one motion, his arm threw back the covers and his legs spun down to the floor. Before heading to the bathroom, he looked at his bed. A thin smile curved its way onto his lips.

The bed was simple. A captain's bed with two drawers underneath and a bookshelf at the head. White paint peeled away in spots where he had played a little rough with some of his toys. The nondescript bed had been made by his father's hands. Hands that hadn't been in the same house as him since before his third birthday, just over four years ago. He touched the headboard before leaving the room, carrying on a ritual he'd developed.

Today as he got ready for the day, he uttered no complaints to the walls and grinned at the bathroom mirror.

"So you can get on the plane to Alaska," Mama had said. Dad had completed his studies in engineering at the local university and taken his first job in Alaska. He was overseeing several projects upgrading roads and a campground facility.

I get to see him today!

Mama had come from Germany to the United States when she followed Dad home after he'd served in the army there. Rafael understood she was a single mother without something called a college degree. He heard adults on the news talking about things called inflation and unemployment, and people named Jimmy Carter and Ronald Reagan. Mostly, he ignored it and smashed his toy cars into each other while she watched from the couch.

There were nights she didn't know he heard her crying and asking God how to find enough money for gas for the car and food for their stomachs. He once questioned why they didn't ask her family for help.

"My family didn't hug me the way I hug you, or say 'I love you.' They were too broken after... well, after a lot of things happened in my country. But it's okay. You and I will make something new. Anyway, your father isn't in Germany and a boy should have his father," she'd said, and he didn't ask again.

Rafael walked from the bathroom to the kitchen, where Mama had prepared him some breakfast. He watched her move slowly, shoulders slumped, head down, packing snacks in his backpack on the counter. She brought her hand to her hidden face several times, and he wasn't sure if she was wiping tears or just scratching an eye.

"Mama, why did Mrs. Richards tell you I shouldn't go to Alaska yesterday?" he asked her before putting a bite of cereal in his mouth.

"Some people think it's too scary to let a seven-year-old fly from Oregon to Alaska by himself. Are you scared, Rafael?" she replied with both hands braced on the counter, eyes staring away from him out the window. He thought he saw her shoulder muscles clinch.

"I have a funny feeling in my tummy, but I'm not scared. I just want to play with my dad."

"That funny feeling is excitement, little *liebchen*."

"But I'll miss you too, Mama. Will you miss me?"

"Very much, Raf. But I'm happy your father invited you to be with him too. That's worth it to me."

She put the last of his snacks in the backpack before leaving the room. From down the hall he heard her blow her nose a few times. She returned with a slightly redder face and his favorite stuffed animal—a little dog he slept with, played with, walked with, and rode in the car with. The two were inseparable.

"Benji!" he yelled with wide eyes and a wider smile.

"You have to have your friend with you, right?"

"Yes!"

A little while later, she helped him into their beat-up car and turned back to the front steps of the house, where his backpack sat ready. She froze in place long enough that something didn't seem right. Eventually she closed his car door and walked to the pack, shoulders slumped again, her feet barely making it off the ground. Slowly, she returned to the driver's side and gently placed the pack beside him on the back seat. Why had she seemed to take extra care of the pack?

The two-hour drive north to the Portland airport was uneventful, though a little rainy. When they were near large trucks, spray from the road and rain from the sky covered the windshield.

Mama's shoulders tensed and her hands gripped the wheel tightly. "I hate driving in the rain," she muttered.

"Sorry, Mama."

"Oh, baby boy, you're worth it to me. You'll see one day. Moms and dads do things for their children even when they don't want to. Especially if it means they can give them something good."

He knew she meant it. She'd made many sacrifices for him.

"So what are you giving me today?" he asked. He meant it as a tease and a way to ask for a treat.

"A father," she said.

Both were silent as they neared the airport, and Rafael stared out the window at the planes coming in for a landing. Mama seemed sad. It would be great if Dad would give him a twirling hug, but couldn't he just come here?

His arms clutched the stuffed dog to his chest tightly. Keeping his gaze out the window at the planes, he broke the silence. "I'm still your buddy, Mama, right? Even when I'm gone, we're still buddies." He clutched Benji even tighter. "I'll miss you a lot."

The control tower and the airport terminal came into view.

"Of course we're buddies! You'll always be my baby boy." He could hear her smile behind it, but also heard a catch in her throat, which she passed for a tickle she pretended to cough away. "I'll miss you too, but you're going to love it!" Another small cough. She wiped one of her eyes.

After parking, she walked him to the gate and checked him in. They were introduced to the flight attendant who would be his guardian for the trip. "This is Rafael, and I'm his mother, Aila," she said to the kindly woman.

The attendant looked at him and said something about how cute he was and how she liked his eyes and smile. He'd heard this many times, even been pinched in the cheeks sometimes when it was said. He always replied the same, looking down to his feet shyly and saying a quiet, "Thank you."

He stole a glance at Mama, whose furrowed brows and pleading eyes looked back at the woman.

"We're going to take great care of him," she assured Mama. "We'll make sure he's comfy and has plenty of snacks and drinks." Then she turned to Rafael with a broad smile and bright eyes. "You're in good hands! Do you like soda pop? We can give you something yummy to drink."

He let out a sheepish "yes" and looked to his feet again before looking back at Mama. Part of his vision was obscured by tears.

She put a hand to her heart before resting it on his head. Her mouth hung open, wordless. Her tongue looked like it was waiting for the command from her mind for the words to speak.

Something moving just outside the windows surprised them both, and Mama shifted her gaze to it. A crane was landing near them, its wings sweeping and majestic. It moved with such grace, almost like it was slicing through time in slow motion.

Rafael's nostrils took in the hint of diesel fuel surrounding the airport. Around them were the sounds of planes, people, intercoms, and conveyor belts. Yet through the window, the bird was quiet and beautiful.

"You know, the most rare and special birds fly," his mother told him, stroking his hair and wiping a tear from his face. "And you have to work very hard to find them, but when you do, they're beautiful, and you feel special for getting to see them. It can even involve risky journeys through jungles and wild places to find them. Rare birds are worth the effort and the risk. To see them, free and beautiful, can change one's soul."

He looked down at his shoes and wiped his face.

"Do you know what I'm saying, Raf?"

He shrugged his shoulders before looking up with a forced

smile. The muscles on his face must have betrayed it as a pained lie.

"I know that look, Raf. I'm okay, sweetie. Don't worry about me." She looked at the crane once more. "Some birds are in cages, and they can be lovely too. You aren't that kind of bird. I think you're meant to fly high. I'll miss you more than you can know. I'll see you again, though, and you'll have so many new adventures to tell me about!"

She knelt down and held his forehead to hers. Her voice was now just above a whisper. "Our home will be your nest and you can come back, but now you're going to fly away from the nest for a little while."

She stood up and clasped his hand in hers looking at the flight attendant. Ahead of them was the gate, and a line of people shuffling their way to the jetway. She turned and looked behind to the path back to the car.

Rafael felt her arm pull him almost imperceptibly in the direction of the car.

Then she pursed her lips, clenched her jaw, closed her eyes, and let out a half-groan-half-sigh that reminded Rafael of the sound he made when he wrestled with a friend. "The bird is worth it," she muttered. She turned to face the jetway and the attendant. Every movement seemed stiff and forced.

When she'd completed the tortured turn, she spoke again. "Your dad loves you and wants to spend time with you too. And it's important for a boy to have his father. You'll understand some day. And Alaska is beautiful. Send me some postcards and tell me all about it."

"Then why is he so far away?" Rafael asked. "If he wants time with me, why is he in Alaska?"

"Rafael, your father is chasing a different kind of bird. But I think he'll see how special you are."

He scrunched his face in confusion.

His mom's face dropped in resignation. Rafael's eyes remained glued to hers for clues, searching for the unspoken words. They didn't come.

"He got a job there, and maybe he'll come back to our town someday," she said. "For now, it means adventure for you, little bird. You're rare and beautiful, and he should get to see you too." Then she whispered, "Maybe it will change his soul."

What did that mean?

The attendant looked from him to his mother, her expression sympathetic. "I'm so sorry, but we really must go. Rafael, you can meet the captain and see the cockpit," she said, sounding as friendly and warm as she could. She placed a gentle hand on his shoulder.

Rafael reached for Mama, who bent down once more. He wrapped his arms around her neck. "I don't want to leave you."

"You'll always be my little boy," she reminded him.

With that, he was led by the hand down the jetway and onto the plane, but not before turning to wave goodbye one last time.

As RAFAEL LEFT HER view, Aila's body stiffened again. Her eyes grew intensely focused. She turned and walked solemnly back to her car, not once making eye contact with another soul. After getting in and closing the door, she collapsed and clasped her hand over her mouth. Tears poured from her eyes. Five minutes later, she turned the key and heard the engine turn over.

A simple prayer escaped her lips. "God, be with my little boy."

~~~

RAFAEL WAS SHOWN THE cockpit and given clip-on wings before being led to his seat. He placed his backpack under the seat in front of him and sat down by the window, then passed the minutes to takeoff by staring out the window and glancing at the seats next to him, which remained empty.

A little after takeoff, he pulled the backpack up and rested it on the seat next to him.

"What's in there?" asked the kind voice of the flight attendant who'd helped him.

What *was* in there? He began rifling through the pockets and pouches. Snacks, activity books, stickers, notes from Mama, and various items.

"Your mom really loves you."

"Yeah."

Then, for the first time since entering the jetway to the plane, he smiled. *Benji!* He pulled the little stuffed dog from his pack and hugged it tightly. In the transition to the plane, he'd forgotten about his companion. Of course, Mama hadn't, and she'd packed him as well.

"Awww, she even packed your friend," the attendant cooed, then stepped away when someone asked for help.

"I love you, Benji," he whispered in the little dog's ear. "And I'm glad no one is in these seats. We don't have to explain ourselves to anyone. People always ask us or Mama questions. I don't feel like talking today." He put a pillow against the window and drifted off to sleep, one side of his face on the pillow, the other side nuzzling Benji.

When he awoke, he peered out the window across Alaska as they began their descent into Anchorage. Various buildings glinted in the setting sun. "Wonder if we'll be in any of those, Benji." He missed his cars, his living room, and his mom's bed. He squeezed the dog a little tighter.

After letting everyone off the plane, the flight attendant smiled at him. "Are you ready? Let's go see your dad!"

She helped him put on his backpack, then he walked off the plane, holding Benji with one hand and her hand with his other.

"Are you excited to see your dad, Rafael?"

"Yeah," he said quietly.

"You don't sound too excited. Is something wrong?"

"My tummy just hurts and feels all tingly."

"Probably just nerves," she tried to reassure him.

As they rounded the corner, his grimace disappeared and his face brightened. His hand ripped away from the flight attendant's and he was running toward open arms and a wide smile.

His backpack bounced on his back, his arms swung, and Benji waved through the air. Rafael leaped with body, heart, and beaming grin into the bearded man's arms, and his dad twirled him through the air. He held his arms out wide, feeling the embrace of his father and wondering if this was what birds felt like when they flew.

CHAPTER THREE

Rafael's first few days in Anchorage were everything he could have wanted and more. Dad and his girlfriend, Wendy, made Rafael the center of their world. There were trips to playgrounds, a candy shop, and the library, mixed in with board games, bike rides, and play. Wherever Dad was, Rafael wanted to be, and he followed him like a puppy. At night, Dad read him stories until he fell asleep happy and contented.

After those first few days, life began to return to something more normal for Dad and Wendy, as Rafael sensed their adult world demanding their attention again. This was understandable, but it left Rafael looking for connection any way he could find it. The wonderful days were like a car battery receiving a jump and being filled with renewed energy. As they were replaced with monotony and less attention on him, Rafael felt the battery draining.

He stood in the driveway and scanned his surroundings. Across the driveway and to his left, he saw the door of the garage they were temporarily renting and had turned into a dwelling. Inside, orange curtains made from simple fabric hanging on the garage door windows gave the interior a glow, and mattresses laid on the floor softened the room. A makeshift kitchen was set up on a workbench on one side of the room, complete with camping stoves, pots, and water containers. A few children's books were strewn around Rafael's bed, and a sheet curtain hung from the ceiling for privacy between Rafael and Dad and Wendy.

Outside in the driveway sat an old, white Volkswagen van. Most days, Dad spent his time at the back of the van where the engine was. The old van had many miles on it and broke down frequently.

From his spot on the driveway, all Rafael could see were his father's legs peeking out, his torso and head buried in the machinery of the van. The whir of the engine drowned out other neighborhood noises.

As the late-setting Alaska sun began to near the horizon, Rafael stood motionless, watching the half of his father he could see. As he often did, he imagined Benji—who was resting on his bed—could hear his thoughts.

What do I say? Why can't I think of anything?

He stood silently for several minutes, waiting for his father's eyes to see him. Dad continued working on the engine. Why was it so easy to admire the man working at the engine of the VW van, wearing a simple tee shirt and faded jeans, but so hard to approach him?

"What are you doing?" Rafael finally dared asking. He winced in self-judgment at not thinking of something better to say.

Dad peered out around the van, and a gentle smile broke across his face. "I need to fix this old van up. We're going on a trip pretty soon, and we'll be using the van. We'll even sleep in it sometimes. See?" He motioned to the open side doors in the back.

Rafael peered into the van. A wooden frame held up a foam pad that filled the entire back of the van except for a couple of feet between it and the front seats. Under the frame was storage space for gear and food.

"Why does it have a bed?" the boy asked. "We already have beds in the garage."

"We'll be able to be comfortable when we travel around," Dad answered. "Once I get this fixed up, we'll be moving from this place. I have to get it done soon."

"You made all that, Dad?"

"Yeah, I did."

"Cool!"

"Ha, yeah, cool, I guess."

Rafael stared at the van, analyzing his father's handiwork with the same look he gave to his captain's bed at home. "Can I help?" he asked.

"Sure. Hand me the 5/16ths socket." He motioned to a toolbox.

Rafael hesitated and his stomach knotted up. Why didn't he understand?

"Do you know what a socket wrench is, Raf?"

"Ummm, I—"

"It's okay, buddy." Dad stepped to the toolbox and held up a slightly worn set of sockets with bits of rust on them.

"They look like shiny, silver treasures, Dad."

"Ha. These worn things?" Dad laughed. "See, each of them has numbers on them that tell me how big they are. Each one is made just the right size for turning different sizes of nuts. Without the right socket, I can't tighten them correctly and the engine might break down. This tool gives me the strength I need to fix this engine. Without it, I'm not strong enough."

"Can I get you the sockets whenever you need them?"

"Sure. I'll tell you the numbers and you get them for me. Can you please get me the 5/16ths socket now?"

Rafael searched the numbers on the set, and his right finger pointed to each one until he handed the correct one to Dad.

"Thanks, son." He patted Rafael on the head.

Son. The word washed through Rafael's insides like a roaring wave of electricity. Pride swelled in his chest, and a strange feeling began to take root. One he hadn't realized had been taken from him these past several years since Dad had separated himself from their home. It felt like security and surety and gave him a sense of confidence.

Rafael had a flashback to something Mama had said before he left. They'd been at a friend's house for a playdate, where he and his friend were playing with cars in the living room while their mothers chatted in the dining area nearby.

"I have to let him go," she'd said to his friend's mother.

"But a little boy traveling that far by himself? And how do you know he'll be safe all summer?" his friend's mother asked.

"There's just something in the heart of children. I'm convinced of it. It boils down to this. Show me a child whose father claims them as his own and I'll show you a child who is confident.

Being wanted, loved, and nurtured is world changing. Look, I'm not saying I won't give him all those things and more. I'll do everything I can. But there's something about a child receiving that from their father."

"I get that, Aila. We just love Raf and want to see him come back safe and sound. I know you know best. Forgive me for butting in a little."

"I'm more afraid than you could ever know. But I have to do it. I only hope Scott will give him enough time. Who knows, maybe Scott will see what he's missing and come back to live near us. I have my doubts, but I have to keep hope alive. For Raf."

Rafael came back from his memories to see his dad's head buried in the back of the VW van again.

They repeated the scene for the next two days, with Dad working on the van and Rafael on socket duty. In the afternoon of the third day helping around the van, Rafael noticed some neighbor kids. He missed playing. He'd loved being needed and feeling he brought value, and every time he grabbed for a socket or another tool, he tried to see if he could do it faster than the last. Still, seeing other kids playing reminded him of running and laughing.

"Dad? Can I go play with those kids?"

"Sure. Go for it! Just be home by dark."

He walked right up to them in their yard and said, "Want to play?"

Together, the two brothers and one sister who lived next door all replied, "Sure!"

With that, they ran around the neighborhood playing various games. The one he liked the most was when he and one of the neighbor boys pretended to fly.

"How do you do that?" the neighbor boy had asked him.

"Well, you spread your wings and just fly all around!" Rafael said it with a kind of confidence and enthusiasm that made it sound as if he believed he really could do it.

For the next week, his days consisted of grabbing tools for Dad, flying around the neighborhood with the other kids, and trying to sleep in the orange glow of the garage when the sky was still light at night. On one of those evenings, when Dad was rushing to finish his work on the van, Rafael was invited to dinner at the neighbor kids' house.

Their mother placed a bowl of chicken and dumplings in front of him. He looked at the food he'd never tasted before and smiled, then looked up at her.

"Is something wrong, dear?" she asked after a few moments.

"No. I just like nice moms. Thank you for the food." He looked back at the bowl and thought about nice spring mornings with Mama's arm for a pillow. And sitting by the fireplace when she would make them a fire some winter nights to be cozy. That night he lay in his bed picturing the orange glow of the room was the glow of a fire. He drifted off to sleep with thoughts of dumplings and Mama.

CHAPTER FOUR

The next few days after the dinner at the neighbors' house seemed identically monotonous and lonely for Rafael. The neighbor children had left on a vacation, and Dad worked nonstop to get the van ready to move to a picnic area at Blueberry Lake. Rafael knew something about Dad being the head engineer overseeing the creation of a campground and improvements to the road over the pass in from Anchorage and other places. They were to spend most of the summer there, then he would drive Rafael back to Mama in Oregon.

Rafael stood in the driveway again, this time scowling. "Can't we *do* something, Dad?"

"Sorry, buddy, I have to get this done by two days from now. I know you wish we could play."

Rafael balled his fists at his sides and remained silent. How could he put words to the feelings churning within?

"It's going to be great, Raf," Dad called from behind the van as tools clinked on engine parts. "We'll have a beautiful drive there, then we'll have lots of time together when I'm not working. And there's a lake there and places to explore. It'll be great!"

"Do we have to wait until then to have time together? I miss home and I'm bored. The neighbors are gone, and I'm tired of the books we have."

Dad peered out from behind the van's engine. Rafael still gave no answer and held his fists clenched. Dad looked at a wrench in his hand, then back to Rafael before he sighed and lowered the wrench. "I guess I'm almost done with the van. Sure, Raf, tomorrow. Let's go to a bookstore and get you some books for the trip. We can read some together there too."

Rafael let out a breath and relaxed his hands. "Can we go, just the two of us?"

"Sure! We'll make it fun."

"And can we get a treat?"

"Sure we can," Dad laughed.

The next afternoon, when it was time, Rafael approached Dad who was working on the van again. He fidgeted in the driveway, coughed a little, and kicked a rock or two. Dad's head didn't appear.

Rafael couldn't take the waiting anymore. "It's two ten, Dad. Can we go now? You said we would leave at two."

Rafael couldn't decipher quite what his dad said but knew he was cursing at the van under his breath. "Son," Dad said.

Usually Rafael delighted at being called "son." This time, his whole body tensed up.

After an awkwardly long pause, Dad finally continued, "I have to get this van ready in time for my job. I thought I would be far enough along, but I have more to do." He looked at Rafael as if pleading for understanding. "I promise we'll do fun things on other days. You're really going to love Blueberry Lake. It's beautiful up there and... Hey! Do you like glaciers? There's a big glacier nearby. We can go hiking on the ice! Won't that be great?"

Rafael pressed his lips together. His mind felt frozen. He opened his mouth to let out what was inside, then instead looked down at the stack of books hugged in his arms. His mouth closed again and his shoulders dropped in resignation. Mama was an eight-day drive away. *She would play with me.*

He opened his arms and let the books drop to the ground, then turned and walked sullenly up the driveway. Before entering the garage's side door, he looked at Dad one more time and his jaw dropped. What was that?

He could swear his dad's hand flickered. It seemed like it was going to disappear for a moment, and little wavy lines washed through it as though it were becoming a hologram.

Dad nearly dropped his socket wrench and stared at his hand with wide eyes. He must have seen it too. Rafael shut his eyes hard, then peered at Dad again.

Dad glanced at Rafael, then back at his hand. "R-Raf, w-why don't you come back? Let's go to the library after all." He picked up the books, then walked over to Rafael and put his very real hand on his shoulder.

Rafael could feel the weight and warmth of it through his T-shirt. He must have been wrong. Hands didn't do that.

That night, he heard Dad speaking to Wendy in hushed tones.

"It's starting already."

"What is?" she asked.

"The disappearing. I thought I had more time. I *need* more time."

"Scott, be serious. I thought you let that silly thing go. You're starting to worry me. It was cute at first, but now you're sounding a little weird."

"Look at my hand."

Wendy gasped and Rafael heard Dad shush her and whisper, "Rafael."

"That can't be real!" she said in a hushed voice. "You understand how hard it is to believe, right?"

Had his hand done the thing again? Had she seen it too?

"It's an old legend. A myth really, but now you know why I take it seriously," Dad said.

"Tell it to me again, but tell me the whole thing this time. I've never paid close attention to it before."

Dad drew a deep breath. "Many, *many* generations ago, one of my ancestors went on a journey in the Highlands of Scotland in search of a magical treasure. It was said if someone could get one of the feathers of the most ancient of the golden eagles, they could use it to choose either the power to fly or to heal. My ancestor spent years searching the Highlands. One day, when he had nearly given up, he saw an eagle with its foot stuck in some brambles, and he approached the eagle.

"'You seem to be stuck, eagle,' he said. The eagle replied, 'Please help me. I'm the ancient mother of the eagles and need to go and provide for my offspring.' When my ancestor realized he had the ancient eagle trapped, he knew he had found, at long last, what he had searched for. He told the eagle he would set her free if she would give him two feathers. 'With the one I'll choose to gain the power of flight and soar as you do, and with the other, I'll choose the power to heal others,' he told her.

"'You may only have one feather,' the eagle said. 'All others will be useless to you. The power of my feathers only works once, and you must choose wisely.' My ancestor freed the ancient eagle-mother, who kept her promise and gave him one of her feathers. He kept it safe, wearing it around his neck while he decided how to use it. On his journey home, he came by a cottage. The woman of the house came out and approached him.

"'Sir! Please, sir, you must help us!' she pleaded. 'I'm a poor widow and my son is very ill and will die by morning's light if he doesn't receive help.' She got down on her knees to beg. 'Sir, I see you're the first to finally retrieve the ancient eagle's feather. Please, sir. Please heal my son!' At that moment my ancestor's decision was made. He thought of generations to come after him and told her, 'Madam, I'm sorry, but I know my choice. I'm dearly sorry for you and your family, but with the gift of flight I will be able to search the world for every treasure. I, and generations to come, will be wealthy. I can't take this chance away from my people. After we find the treasures we seek, we'll help people like your son, as we'll have enough to share.'

"With that, my ancestor walked away, ignoring the pleading and crying of the woman. That night, as he slept by a fire, there was a magical breeze. He felt it deep in his bones and it woke him. Just as he awoke, he realized a man had appeared. My ancestor sensed this was a powerful man who had magic about him. 'Why are you here and what can I do for you?' my ancestor asked. 'I'm the protector and provider for many people,' the man replied.

'I've just come from speaking with the ancient eagle-mother and the poor woman you passed earlier today. Her son has died.'

"'I'm sorry to hear that,' my ancestor replied. 'It's truly sad, but I hope you can understand why I've chosen to seek the treasures of the world on behalf of many future generations. This way, my family will always be wealthy. There will always be other widows and other sons to help.'

"'I understand your choice perfectly,' the man replied. 'But I don't agree with it. That woman's son was her treasure. It would have been better for you to teach future generations what really makes a family wealthy. Wealth of the heart. Because you have chosen to seek the treasures of this world and did not value another in need, the gift of flight will be taken from you and a curse will be on your family. Since you desire flight so greatly, from now on, until a male in your line teaches his children to fly, all the males from generation to generation will disappear, leaving their children behind. Understand, I'm not giving you this curse as a punishment. You have chosen the curse upon yourself.'

"'Sir, please, this is too much to bear!' my ancestor pleaded. 'How can we teach children to fly? No one has taught us, and there's no way to learn it! It's impossible! There must be another way!'

"The man remained still a moment. The breeze blew again, blowing out my ancestor's fire. In the darkness the man seemed to glow of his own light. He pulled something from his cloak. 'This is the Talisman of the Crane. It carries the grace of the crane to slow the effects of time. With it, you can slow the curse. Your male children, for all generations, will disappear around the middle of their life, or a little earlier, without the talisman, until they can teach their children to fly. Then they won't need the crane's wings, and the curse will be broken.'

"The man disappeared, leaving my ancestor holding a small charm of two crane's wings. When the sun was up, he continued his journey home. For generations, the talisman was handed from each father to the oldest son. The men disappeared but were able to try to learn to fly until they were sixty or so. Of course, no one was successful. How can anyone learn to fly, much less teach it to their children?

"Then, about sixteen or seventeen generations ago, somewhere in the 1500s, the talisman was lost, and the men started disappearing in their thirties and forties. To this day, the men in my family have been disappearing before their fiftieth birthday. It's why I took this job. I think I have a clue about where the talisman is. I've been chasing clues my whole adult life. There's a rumor it's actually hidden somewhere not far from Blueberry Lake."

"That's all of it. I know how bizarre it all sounds, but you saw my hand. And you know my dad has been gone since I was young. Please don't look at me like I'm crazy, Wendy. You saw my hand, right?"

"I-it's a lot to take in, but yes," she stammered. "I saw your hand and I've never seen your dad."

That night, Rafael fell asleep still not believing what he'd just heard. He dreamed of a crane and of meeting a mysterious and wonderful magician who taught him to fly.

Four days later, the crackling sounds of fire stirred Rafael from sleep. He rolled over on his foam pad on the floor of a tiny campground cabin and pulled his sleeping bag and blankets close to his chin. It was the second morning waking up at Blueberry Lake.

"Good morning, Raf," Dad greeted him. "There's some oatmeal almost ready for you."

A slight draft drifted across his face. Rafael glanced toward the doorway, and the cracks letting in light and air all around its frame. He turned away from the doorframe, then moved reluctantly out of his warm sleeping bag and blankets before quickly putting on warm clothes.

He sat down on the bench of the picnic table Dad and Wendy had brought into the one-room hut to be their dining table, then glanced around the room. In the middle of one wall was an open, rock fireplace with a bright fire already crackling, sending its heat radiating as best it could against the drafts. To the left, his foam pad and sleeping bag and blankets lay on the floor inviting him to return. Nearby that, a kerosene lantern hung from a rafter. To the right, some empty cardboard beer cases sat on the hearth, and another larger foam mattress lay on the floor where Dad and Wendy slept. Around the room he saw another lantern and various supplies on temporary shelving.

Decks of cards with a cribbage board in a windowsill and books around his pad on the floor served for entertainment. There was no television, no phone, and no electricity. No sink or toilet either.

Dad lifted a pot of oatmeal from a hissing camping stove that rested on part of the stone hearth. After shutting off the stove, he stirred peanut butter, honey, raisins, and a dash of cinnamon into the pot. The more his dad tended to the oatmeal, the more Rafael's body relaxed. His insides felt warmed, even before the heated meal hit them.

Rafael cocked his head to one side and rubbed his eyes. He could have sworn something was happening to his father. It was as though he was becoming more solid.

"Here you go, son," Dad said, handing him a bowl.

He took a bite of the oatmeal. The warm, dense meal filled his stomach, and feeling cared for by the work of his dad's hands filled him much more. Now Dad's hands were not in the back of a VW van. They were at work taking care of Rafael.

They ate together until Dad stood from the table. "I need to go start the day's work with the construction crew." He gave Rafael a hug and put his hand on his shoulder, then opened the door. "Have a fun day, son."

Rafael couldn't be sure, but the hand on his shoulder seemed warmer and firmer than it had that day in Anchorage.

CHAPTER FIVE

The little temporary home by Blueberry Lake provided shelter, if not luxury, and the surroundings offered some compensation for any comfort the stone hut lacked. Each day Rafael was greeted by hills and mountains surrounding him and leading down to the lake basin and its marshes, bushes, and grasses. All was a sea of green. The landscape was grand and the people small in it.

Dad tried to make the place as much of a home as it could be. One midafternoon, he came by the picnic hut, his hardhat and orange construction vest still on. "Rafael, are you around?" he called.

"I'm in here!" Rafael said from the hut.

"Come on out, son! I have something I want you to see!"

Rafael could hear a rumbling noise not far off. It sounded like rocks being split open. What could make such a noise? He opened the door to see a large bulldozer rolling up the gravel road laid for the machinery and trucks. The yellow beast belched noises and crunched the rock under it as it drove closer.

"Step over here, out of the way, and watch!"

Rafael moved to where his dad had motioned as Dad gave the driver some instructions. With waves of his hands, he appeared to be marking out an area next to the house. Amid new sounds and more noises from the engine, the hydraulics of the machine began working.

Rafael's mouth hung open. His eyes locked on the yellow dinosaur pivoting and jerking forward. The dozer's bucket tilted, and a pile of dirt poured out a few feet from the hut.

Rafael looked up at his dad with excited curiosity. What was happening?

Dad gave a thumbs-up signal, and Rafael looked back to the driver, who turned the yellow contraption and headed back down the gravel road.

"What's happening, Dad?"

Dad smiled. "You'll see."

The bulldozer reappeared after a couple minutes and dumped another pile of dirt on top of the first. This was repeated until the dirt pile was about thirteen feet high.

Rafael nearly shook with curiosity. He tugged at Dad's sleeve. "C'mon, Dad! Tell me! What are they doing?"

"They're building you your own hill!" Playful enthusiasm spread across his face.

A hill? But for what?

Dad grabbed a shovel and tamped the dirt down with the backside to solidify the hill a little, giving extra attention to a line down the middle. After a few minutes he turned to Rafael. "C'mon!"

Rafael grinned at how Dad looked like a playful child when he gathered up wooden stakes normally used as markers for the construction workers. His energy was joyfully chaotic and his pace quickened. What was he doing? Dad lined up two rows of stakes from the top of the hill to the bottom along the line he'd spent the most time on. "I'll be right back!" he said and rushed inside.

Rafael stood, confused and contemplating why there were two rows of stakes running down his hill and what he was even going to do with a hill.

Dad burst through the door with two toy trucks in his hands and a wide grin across his bearded face. "Let's see if it works!"

Things were starting to make sense. Rafael gladly took one of the trucks and ran to the top of the hill. At the top, he looked at Dad beside him, both of them smiling. Dad knelt, then the two of them held their trucks on the ground.

"Ready, set, go!" Rafael exclaimed, and they released the trucks. One of them went careening down, toppling end over end, while the other drove wildly, bouncing off the stakes from side to side until it went shooting out the bottom of the hill out toward the road.

Like magma building in a volcano and then erupting in earth-changing upheaval, Rafael felt laughter build. It first grew in his belly, then filled his lungs, then sprang with abandon out his mouth.

It was infectious. Dad couldn't contain himself either, and the two of them laughed so hard they cried. After a moment, they both ran down the hill laughing. Rafael ran into the cabin and found every toy vehicle he had. Plastic and metal. Tow truck, fire truck, ambulance, police car, race car. All of them. He lost all sense of time as the two of them raced the cars. They devised a ladder system of head-to-head races to see which car would be the ultimate champion.

Rafael forgot all about not having a television or friends to play with. For days he entertained himself playing with the cars. For variety, Dad and Wendy made swords by nailing some of the stakes together and fashioned pirate hats from empty cardboard beer cartons. Rafael played cars, pirates, mountain climbing, and any and every game he could think of on and around the makeshift hill. He played with Dad when he was available. Wendy would join in too, especially when Dad was working. Even when he played by himself, the hill was a place he enjoyed. A place that was his in the middle of this big country, far away from home.

As the days went by, Dad's job demanded more and more of him. Rafael tried protesting his busyness only to receive the same answer each time. The crew had deadlines to hit, and inspections with various officials to pass. He'd also been told the job needed to be done in time so Dad could drive him home to start second grade. Dad became less and less available for games and morning oatmeal.

One morning, Rafael woke to the sound of crackling fire in time to see Dad opening the door to leave. He braved the question, "Can't you stay and make me oatmeal today before work?"

"Oh, it's not a workday today, son," Dad replied. "I'm going on a hike and I'll be back around bedtime."

"Can I go with you?"

Dad looked out the door to the distance, then back at Rafael. His face looked pained, like he was holding something back. After he thought for a moment, the blood drained from his face. Clearly something was tearing at him.

"Not this time," he said with a voice that belied the tensions on his face, then looked back at the distance outside the door. "I'm sorry, buddy. There are things I can't explain to you until you're older. It's a long, hard hike. I better hurry. I need to get going to make it back by dark. But you can go exploring. Just don't go too far, and let Wendy know where you'll be."

Rafael missed Dad on workdays. Now he was watching him leave on a day they could have played. He was nearly a continent away from Mama and home. He rolled over in his bed and faced the other way, staring sadly at the fire. His chest felt swollen. His throat felt like there was a rock in it he couldn't swallow, and his stomach turned in knots. His lips pressed together.

He heard Dad take one step toward him. The door creaked slightly. Then Dad sighed and stepped outside.

Rafael stared at the fire long enough to give up on the hope of Dad changing his mind, then emerged from his warm bedding and ate some of the breakfast Wendy made. While she was outside gathering wood, he had a moment alone with Benji.

"Dad said I could go exploring, Benji. The cars and swords and stuff are fun, but I'm kinda tired of that. You stay here and I promise I'll be back later."

He checked in with Wendy, who gave him boundaries, then

headed out. He walked through tall grasses with moss underfoot until he reached a marshy area by the lake. He skirted the lake as close as he could without getting wet and wandered around, lost in his thoughts, as one or two clouds passed overhead in the expansive Alaska sky.

As he walked near the marshes at the edge of the lake, grass to his knees, a breeze began rustling the growth around him. His heart quickened and his feet felt lighter. A faint whisper swept across the grasses toward him and the lake. The breeze reached the lake, which appeared to him to shiver like a person does when deep inspiration gives goosebumps so tingly one can only shake them out.

Rafael's wide eyes felt dry from staring. Still he didn't move. He stood, enrapt, watching the tall grasses bowing to the breath. The lake shivering in inspired wonder. The mountains gazing down approvingly.

He finally blinked when an eagle splashed the water, and watched it climb its way into the sky. Then he realized he was not alone. Across the lake, a man was sitting on a boulder.

Their eyes locked, and in that moment he felt something he was sure was similar to what he'd seen on the lake moments ago. This feeling was unlike the volcanic laughter with his dad on the hill. It didn't rise and explode out. It found its way within. It moved through marrow and bone. It triggered adrenaline and woke something in the heart. The two of them stayed still, both looking across the trembling lake, until each of them shivered simultaneously.

"This really is a beautiful spot," a man's voice said from behind him.

The voice almost matched the breath of the breeze. It was calming and reassuring. It belonged.

Rafael looked back across the lake to the man on the boulder. He was standing now, and it looked like he shivered once more. Did he feel it too?

"Is this what magic feels like?" he asked the man who stood close by.

The man across the lake appeared to be watching intently. Rafael judged he was too far away to hear, or he might've asked who he was.

The nearby man replied, "There is a sort of magic here, isn't there?"

The eagle cried above, and both looked up at it.

"Amazing sight," the man said. "She's a mother. She's taking food back to her nest, way up high in the hills. I love watching her. This is a place I enjoy a great deal."

He wasn't supposed to talk to strangers, but this man didn't feel like a stranger.

Whether the man could read his thoughts or just guessed, he answered, "Sorry, I should share a bit about who I am. I spend time here frequently, and I noticed you and your family these past weeks. I gave your dad the idea for the hill. Looked like you needed some fun."

Rafael opened his mouth to ask where the man came from and how he'd seen them, but he stopped when the man continued, "I think more than a hill to play on, a boy needs a friend."

Fifty yards to his right, Rafael heard rustling through the reeds. The stranger whistled, and the rustling grew faster and bigger. The grass was bending this way and that, and something was approaching quickly—or rather, two somethings.

Rafael forgot the eagle, the shivering lake, and the man on the boulder. His heart raced and muscles tensed. He was about to run when the stranger shouted with a friendly voice, "Good girls! C'mere, Sheba! Here, Cinnamon! Come on over!"

A blur of white fur stood up and tried to lick the stranger. He grinned and petted her. "Atta girl, Sheba. Good girl."

The dog was covered with thick fur that the stranger's hands disappeared into. Rafael loved dogs. *Her fur looks so soft! She reminds me of Benji.*

"Oh, you too, Cinnamon! You're not forgotten!" The stranger chuckled, tussling her hair too. "Good girl. I love you too."

Cinnamon had a beautiful orange coat that shined in the sun. Her tongue hung to one side as she pushed her head toward the man's hands.

The stranger addressed the dogs as though they understood his every word. "Girls, this is Rafael. I want you to keep him company until he leaves. Play with him and watch out for him."

Had the dogs nodded back in understanding? That couldn't be.

No sooner had the man finished his commands to the dogs than they ran to Rafael and snuggled up against him. He stroked his hands over their fur and fell to the ground, rolling around with them as a pup would. For the first time today, he grinned.

"You can play with them every day, Rafael," said the stranger. "It'll be much more fun, and a little safer, I think, if you have them to wander with."

As he lay on the grass he and the dogs had already matted down, Rafael didn't question how the stranger knew his name. Cinnamon's head lay on his chest, and Sheba's paw was on his leg. His arms were folded up behind his head, eyes squinting out the sun beaming down on them. "Thank you! I promise to be good to them!"

Wait! The man on the boulder! Would he like the dogs? And the eagle? Did he see her? He'd probably enjoy seeing them.

He stood, patted each of the dogs on the back, and scanned the far side of the lake.

"He'll be back," the stranger said.

Rafael relaxed a little. But why was he relieved the man would return, and why did he care if the man met the dogs or saw the eagle? "He will? Who was he?"

"Like I said, a boy needs a friend."

He hadn't meant the dogs? "But who—"

"Rafael, when you first heard me, what did you think?"

He blurted out the first thing he thought of: "I thought you made the lake shiver." It sounded so silly when he heard himself. His face heated and he looked at the ground. But why fight his thoughts? Why not just share them? What could happen? He shrugged his shoulders. "I don't know. I-I...well..." He threw up his hands. "I guess I thought I already knew you. I don't know why."

"I've been watching you for some time, Rafael. You could say I care about you. I know that's probably strange sounding and hard to understand."

It wasn't. Nothing felt uncomfortable. He felt safe when the man spoke.

"Let's just say I'm someone who notices people and I like to help them. I helped give you the hill and the dogs, and, well, actually *you* chose him." He motioned toward the boulder across the lake.

Rafael's mind raced with so many questions. Cinnamon sat by his side, licking his hand. Sheba sniffed the ground nearby.

"Enjoy the dogs, Raf. I can see they've taken to you already. Don't worry. The man will be back again. You'll decide when it's time."

Rafael looked back to the boulder. *When it's time? I'll decide? Time for what? How do I know when?*

He lay back down in the matted grass, put an arm behind his head, and called the two dogs, who both nuzzled in. Then he closed his eyes and felt the warmth of the sun.

He was lost in his thoughts when he realized he'd forgotten to say thank you for the dogs. He sat up and opened his eyes, but the stranger had disappeared.

RAFAEL CAME TO THE lake day after day, telling the dogs stories and sharing his thoughts with them. He would return and lie embraced by the two dogs and the warm sun. He missed Mama greatly, but the dogs comforted him.

Once he heard Wendy tell Dad, "The boy should have real friends. Dogs are great, but people are really man's best friend." Here, relaxing by the lake with these two, he wasn't sure she was right.

He sat in their usual spot—where he'd first met the dogs and the stranger—while Sheba sat by him and Cinnamon followed the smell of some small animal nearby. "Sheba, you and Cinnamon are my best friends here."

Sheba licked her paw a moment before looking back at him. Cinnamon, though close by, was sniffing so low to the ground, only her noises and the rustling grass betrayed her otherwise hidden body. She stopped and poked her head above the grass, then stood and stared toward the lake.

A man was walking toward them.

As Rafael got up, the dogs moved to his sides. They watched intently, but their calmness told him they trusted the man.

CHAPTER SIX

I rolled over in my sleep. In the darkness of the bedroom, I groaned, and my own voice woke me from a dream. On the other side of the bed, my wife, Krynn, shifted.

What was that dream?

I grabbed the phone from my bedside. Despite dimming it as low as it would go, the glow was too bright this early on a dark, wintry morning. Through squinting, sleep-crusted eyes, I saw that it was time to leave the comfort of my bed. I dutifully dropped my feet to the floor and shuffled to the bathroom. Thoughts of work, my kids, my wife, and the pressures of life crowded out the memory of a sunny lake, shivering grasses, a lonely boy, and a mysterious stranger.

A few minutes later, Krynn joined me. While she was applying her makeup, she asked, "Did you have any dreams last night?"

I paused shaving and stared at myself in the mirror. *It was so sunny and so real.*

"Honey?" she said. I drifted off frequently, and she was accustomed to it.

"Oh, yeah. I did, actually. It was really beautiful."

Outside the bathroom window, early hints of daylight revealed all that could be seen was under a veil. Clouds covered the sky, and the rain coming down turned even the air gray. A normal February morning here in the Portland suburbs. Cold, wet, and dismal.

"What was beautiful, babe?" A voice that was anything but gray brought me back out of my thoughts, which had returned to the responsibilities of life.

My eyes returned from their distant place and my shoulders lowered. Krynn stood at her sink a couple feet from mine. "I love the sound of your voice, Krynnie. You know things have been hard for me for a while, but you're a bright spot. Everything just feels like those clouds outside. Just gray. But you aren't." I winked at her.

Her mouth smiled but her eyes betrayed unease. She'd never been good at hiding her feelings from me. I knew her concern for me had been growing.

Not just concern for me, but for us.

"Awww. Thanks, baby," she said, then finished applying her makeup.

I looked at myself in the mirror again. Heavy shoulders and under-eye bags looked back at me. *What's wrong with you, Benjamin?*

I'd worked for a large corporation for twenty years, climbing the ranks to a mid-level executive position. Krynn and I had beautiful children, had done well enough financially, and generally had what we wanted. Yet the gray covered everything.

I finished a last stroke with the razor and sighed. Another day in a job I didn't care about anymore. I wiped down my face and walked by my nightstand, stopping at a framed photo of my family. I kissed two fingers to my lips, then placed them on the picture three times, touching Krynn, ten-year-old Abigail, and seven-year-old Lucas.

"You make me clean that darn picture every day." Krynn feigned annoyance with a sweet smile and happy eyes.

"Just reminding myself why the work is worth it, babe."

"You drifted off again, sweetie. What was beautiful in your dream last night?"

I looked her up and down. *She's still so beautiful.*

The idea that I still loved her comforted me. She had a special way about her. A grace that set me at ease. She wasn't fragile, though she was soft in good ways. She had an inner strength that I could see, though she didn't fully perceive it herself.

"It was a strange dream, but it was nice," I said. "I was at a lake. It was so beautiful and so peaceful. I watched an eagle catch a fish. The way the mountains surrounded the lake was so amazing, and there was this long grass that swayed in the wind."

"That's nice, babe. You talked in your sleep a little, but I couldn't understand it."

"Yeah, I, uh... well, I think I was trying to talk to someone across the lake."

What was it, exactly, that I'd felt? I wanted to run to the boy. I wanted to wrap him up and shield him. And the man—I didn't just *want* to talk to him, I *needed* to.

How could I tell her the dream felt real? Not like any dream I'd ever had. That wasn't even possible.

My stomach turned.

I looked down at my watch. "Looks like I better get going. Probably just a part of me that wishes it wasn't the middle of winter. It was so sunny and green in the dream."

She smiled at me. "Well, maybe it's time to book a vacation somewhere sunny."

Outside, all was still gray.

It did sound nice, but it would cost us too. "I don't know. We'll see."

"Benji, I know you. You're thinking of the budget and work and meetings and everything. You'll have to just have some fun soon and let it go."

"I think you're right." My mind raced with responsibilities and pressures while trying to forget the dream. I gave her a kiss and a hug and left our room.

I walked by the hallway bathroom, and Abigail brushed her teeth and waved at me. She reminded me so much of Krynn. She had a light and a grace to her that brightened my heart. I gave her a hug and wished her a good day, then went downstairs to where Lucas sat on the couch watching cartoons. I dropped to one knee and held out my arms.

He hopped off the couch and put his arms around my neck. "Good morning, Dada."

"Good morning, bubba."

"Dada, can we do something fun together this morning?" He asked me this nearly every morning, though he knew the answer would usually be no.

"Sorry, buddy. I have to go to work today."

"Okay. Can we do something fun soon though?"

"We'll see, buddy. Maybe one day soon." My life was so perpetually busy that I wasn't sure when I could make such a promise.

"Dada?" Lucas said again. He called my name so frequently, I'd become accustomed to it. A constant searching for my presence that I didn't yet comprehend. "Can we at least be cereal buddies before you go?"

"Sorry, bud, not today. I have to drop my car off at the shop on my way to work."

"How come? It's still working, right?"

"Well, yes, but there's a part in it that's breaking. If I don't get it fixed soon, it won't work."

"Okay, Dada. Maybe you can take me for a ride when the car is fixed." Lucas returned to the cartoons.

"Sure, buddy." I slowly walked out to the car.

My feet dragged. Why was everything gray and heavy? If only a mechanic could fix whatever was broken.

I didn't have time to dwell on it. Another long day called. Most of it passed by in a blur until my head hit the pillow again that night so I could do it all again the next day.

From near the edges of unconsciousness, I heard Krynn's voice next to me. "Hope you dream of sunny places again, sweetie."

CHAPTER SEVEN

A fresh breeze and warm sun on my skin acted in perfectly balanced harmony. I breathed deeply, expanding my chest, as my heart slowed. The lake before me lapped at the edges with musical sounds. I had no recollection of arriving, not that I cared. I knew I'd returned. Something like hope hung in the air.

What is the magic of this place?

To my right, across the water, I saw the boulder I'd been sitting on the last time I was here.

The boy! Is he here? And the man?

A ways off to my left, on the near side of the lake, grass rustled, but I made out no visible form.

There must be some animal there.

Then I saw him. The boy stood facing the water, turned just enough in the other direction that he couldn't see me. My heart caught in my throat, and I chased tears away. My stomach turned. A white dog stood at his side. The grass nearby kept rustling.

I need to make sure he's safe. And maybe he can tell me who the man is.

I made my way toward him, walking near the edges of the lake, carefully staying far enough away to keep from sinking in marsh and mud. The rustling of the grass and lapping of the waves faded away, drowned out by the pounding of my heart in my ears.

Why was I scared of meeting a boy, and why did I need to meet him so badly?

A couple more steps and I knew what was rustling the grass. First a snout, then the rest of the head of an orange dog emerged, and stared at me intently. The orange dog moved to the boy's side where the white dog already stood. They were like two sentries. Though they looked at me unblinking, they didn't look menacing.

The boy grinned and fidgeted like he was excited to see me.

Why?

"Hi, I'm Benjamin," I said.

"I'm Rafael." The boy's eyes glinted with joy. "Did you see the eagle? Wasn't that so cool?"

I grinned despite my efforts to fight it. I'd developed a habit of holding back smiles. This time I lost the battle. The little boy's enthusiasm was disarming.

Who is this boy?

My smile faded quickly. I looked away, across the lake. Why did he remind me of things I had carefully put behind walls and buried under the dirt?

I became unsure I wanted to meet him after all. My insides swirled with contradictions. Resentment pricked my heart.

Resentment that was being overcome by a longing to protect him. I looked at him again. "I saw the eagle. It was so cool. Your white dog sure looks furry. And your orange one is so pretty." My face was a full smile again.

"They aren't exactly my dogs, but they *are* my friends. This one is Sheba." He petted Sheba's thick fur, then put a hand on the other dog's head. "And this is Cinnamon. Want to pet them?"

"Sure." I stepped toward Sheba. The dog graciously watched my hand approach her shoulders. My fingers slid into thick, fleece-like fur.

I looked at our surroundings again. It was brighter and quieter here. Taking in another deep breath, I realized my neck and shoulders hurt less than usual.

The little boy looked up at me, and a blur of words poured forth without a pause for breath. "I love the outdoors. When you're inside, there are rules. Don't eat on the couch. Pick up your shoes. Change your socks. Outside just feels free. I'm kicking soccer balls, smelling the forest, throwing rocks, and exploring. I wonder if we can be friends."

The world screeched to a halt. I nearly crumbled into a ball, and my heart stung with something hot piercing it. He deserved a friend. I could be his friend. I fought feelings growing within me for fear they would be so big I could never hope to contain them.

He didn't seem to notice and still hadn't paused to breathe. The entire time he spoke, light filled his eyes. Goose bumps covered his arms. There was a magnetism to him. He was inspiring, though I didn't understand why. I didn't dare to interrupt him.

"It's also easier to make friends outside. That's another reason I like it outside. Or by a good fireplace. There's nothing like staring at a fire and drinking hot chocolate and talking about good memories. Anyway, there's something about you I like. I think you feel safe, for one thing. Well, mostly safe, I guess. I bet you're smart too. Mostly, though, you seem like we could have fun together. I wonder if you could be a good friend."

There it was again. Why did it move me and bother me at the same time? I sighed and pulled my hand away from the dog. It was all confusing and overwhelming. This invitation to be his friend was a reminder of places hidden away against the gray of my life, locked up and kept secret.

I looked at the boy still grinning back at me. Though it defied reason, I felt love for him. I thought of the heaviness of my life. Though I didn't know who this boy was, I wanted a world where he never felt heavy.

A gut-wrenching desire to wrap my arms around him, protect him, and shut out the dangers of the world pushed away my discomfort. I wished to keep him here on the sunny shores of this dream-world lake, with the breeze waving the grass around him and the dogs to play with. I would never let the gray touch him.

At noticing a little peanut butter on his face, I snorted a laugh. "I'm sure we can be friends."

He grinned. "Great! The man told me you'd come again. I'm glad you saw the eagle and I'm glad you got to pet Sheba. Better say hi to Cinnamon too, or she'll get jealous."

Cinnamon, who had decided I wasn't a threat, was in the grass sniffing and seemed more content than jealous.

I looked once more at the beauty surrounding me. A new urge swelled. I wanted to spread my arms and feel the breeze. Then my smile disappeared. What if it swept me up into the air? Where would it take me? What if I lost control? I held my arms a little tighter to my sides.

"Where are your parents?" I asked.

"My dad is on a hike and won't be back until around bedtime, and Wendy is around somewhere," he said matter-of-factly, as though it wasn't strange for a little boy to be wandering around the lake on his own with no companions besides the two dogs, the eagle, and the fish.

His eyes lit up again. "Hey, if we're going to be friends, I want to show you something!"

A chuckle escaped my chest.

Without a word he started away from the lake. Sheba and Cinnamon followed. The three of them looked carefree. There was lightness in their steps.

Curiosity swirled as I followed a few steps behind. What was I to make of the boy and these dogs that followed him everywhere—and this desire to protect a boy I'd just met?

As I drew near to a hut, Rafael ran inside. Sheba and Cinnamon fanned out, casually sniffing the grounds around the hut. I reached the front door just in time for the boy to burst outside.

"I got all my cars and trucks in this bucket! Let's race them down the hill! Have you ever raced cars down a hill? It's super fun! I'll give you half of them, and I'll take half. We'll each race one at a time, and the winner each round gets to keep them both until one of us has all the cars! It'll be super fun!"

He scrambled his way to the top of the hill, carrying the bucket full of cars with two hands. His little arms worked hard to keep the bucket from dragging on the dirt and spilling all its contents.

How could I say no? I joined him at the top of the hill, where the two of us raced every car until he eventually won.

"That was a lot of fun!" he said. "I love racing cars down the hill. Next time I'll try to give you more of the fast ones and maybe you'll win."

"No problem. I'm glad you won, friend." I winced, hoping it was imperceptible to the boy, but I felt it. What was this conflict? One moment the little boy made me laugh; the next, discomfort grew.

I wouldn't get too attached. Not to the boy and not to this place.

"Listen, I've got to go soon," I said. "Maybe you should stay close to the hut until your dad or Wendy shows up. Before I go, I wonder if you could tell me who the man was you were talking to the last time I was here?"

He shrugged. "Well, I only talked to him that one time I saw you across the lake. He was nice. He gave me the dogs. He also told me you'd be back, and here you are!"

Told him I'd be back?

I brushed that aside, sure I'd misunderstood. "Do you know how I can find him?"

He collected a few cars into the bucket. "Not really, but I feel like I'll see him again. I feel like I'll see you again too."

I didn't have the heart to tell the kid I didn't think I'd be back here again. I slid my hands into my pockets and found one of the cars we'd raced. Before I could hand it to him, thoughts of my world crashed in. The hut, the mountains, and the lake faded away, replaced by budgets, projects, meetings, and the gray.

My hands fumbled in the dark to find my phone and shut off a blaring alarm.

I opened bleary eyes and took a disoriented moment to comprehend where I was. Grogginess and confusion filled my head. Everything was dark on this early February morning, in stark contrast with the beautiful lake and mountains.

My bedroom. Time for work.

I rubbed my eyes and shuffled my feet to the bathroom for the morning routine, fighting a gnawing thought in the recesses of my brain. *Didn't feel like a dream. Felt so real. Snap out of it!*

I splashed cold water across my face, which helped me forget. It was absurd. I dried my face, feeling a little better.

"What was that for?" Krynn asked.

"Just waking up a little more. I'm extra tired today."

It was a passable lie. I kissed her goodbye and left the bathroom to say good morning to the kids. All my thoughts focused on the day ahead to avoid dwelling on the two dreams at the lake.

As I walked out of the bedroom, I noticed a toy car sitting next to my pillow on the bed. I'd have to tell Lucas he'd left it there.

CHAPTER EIGHT

Rafael stood stunned. Benjamin had just disappeared! He shook his head and replayed the kind stranger's words: "The man will be back again. You'll decide when it's time."

"Do you think I can really bring him back, Cinnamon?" he asked the dog, who sniffed where Benjamin had stood only moments ago. "What if it doesn't work? I wish he could stay and play."

He looked at the bucket of cars resting on the ground. It had been so much fun. He hadn't even shown him everything else about their surroundings. Then he looked across the grass to his favorite spot where he'd lay and talk to the dogs. Cinnamon would shake her leg if you scratched the right spot. Benjamin would probably think that's funny.

A little farther still, he watched part of the lake where fish gathered near dusk to jump and catch bugs. "Maybe we'll show him that next time, girls."

"Hi, son!" came a voice from the road behind him.

"Dad! You're back! How was your hike?"

Dad looked up toward the hills pensively. "It was good. Listen, I was thinking. We should go to the library in Valdez tomorrow and read some new books. We can make a day of it. And, yes, before you ask, we can get a treat!" He winked.

"Yay!" A drive over the pass together meant he'd have time alone with Dad's undivided attention.

Did Benjamin like libraries and books?

He decided not to tell Dad about meeting a disappearing man. How could he ever explain that?

~

That night, after making a fire and tucking Rafael into bed, Scott replayed the day in his head.

He'd stepped out of the hut in the morning, leaving Rafael behind. The knots in his stomach and the pain in his chest begged him to return, and when the door closed behind him, wavy lines passed through his hand. He clenched and unclenched his fist, for a moment and considered going back inside. Maybe he could make the little boy oatmeal. He looked up to the hills and a grunt not much louder than a whisper emerged from his chest.

There was no real choice. What if he couldn't find the talisman? What if he disappeared soon, leaving Rafael behind for more than a day's hike? Would any man in his family ever learn to fly and be able to teach his children? He set out on the day's trek.

Though it was summer, the Alaskan morning air was crisp

against his face. A mist rose from the lake enveloping the grasses and marshes in wispy fingers of fog. A breeze as slight as his own breath might clear the vaporous trails. He considered walking through the grasses and marshes to blow it away, then shook his head at such a silly idea. In a strange twist of timing, a light breeze blew through. The thin, gray tendrils were pushed back from the grass, yielding to the breeze. The lake rippled, and an eagle could be heard above.

So much for the fog. The eagle would be lucky to get a clear view of the fish now.

It turned into a wonderful day for a hike. He climbed in elevation, leaving the lush, tall grass surrounding the lake and passing into rocky trails, which climbed up switchbacks. After a steep climb, he passed into fields of wildflowers and stopped to collect some for making tea.

He surveyed the wildflowers surrounding him, in and among mostly rocks. They lived in hard circumstances but refused to disappear. They returned, year after year, regardless of the harsh conditions they faced. He closed his eyes, drew in a deep breath of fresh air, and released it with a long sigh. What would it be like to keep returning and never disappear?

Good for them, but he needed that talisman.

He climbed farther up the hillsides to the top of the pass. This lofty perch afforded a view of all below, and a pair of binoculars would help him in his search. Cold air blowing over the pass nipped at his fingers.

First some tea to warm up.

He picked a spot to sit among juniper and wild huckleberry bushes near a small stream, then reached into his pack and pulled out a camping stove and a worn aluminum pot. After lighting the little stove, he carefully placed the pot full of water on it and emptied little bags of wildflowers, sage, and juniper into the water to boil.

In a few minutes he was holding a warm tin cup near to his face with both hands, as he sat atop the hillside. The smell of the fresh wildflower and wild herb tea wafted from the cup to his nose. The view stretched for miles around.

Where are you? You're out there somewhere, I know it. He'd searched for it his whole life. It had to be out there.

He pulled out the binoculars. He'd come up to these ridges to search for the clue to the talisman's location. Somewhere, he hoped, in the valleys beneath these passes, there should be a boulder shaped like a wolf and there, he prayed, would be the talisman. Before continuing his hunt, he surveyed the campground far below and the progress the construction crew was making. The hut and the hill appeared tiny from up here.

Another deep breath was an attempt to chase away frustration. He thought about Rafael and how glad he was to have him here and of all the fun they'd had. A bug landed on his hand, and he swatted it away.

His hand. Twice now it had scared him half to death.

He had to find that talisman. But what if it wasn't real? What if he disappeared soon? He squeezed the binoculars harder, feeling their solid frame in his hands.

A breeze swept over the top of the hillside. The juniper and huckleberry branches moved as though dancing and playing. A sense of joy filled the place—something Scott hadn't experienced in a long time. Mostly what he knew was an emptiness he tried to avoid.

He'd been following leads on the crane for years. When he heard it had been seen in Europe in the 1600s, he enlisted in the army and got assigned there. That was where he met Aila. Joining the army served the dual purpose of making ends meet and distracting himself from thinking about missing his father, who had disappeared when he was young.

After a few years in Germany, having found no sign of the crane, he followed a lead to Texas. There was rumor of a shipwreck in the Gulf of Mexico and a magical talisman a sailor had carried. He took up diving to scour the Gulf waters for the crane.

When that lead dried up, he was left with only the emptiness. Adventure and travel had failed both at finding the crane and as a salve for the hurt, so he turned to education. He moved with Rafael and Aila to Oregon to study engineering, shortly before moving out to his own house without Aila and Rafael. Now he was using alcohol and Alaska to chase the emptiness. At least he had a new lead to follow. That provided some solace.

For a moment, he sat in the breeze and forgot the emptiness. It was like being filled for the first time in a long time.

"It's a beautiful spot," a voice said behind him.

Scott turned to find a familiar face approaching him.

"Hey! You're the guy who gave me the idea for making the hill for my boy. He *loves* that hill. He plays on it all the time. I've had quite a bit of fun myself."

"Great! That's good to hear. I noticed you and him playing on it a couple times. You two looked pretty happy together. This is a great spot for a hot drink and reflection."

"An amazing spot," Scott agreed. "And I'm sorry I didn't ask before, but who are you?" Something intrigued him about the man. Why did he want to know more?

"I like hiking through these areas. I'm around here often. Seems like you've got a big project going on."

Scott looked at the campground. His chest filled and he smiled with satisfaction. "It's nice that people can come enjoy this place for years to come. I like the idea I'm doing something bigger than myself."

Something that will last, and not disappear.

"Is that why you came up here?"

Scott eyed the man, confused. "I'm not sure I follow."

"For yourself."

He scowled.

The stranger offered an explanation. "You look like a man looking for something. Maybe you feel if you find it, this one special thing, it'll chase away everything wrong. I've seen the look before. A lot of people are looking for something 'out there' to chase away what's wrong."

Scott's eyes searched the valley below. Who was this man, and how had he poked Scott in such a soft part of his heart? There was no harm sharing wild thoughts with a stranger. Someday they'd leave this valley, never to see him again, and it seemed the man had already guessed at his thoughts.

Why not?

"Well, you wouldn't believe me if I explained it, but yeah, there's something very important I need to find. Something"—he searched for the right words—"something I lost. I think if I find it, it won't necessarily stop what's wrong with me, to use your words, but I can slow it down. Maybe pause it a while. I've basically devoted my life to finding it."

"I wonder…"

The words hung in the air long enough Scott nearly asked him to finish.

"You might find the treasure you're after. I've found people seem happiest when they've stopped searching for things 'out there.' Life's funny that way, isn't it? Sometimes when we find what we want, we find we don't want it, and sometimes when we give away what we want, we find it and realize we can't lose it."

Scott raised an eyebrow and squinted. "Now I *really* can't follow you."

The stranger laughed. "Ha! It's a hard concept. Figuring out what you want and how to get it. People make it harder than they need to. Take that little boy you've got. You know what I think he might want?"

Scott smiled wryly. "Well, I know a few things he wants, but I suspect you're about to tell me something."

"I think he might want you to read him some new books. I saw him looking at the pictures in his books once, when I walked through the campground. He seems to enjoy those."

Scott nodded. "For sure. We don't have any electricity or TV here. That's his entertainment. He likes when I read to him too."

"I'll bet he does."

An eagle appeared in the air between them and the lake.

"I like watching her." The stranger's voice sounded pleased. "She flies alone, but it's with purpose. She's hunting a sort of treasure too, but it's not for herself. She's gathering for her young and will return to provide for them. Then she'll keep them warm and secure."

Scott watched her circling in the air currents above. He drew another deep breath of the wildflower and herb tea and sighed.

What would it be like to soar above the problems of the world? To spread his arms and feel the breeze carry him. It was both wonderful and impossible.

"There's something so tangible about her providing for her little ones, isn't there?" The stranger added. "Such a practical demonstration of her care. Yet she's most real to them when she's there, in the nest with them."

Scott kept his eyes glued to the bird, feeling special to see her soar on the winds. He took a sip of the tea in contemplation, then turned to say something to the stranger.

Gone? How had he disappeared so quickly?

The breeze stopped, and the eagle flew off.

Emptiness encroached on him, feeling like the morning's fog returning to reclaim the land. He wanted some beers and the comfort of a woman's arms for the night.

The sun glistened off the metal roof of the hut far below. He remembered laughing with Rafael. His eyes moved from the cabin to the binoculars and back several times. How could he reconcile two paths ahead of him?

He needed more time!

Time to chase away the emptiness and find the talisman. Time to figure himself out. Time to stay and not disappear. And he needed time to enjoy laughter and fun with Rafael. He liked that so much, time didn't seem to matter when they were having fun.

He scanned the valley for several hours alone with his thoughts, eventually dropping the binoculars to his lap in defeat.

He gathered up his things slowly. With a last look below, he started the hike back.

Another dried-up lead.

Feeling so close made the sting of failure worse. His feet trudged forward, dragging his body down the trail. Behind him, his spirit remained on the ridge, frozen in mourning. How could he ever learn to fly or teach Rafael? Was he destined to fade away?

It must just be the wrong valley. It *had* to be close. He'd have to try at least one more time. Maybe figure out the right valley and try again.

The man was right about the books though. They both needed a trip away for a day.

THE NEXT MORNING, RAFAEL lay awake in the quiet of the cabin eagerly waiting for his dad to wake. The minute hand of a little clock stubbornly refused to move quickly enough.

C'mon! Let's go to the library and the glacier!

When Dad finally stirred to make a fire and prepared oatmeal for everyone, Rafael nearly jumped out of bed. They sat near the fire, eating on the rock hearth warmed by the radiant heat.

Rafael fidgeted. "Can we go now, Dad?"

"Yes! Let's go."

The day was everything Rafael wanted. On the hourlong drive to the library he could barely find words to carry a conversation, but time alone with his dad seeing a world outside the campground, lifted his spirits. They got a treat at a local bakery which filled his stomach.

As they left the bakery, Dad exclaimed, "Hey, I see a bookstore there. Down the street. How about we go buy a book or two together?"

Together.

That was all Rafael wanted. "Yeah!"

He pictured relaxing in the van with a peanut butter sandwich, a blanket, and the orange curtains where he could listen to the soothing sounds of his dad's voice reading.

A small glacier hike added adventure to the day. Rafael could hardly believe he was walking on ice in late summer. How amazing! And, before the final stretch of the drive, Dad pulled over at a lookout point at the top of the pass.

Just off the road was a spot to enjoy a view not too unlike the one his dad had hiked to. They sat among the juniper and wild huckleberry to watch the sun move over the expanse of Alaska below. Dad put his arm around Rafael.

Rafael sat silently, absorbing the warmth from his father's side. Maybe if he stayed quiet, he could stretch the day out a few more minutes. The strong frame of his father next to him felt solid and safe.

CHAPTER NINE

Over the next several weeks, Dad spent most of his time alternating between working to finish the construction project and searching for the talisman. Rafael settled into a daily routine to keep himself entertained. He wandered through the campground, played on his hill, and spent time at the lake.

Cinnamon and Sheba were his inseparable companions, following him everywhere, and their closeness eased any loneliness. The dogs were great listeners, and the only creatures who knew how much he wanted to see if Benjamin could return to give him someone to play with. "What if I call for him and he doesn't appear?" he asked them.

He chose to wait and hope, rather than confirm he didn't have the power to bring Benjamin back. Believing he could see Benjamin again, but not knowing when, was better than finding he was gone for good.

A little over a month had passed at Blueberry Lake, when Rafael settled into his bed for the night only to be awakened by unusual noises a few minutes later. The dim light of several candles, the fireplace, and a lantern cast Dad's shadow on the cabin walls as he gathered up their belongings. Rafael watched in confusion as his father packed bags and boxes, took them outside, and returned. It became evident he was putting everything in the old van. He wasn't sure what to make of it all as Dad and Wendy quietly packed everything up for a little over an hour. Hardly a word was spoken between them.

Rafael tried to figure out what was happening, but his eyelids drooped further and further in the dimly lit hut. Just as he closed his eyes to sleep, he heard Wendy's voice outside.

"You're doing the right thing," she said.

"I know," Dad replied. "It's just so frustrating. I *need* to find that talisman. You understand how important that is to me, right? We're talking about years of my life potentially lost! I *have* to find it."

"Of course. I understand, and I'll come back here with you and help you. But we talked about this. School has already started and he's late getting home. Aila must be worried sick. There's no phone around here, and you haven't been updating her. Can you imagine how she feels right now?"

He sighed and dropped his head. "She's going to let me know about it too. I need to stay focused on this search, but I do feel bad for her sometimes. We'll call her from the road, I promise. Speaking of the road, we'd better finish packing so we can get a move on in the morning. I figure since we're late anyway, we can make it a fun trip. If we were to drive hard, we could get there in five or six days, but I figure we can make it fun and take an extra week. It's just elementary school. It's not like he's going to be studying nuclear physics. He's smart. He'll catch up."

Wendy nodded. "When we get him home, we can come back here and look for the rock and the talisman. I'll help you."

Rafael heard them give each other a little kiss before they went back to their packing, and he fell asleep.

He had sweet dreams of seeing Mama that night, and in one dream he and Benjamin were flying. What fun that would be!

In the morning, Dad made them all oatmeal one last time before loading the rest of their belongings into the van. The van's engine sputtered to life, and the gravel crunched under its tires.

"Wait!" Rafael yelled.

Dad hit the brakes, and all three jerked against their seatbelts. He whirled around. "What's wrong, Raf?"

"Sheba and Cinnamon! I didn't say goodbye to them!"

Dad sighed. Rafael saw red, sleep-deprived eyes staring at him. Not just sleep-deprived though. Was there fear in his eyes too?

Dad pinched the bridge of his nose and squeezed his eyes, then held up his hand. "Raf, buddy, I'm sorry. We've got to get going. We have no idea where those dogs are right now. Sorry, buddy."

"No, please! Please! Just a few minutes! Let me call for them! I know they'll come!"

Dad looked at Wendy, who shrugged. He turned off the ignition, placed both hands on the steering wheel, and slumped forward. "Okay. Ten minutes. I can check a couple things on the van's engine again and make sure she'll get us to Oregon. Don't go far. And come right back. Understood?"

Rafael was already heading out the door. "Yes! Thank you! I promise!" he yelled over his shoulder. "Sheba! Cinnamon! Come, girls! Where are you? Sheba! Cinnamon!"

Frantically he turned in a circle, calling for the dogs again and again. He searched the grass for even a faint sign of movement and strained his ears for any sound of the dogs. The air was still and all was unbearably quiet.

Where were they? He couldn't leave without saying goodbye!

An eagle called out above, breaking the silence and his concentration. He spun in its direction. There was a man standing near the lake, in the tall grasses. The air moved with a new breeze blowing through, making the grasses and the lake dance. Could it be Benjamin? Or maybe the kind man? Rafael jogged to the lake, hoping it would be one of them and calling for the dogs every few steps.

As he drew closer to the man by the lake, his heart leaped and he broke into a run. "Sheba and Cinnamon!"

"They've been waiting for you," the stranger said. "They're sad you're leaving, but they're happy you're returning home. I know your mother misses you very much."

Rafael was already on his knees with dogs swirling around him, nuzzling and licking him in between hugs.

"I miss her too. Okay, girls, too many licks!" he laughed, pushing himself back up. "Thank you for letting them play with me so many times."

"Of course, Raf. Of course. They tell me you were a wonderful friend and that they're thankful too."

How could the dogs tell him all that? Of course it couldn't be true. But then, there *was* something magical about the man and about this place. And hadn't he talked with the dogs all summer? There were plenty of times he was certain they understood him. Maybe it wasn't so hard to believe the man could have a special connection with them.

For now, Rafael had more pressing thoughts. "Benjamin came back one time. I wish he had come more, but we had a lot of fun. He asked about you too. Will I get to see him again?"

The stranger watched the eagle circling above as she effortlessly lifted ever farther upward on unseen air currents. Then he looked at Rafael with intensity and gentleness in his eyes.

It comforted Rafael in much the same way as a hug from his father would make him feel. Still, he wasn't certain what the stranger might say or do next. There was an air of both love and power to this man, and something unpredictable.

"Rafael," the man said, pointing at the eagle, "do you see the way she lets the wind carry her?"

Rafael looked up at the eagle, now seeming to meet the sky itself.

"She lets the air currents do the work and she trusts. See the way she has her wings out? She accepts what the wind will bring her. Like when you open your arms for a hug and receive an embrace back. It's lovely to watch, isn't it?"

Rafael pictured himself rising above the earth, embracing the wind. He closed his eyes and saw a vision of himself flying near the sea. A tingle coursed through him, raising the hairs on the back of his neck, and then ran through his face and arms. He almost felt himself begin to rise off the ground.

"When Benjamin was here, he noticed the same breeze you did," the man said. "Do you remember the first thing you said to me?"

"That I thought you made the lake shiver?"

"Yes. And do you remember what you felt when the lake 'shivered'?"

"I felt all goose-bumpy and like something was happening in my insides. And I-I wanted to talk to you." Why did thoughts come spilling out, and why couldn't he stop from telling this man so much? It wasn't Rafael's usual way. Usually he guarded himself and his thoughts.

"Good for you, Rafael," the stranger replied. "You know, some people forget about magic like that. They stop feeling it and they stop believing in it. It hasn't gone away, but they've stopped looking for it. Sometimes they'll notice for a moment, but it's not quite the same. Something special happened that day. Benjamin is one of those people who is forgetting what the goose bumps feel like and where they come from, but he felt the same shiver you did that day. He'll need some help to understand what he felt. He's scared of it."

What did that mean? "Scared of what?"

"Of feeling. And of giving up control. Some people decide it's safest not to feel too much, so they control their world as much as they can. They hide their heart away and feel it's safest never to fly. Never to let the breeze carry them. They stop trying big things and stop daring to dream or to try. Some get wrapped up in pursuit of self and begin to disappear. I think Benjamin might need your help."

"Help with what?"

"To fly." The words weren't so much spoken as they were breathed.

A rushing wind filled the area. It was strong enough to blow Rafael off his feet, yet instead of being knocked over, he was being filled up. Waves of energy surged through his veins, and it seemed the world was disappearing. Deep joy and contentment swelled in him. It was bewildering and exhilarating, and he didn't want it to end. He stood quietly, eyes closed, letting the feeling remain for whatever time it would.

The wind subsided and he reopened his eyes.

"Rafael, it's been fun to watch you. You're very special to me. You've been very kind to Sheba and Cinnamon, and you have a kind heart. You have the heart of a healer. That's a special gift. You might even know things about people before they tell you and think things that don't make sense for your age, but don't be shy about that. People always need to hear healing words.

"Don't worry about Benjamin. He might be forgetting about the magic, but he felt something powerful that day, and I think he'll want to feel it again. It's not too late for him. And don't worry about how he feels about you. He felt something deep for you as well. You can call him when you want to, I promise. He'll come again. Maybe not every time, but he'll come. Right now, you'd better run back to the van. I think your ten minutes are up."

Rafael didn't bother to ask how the man knew about his ten minutes or how he knew so much about himself and Benjamin. He gave Sheba and Cinnamon each one more hug and turned to walk away.

"Raf," the man said after he'd taken a few steps. "One last thing. Keep dreaming of flying."

Rafael nodded and resumed walking. About halfway back to the van, he turned to wave but couldn't see the man or the dogs anywhere.

"Did you find them, Raf?" Dad asked as Rafael climbed back into the van.

"Yeah." He didn't share anything more about his conversation with the kind stranger or even about the stranger at all. As they drove away, he stared out the window toward the lake, hoping to catch a last glimpse of the man and the dogs. They were nowhere to be seen, so he watched the grasses swaying.

The van began to climb the road to the pass. Just before they turned out of sight of the lake for the last time, he watched a crane take off in flight from the marshes. Its wings moved so beautifully and gracefully, the sight sent a shiver through him.

CHAPTER TEN

The alarm blared, but I was already awake, staring at the ceiling. I turned it off quickly to let Krynn sleep a few more minutes beside me.

What had it been, about three months since I had dreamt about the boy? It was a little easier to focus on meetings at work when I didn't think of the boy, the man, and the lake.

I'd been less distracted without him on my mind. It was for the best. So why didn't that feel like the truth?

Maybe I did want to go back to the dreams.

Wandering with the boy and the dogs around the lake sounded peaceful. I breathed deeply and let my chest drop with a slow breath out. It would be fun to play with those three.

Since when do I want to go play?

And there was the stranger. What was it about him? Why did I want to meet him so badly?

It was too much time spent on thoughts I'd been trying to bury. The veins in my throat and my temples warned me my blood pressure had risen.

Better to keep that buried and move on.

I checked an email on my phone, reading the instructions for entering a home we rented for a long weekend at the beach, then took another deep breath and smiled.

No boy and no work today. Just me and the family.

Krynn still slept peacefully next to me, and my heart warmed at how much her cup would be filled with a weekend of family togetherness at the small beach cottage we'd rented.

I gently rolled out of bed and went downstairs, where I found Lucas and Abigail on the couch. "You two look so sweet, wrapped in that shared blanket," I greeted them.

They both smiled, then paused their show to get up and give me a hug.

I got down on one knee and wrapped an arm around each of them. They lingered there. Life wasn't so gray when my arms were around these two little ones.

I hoped my arms felt like safety and comfort to them. And it felt good to give them the hugs and morning cereal times I never had.

"Dada, can we do something fun today?" Lucas asked, as he nearly always did.

"Actually, yes. We're going to the beach for a long weekend," I said.

They looked at each other, both with impossibly wide eyes and grins. "Yay!" they shouted, dancing and jumping around.

"That means Vacation Dad!" Abigail exclaimed.

"Ha. Yeah, extra treats for everyone." I winked at her.

"And more fun!" she said. "You play with us more and you're happier on vacation. And you're with us! We get to be together."

That hit me in the gut, and I tried not to show the sadness on my face while the two of them were doing their happy dance. They moved around the room chanting "Vacation Dad this weekend," to a conga rhythm.

Look at their faces shine. They deserved more fun and less heaviness from me.

Abigail's word "together" kept ringing in my ear. These two wanted time with me so much. The promise of a couple days without distraction was enough to make them dance around the room. I'd have to play some extra games with them this weekend.

Their excitement was spilling over onto me. "First, let's have breakfast!" I said as I headed for the kitchen.

"Cereal buddies!"

They ran to the cabinet to get the cereal boxes, while I got bowls, spoons, and milk.

"Dada, can we run from the waves right away when we get to the beach? *Please*?" Lucas pleaded with eyes, hands, squealing voice, and every other energy he could send my way.

Abigail watched for my response.

"Of course. That sounds great."

After packing and prepping—with no small amount of "are you done yet?" interruptions—we loaded up and made it out to the beach house. "Can we play yet?" the kids asked countless times as we unpacked our clothes and food for a four-day weekend.

When we were finally ready to go outside, the kids could barely be contained. They ran around the beach aimlessly, the sand squishing between their toes, leaving two sets of footprints. I walked a little ahead, making my way toward the ocean. Lucas followed my footprints in the sand, his little legs jumping from one print to the next to match my stride. Abigail, seeing the game, followed suit.

I neared the water where a man stood with a baseball cap pulled low, his bare feet in the wet sand and jeans rolled up. He watched my two little ones jumping, following my footprints fifty yards back on the beach. "They look like they enjoy following in your footsteps," he said, smiling.

He seemed nice enough, and I smiled back. "I guess they do. They tag along wherever I go."

"That's sweet. I come to the beach often. I like when a father leaves good footsteps for his children to follow. If they're too far apart, they can't reach each step. If there aren't any around, they tend to wander." He nodded at the kids. "Yup, a good set of footprints set just right, and they'll follow them and have a little fun in the meantime. They might act like they want to do their own thing, but they love following a good set of footprints. Makes them feel secure. It takes care to set them just right. Care and thought."

It seemed a little peculiar that someone would go on and on about footprints in the sand. But I was in a good mood, and here at the ocean with my family, so I didn't mind. I attempted to make friendly chit-chat, only to see he had walked off far enough I'd have to shout after him.

Something seemed familiar about the man walking away.

Did I know him from somewhere? And who would take time to develop a philosophy on footprints?

I chuckled. "Must be someone who's had the time to study human behavior."

"What, Dada?" Lucas asked.

"Oh. Nothing, buddy."

Abigail followed after him. "Come play with us in the waves, Dada!"

"That water is super cold," I objected. "I'll stay here and watch." The ocean in Oregon could be so cold, the water felt it was biting at your bones.

"Please? Come play with us!" she invited again.

Again I declined, so she ran out with Lucas, laughing and playing. They waited for the waves to come crashing in toward them and, whenever one got close, they'd run shouting and giggling.

Krynn arrived by my side and made it clear she wasn't going to let me off easily. "They would absolutely love it if you played with them. They adore you."

I looked at her, begging not to have to go in the cold water, but she just gazed steadily back, unmoved by my pleading eyes.

Then I heard it. "I wonder if you could be a good friend." Rafael's voice. I watched for Krynn's reaction to see if she'd heard it too, but she just watched the kids as if nothing happened. It was startling, but unmistakable.

On instinct, I ran full speed toward the children. Veering toward Lucas, I stretched my arms out wide, giggling as I could see him bewildered by the wildness in my eyes and approach. Not knowing what to do, but sensing the beginning of a game, he turned and ran away. Every few steps, he looked over his shoulder with a mix of fear and laughter. I caught up to him and swooped him up with both arms before pretending to throw him into the ocean.

Krynn watched with a smile as the kids and I spent the better part of an hour running and splashing together until one large wave came and knocked them over. I reached down and snatched them both up. They were soaked and cold, but it didn't matter. The joy of playing with their father filled their bellies with laughter.

I carried them, one in each arm, and walked toward their towels to dry off and a beach blanket to sit on.

I wasn't yet done with whatever had grabbed hold of me. Grinning mischievously at Krynn, I stalked closer to her. She raised hands in protest, but it was too late. The kids understood what was happening and joined. We gave her a cold, wet hug that she pretended to hate, although we knew she loved it.

We lay warming in the sun for some time, each of us feeling refreshed and happy. At some point the children began digging in the sand while I watched a few lonely clouds roll across the blue sky, wondering how fast the wind traveled up so high and how far out to sea the gulls traveled.

In the evening, after getting the kids to bed, Krynn and I opened a bottle of red wine and sat on the couch, watching out the window at the reflection of the moon on the rolling waves. I absentmindedly rubbed my fingers on a toy car in my sweatshirt pocket. Lucas must've left it on my pillow when I was in the bathroom. I'd have to give it back to him.

"The kids had so much fun with you today," Krynn said. "I love watching you play with them and watching you be a kid. They really love you. You're a good dad."

A good dad. I didn't always believe that myself.

"Thanks," I sighed. "It was fun with them today." Holding my wine glass, I stared out at the ocean. Out past the breaking waves, the ocean rolled, and the moon covered it with a silver blanket. The view was romantic and calming.

"What are you thinking about?" Krynn asked.

"I was just hypnotized by the waves and the moonlight on them."

She studied my face. She must have wondered what was being left unsaid. "Where do you go? When you get quiet and stare off? Where is it you go to?"

I shrugged. "Lots of places, I guess. I think about the kids and what they need and who they'll be. I think about you and how I enjoy your company." I winked at her. She sat with her feet pulled up on the couch. "You're cute, you know? Even just how you sit. I kinda like you, ya know?"

She blushed a little. "Aw, thanks, baby."

I leaned in for a kiss before opening up more. "I think about work and how unhappy I am there. I'm glad it provides for us, but it's hard. My boss stresses me out, and I just don't care much about it anymore. And I think about our future. How to pay for college, and new cars, and our house, and retirement, and all the things."

The veins in my neck and temples tightened up again. "And, well, just this weird feeling I haven't been able to shake about something just being 'off' with me. But I try not to think of that very much."

And Rafael. I think of Rafael, the man, the lake, the dogs and whatever that breeze was.

Why had I felt the impulse to close my eyes, spread my arms, embrace the breeze and see where it would take me? I squirmed imperceptibly, or so I thought.

"Where'd you go this time?" she asked.

I blinked, returning to her. "What's that?"

She put her wine down, moved close to me, and rested her head on my shoulder. "You got quiet again and then looked a little stressed. Let me in. I feel like you've been distant lately."

I didn't like explaining the dreams to myself. How could I even start with her? "Sorry, I've just been fixated on work. I'll be better."

I didn't know whether the lie was for me or for her.

A little later, as we were falling asleep in bed, Krynn turned to me. "Thanks for taking us to the beach. I love family time." She put an arm around my side as I lay facing the other side of the bed. "When you play with the kids, I like picturing you as a kid. I love that picture we have from when you were little. The one from your hike with your dad. You're lying in the grass without a shirt, and there's peanut butter all over your face." She let out a tiny laugh. "You were so cute!"

"Ha. Yeah, that's a silly picture."

She'd reminded me of one of my only memories with my dad at that age. I stared into the darkness of the night, wondering what it was like for kids who had more shirtless peanut butter times with their dads than I'd had.

The sound of the waves outside and the warmth of Krynn's nearness relaxed me. Eventually my eyes grew heavy and shut slowly as I drifted off to sleep.

CHAPTER ELEVEN

"*Vroom! Vroom! Honk! Honk!*"

Startled by the sound, I opened my eyes with a jolt. Just down the sidewalk, a little boy was leaning over a large toy truck reaching as high as his knees. He had a hand on each side of the truck and was running it around, honking and making engine noises.

Suddenly he stopped in his tracks and looked up. "Benjamin!" He broke into a run straight toward me and nearly knocked me over with a hug around my waist. "You're here!"

My heart skipped a beat, and nerves churned in my stomach. I was back. Back with Rafael, anyway, but not at the lake.

I awkwardly lowered my arms and returned his hug. Hearing his call was like a summons to a critical task. One so weighty and somber it was an honor and a necessity to answer.

"Rafael!" I shifted him back to look at him and found I couldn't hide a smile.

It was nice to see him again.

"How are you?" I asked.

"Good! This is my home. Where me and my mom live."

I looked at the little cottage on the corner lot. In front of me were a few stairs up to a small porch and the front door. A willow tree gracefully rustled its tendril branches in the breeze.

A shiver ran run up my spine, through my arms, and over the back of my neck.

Why does that keep happening around him? It reminded me I still wondered who the mysterious man was. Why was it all so exciting and unsettling?

"Come on!" Rafael said. "You can meet my mom."

We walked into the small house. There was a little fireplace in the living room and a basket full of toy cars on a bookshelf in the hallway.

"Mom! Benjamin's here!" Rafael called through the house.

A woman with a warm smile stepped into the hallway, setting me at ease. "Oh! Benjamin! I've been looking forward to meeting you." She gave me a friendly hug. "I'm Aila, Rafael's mother."

This surprise meeting should've been awkward, but was comforting instead. "You were expecting me?" I replied, casting a side glance at Rafael.

She smiled down at him. "He hasn't stopped talking about you. With Rafael, I just expect interesting things to happen. I wasn't sure I'd meet you, but he insisted you'd come, and I've learned not to doubt him. Never mind all that. Please sit and eat with us."

In the small kitchen, I pulled up a seat at the table. A wave of nostalgia overcame me. Why did this place feel familiar?

I embraced everything my senses could tell me, soaking in sights, sounds, and smells. Though I felt a deep sense of belonging, there was something haunting about this place. Emptiness hung in the air like a lurking shadow. I didn't want to find out what it was.

Aila served us a simple meal of German pancakes with hot dogs rolled up inside them. We ate until our stomachs were full, enjoying the salty, buttery crepe-like food, and drank strawberry milk. We were so content I hadn't noticed it getting dark outside.

"Benjamin, do you want to go play with my big trucks with me?" Rafael said, wiping a strawberry milk mustache off his face.

Aila smiled at him. "Sorry, but it's time to get ready for bed, *liebchen*."

"Can I have a bubble bath first?"

"Sure, sweetie."

"Can Benjamin hang out with me?"

Aila looked at me. Her eyes seemed like they knew me. As if I wasn't new in their lives. I squirmed in my seat, still wrestling with the dueling feelings of comfort and unease until she broke the silence. "Sure. Benjamin, would you like to help Rafael with bedtime tonight?"

I didn't know why it was easy to answer, but without hesitation I replied, "I can do that."

"Great. Raf, how about you go put on your swim shorts and I'll start the bath." Aila walked to the bathroom and put an exaggerated amount of bubble bath in the tub. By the time Rafael was ready to get in the bath, the bubbles were so thick, he could have hidden under them. He placed his bath toys into the tub one at a time.

It bordered on comical. How many could he get in there, and where was he going to sit with all those toys?

"That's the last one," he said as he dropped a small boat into the bubbles and climbed in.

I sat nearby on the toilet lid and watched him play with his toys. He looked so happy in his imaginary world of boats, deep-sea divers, dinosaurs, and submarines.

"Benjamin, do you like bubble baths?" he asked.

"Well, I haven't thought about that in a long time, Rafael, but sure. They're warm and relaxing, and it looks fun with all those toys."

He splashed with the toys for a moment. "Sometimes I wish my dad were here to make a bubble bath for me. Do you do bubble baths for your kids, Benjamin?"

I forced my face not to frown. "Sometimes I do. How did you know I have kids?"

"I didn't really know. I just guessed. That's what grown-ups do, right? They're moms and dads. Well, my dad's an engineer, I guess, but he's a dad too. He's in Alaska. How many kids do you have?"

I thought about how I'd met Rafael in Alaska. Had time gone by here? He'd come back to Aila while his dad was still in Alaska?

I had so many questions, not the least of which was why I accepted this place as a parallel reality—but the boy was waiting for an answer. "I have two kids. Abigail is nine and Lucas is seven."

"I bet they're really nice. And I bet you're a good dad."

"They are really nice. I'm not sure I'm a good dad, but I love them a lot."

He played with the toys again. "That's what a dad does. He loves his kids and makes bubble baths for them and stuff. So you're a good dad."

Why did I want to cry, and how could he so consistently poke me right in the heart?

He looked at his hands. "They're so wrinkly from the bath. I always think that's so weird, and I like to look at it. I think I'm done now." He looked up from his hands. "Benjamin? Would you listen to *The Night Before Christmas* with me?"

Christmas? It had been a warm, sunny day. It couldn't be Christmas. "Rafael, it's not Christmastime, is it?"

Come to think of it, if this place really was apart from my world, could it be a different time of year? Was it even the same year at all?

I recalled the cars I'd seen outside. It had to be the early 1980s here.

I accepted I'd traveled somewhere other than my own place and time. This should have been alarming, yet I thought nothing of it.

"I know it's not Christmastime, but I like listening to it," Rafael explained. "It's a tape my dad made for me. He gave me it with a tape player for Christmas."

He grew quiet, and I waited for him. "Benjamin?" he said, his face now a little more serious.

"Yes, Rafael?"

"Do you read books to your kids at bedtime?"

The words stung my heart as they hung in the air, and I looked out the open bathroom door to the hallway. I hadn't had a father in my home when I grew up. I understood the depth of the question in a way Rafael couldn't yet.

We both let the question linger and then disappear without an answer.

Rafael got out of the bath, and I wrapped a towel around him, then left the room to let him change out of his wet shorts. When he was done, I sat on the floor of his bedroom and he took a tape player from the top of a toy chest, then set it near us and hit the play button.

Scott's voice, jingling bells, and clippety-clop noises blared from the tape player as Scott performed an amateur production of *The Night Before Christmas*. Scott bellowed "ho ho ho."

The room swirled around me. Every sound filled my inner being with homesickness and nostalgia. I grew dizzy and my stomach hurt. Why was I having such a strong reaction?

I prided myself on never getting too low or too high. I'd found a nice, calm, flat line of emotion in the middle. This was something else that challenged my sense of control over myself and my life.

I needed to get away.

I shifted to stand up, then looked at Rafael, who lay on his belly, elbows on the floor, head in his hands.

Look at him soaking this up. He's so happy.

I decided to linger a little longer. When the tape finished, Rafael put the player on the toy chest and got into bed. "Benjamin?"

"Yeah, buddy?"

"Do you tuck your kids into bed at night? I think kids really like to be tucked in. Even big ones. I think kids really like having a dad tuck them in at night. My dad is in Alaska."

"Yes, I remember that, buddy," I said, smiling. "And yes, I tuck my kids into their beds."

"Benjamin?"

That way he called my name.

A shiver of goose bumps rippled over my face, arms, and neck again. It felt like caring about the boy was doing something to me, changing something in me. "Yes, Raf?"

"Do you tell your kids you love them? When you tuck them in, I mean. Do you say 'good night' and 'I love you'? I think kids want to hear that every night."

I fought back tears and felt like I almost couldn't swallow past the lump in my throat.

A seven-year-old shouldn't be asking things like this.

I felt a new feeling—a spark of determination. No matter how uneasy these experiences with Rafael made me, no matter how much I wanted to run from them, I would keep coming back if it meant Rafael heard a man's voice say, "I love you."

I pulled the sheet and blankets up over him and tucked him in tightly. "There. Now you're a burrito baby. You're all tucked in and I'm going to eat you!" I said with a wide smile.

He giggled and shouted, "Noooo! Don't eat me!"

Aila stood at the door, watching us interact and looking happy. But I thought I saw sadness in her eyes too. Perhaps an understanding that our laughter would never be enough to replace Scott's presence.

I bent down and pretended to eat Rafael around his neck, which tickled him, causing him to giggle more. "Rafael, I know I'm not your dad, but I want you to know I love you."

I could hardly believe I was hearing my own voice. I was never quick to say those words. I said them often to Krynn, Abigail, and Lucas, but otherwise I had a hard time saying that. I was utterly perplexed.

I didn't understand how he'd gotten to me. Still, I was glad he's being cared for.

I heard the slight creak of a door and blinked my eyes open. I was lying in a bed, no longer in Rafael's house. Disoriented, I looked around the room.

The beach house. I'm in the beach house.

Krynn tiptoed across the floor after using the bathroom. It was still dark outside. I rolled over in bed.

As I attempted to nod off, I couldn't stop thinking about Rafael. *It's a dream. It's only a dream. It's not real.*

Try as I might, I wasn't convinced. Some part of me believed Rafael was real, and I wanted to help him. It was the same part of me that badly wanted to find the mysterious stranger and ask him about the goose bumps and the breeze and why I felt the wind could carry me if I would let it.

Maybe he could help Rafael. There was something to him. Some kind of power.

I squeezed my eyes shut in the darkness of the night and tried to focus on the sound of the waves outside.

Maybe I would take a sleeping pill tomorrow to skip the dreams and take a break from all this.

That was the last thing I thought before I heard someone calling my name like one calls for a dog.

"Benjamin! Benjamin!"

I opened my eyes and had to squint. The bright noon sun shined down from a blue sky. Not a cloud could be seen. Various leafy trees were around where I stood on the bank of a small creek. Next to me sat a pair of shoes, and near them, two socks looked like they'd been thrown haphazardly about.

My eyes adjusted to the change from the dark room to the bright day, and I smiled. Five feet in front of me, pants rolled up, standing in shallow water, a little boy came into focus. Rafael was poking around with a stick in the creek.

"Hi, Benjamin! It worked!"

"What worked, buddy?"

"I called you and you came again!"

He called me? What did he mean? How was I here again? Hadn't I just left him in his bed at night? How was it now daylight, and where were we?

"Rafael, where are we?"

"This is the creek just down the street from my house. I came here to play and wanted a friend. Can you play with me?"

"Sure, buddy," I said without hesitation.

I took off my shoes and socks, then rolled up my pants and stepped into the cool water of the creek. Gingerly, I walked across several slick rocks to stand near Rafael, who was moving a leaf around in the water.

I had been feeling deep care for a boy who was nearly a stranger, and was beginning to debate whether dreams were, in fact, reality. Now I was impulsively stepping into a creek and walking in mud and rocks. I was losing control of my carefully crafted persona and didn't like that. Yet, every time the boy invited me—it didn't matter to what—I found myself participating without hesitation.

The boy is like a little Pan. I laughed.

"What's so funny?" he asked.

"Oh, nothing."

"Okay. Let me show you this place!"

We spent an hour playing with sticks, throwing rocks in the water, watching water-skipping bugs, and squishing mud between our toes. I lost track of time, forgetting budgets, deadlines, and meetings. I simply played and didn't even have the conscious awareness that I was doing that.

It was a contented existence that removed thoughts or cares outside the creek, the mud, the sticks, the rocks, and Rafael. The little boy was always in my focus, laughing, playing, singing, and enjoying life. Just as I had during our first meeting at the lake, I wanted to protect him and keep him in this joyful place, never to let the world hurt him.

"We better go home now," Rafael said with sudden urgency. "I'm not really supposed to be here. My mom told me not to come to the creek when she's gone. She went to the store and is coming right back."

We stepped from the creek and struggled our wet feet into socks and shoes, then headed back to his house, walking with light hearts. After a short distance, I could see the willow tree ahead of us in the yard. Its branches and their leaves were still. No breeze could be felt, and an ominous feeling overtook me.

Soon I saw Aila sitting on the front steps. My face drained of blood, and a sense of dread overtook me. She had a hand to her mouth, her eyes fixed on some papers she held in her other hand. She was clearly crying and in shock.

Rafael stopped walking, and I put an arm around him.

"It's okay, Rafael. Whatever it is, it's going to be okay." The words sounded hollow and feeble, but I couldn't think of anything better.

Rafael walked ahead. I stopped where the sidewalk met the

pathway to their front steps, feeling out of place, like I was watching a private moment where those involved were unaware of my presence.

Rafael approached Aila slowly, his face full of concern. He sat by her, put his arm around her, and searched her face. He looked like he didn't know what to do. Braving his voice against the awful silence, it sounded like he forced the words out. "What's happening, Mama?"

Aila looked at her feet.

"Mama?"

Through tears, her voice sounded assuring. The relaxed tone was most assuredly a lie for his sake. "Raf, these are divorce papers."

I'd lived through a moment much like this and knew it too well. Rafael's mind would be full of questions. *What's divorce? Why are these papers so sad? What does this mean? Why is my mom crying?*

"It means your dad and I will never be back together. It's okay, Raf. He still loves you and I will always be with you. *Always.*"

Rafael stared at her blankly and she started crying. He reached his arm up around her neck and hugged her tightly.

Look at him care for her.

I marveled at how strong he could be at such a scary moment, and not run away. Stronger than many men.

He was just a boy.

I couldn't control myself any longer. I wept where I stood, still keeping my distance. Aila took no notice of me. She didn't know I was there. How could that be?

She closed her eyes and dropped her head. I walked the paved path to the front steps and put my arms out. Rafael stood up, moved down the steps, and melted into my arms. Both of us sobbed and held each other.

It was so wrong and so unfair. This amazing boy deserved better!

"Are you okay, Raf?" I asked.

A steel gaze met me. Though he was so young, something hard was forming in him. I understood he was burying feelings that threatened to overwhelm him. This further fueled my growing anger.

A stirring across the street drew my attention. I flinched and my neck grew stiff with fear. Between the hedges, something was peering at us. It looked like a wolf.

No. It had to be a neighbor's dog. It couldn't be a wolf.

A second look confirmed my worst fears. It was indeed a wolf. It seemed Rafael didn't see the animal.

"What do I do, Benjamin?" he asked.

I stepped back and put my hands on his shoulders, unsure what to say. I couldn't shake my focus away from my anger and the wolf nearby. Hopelessness was taking hold all around me.

I heard the faintest of noises in the yard. It was the willow branches, which were now moving. Leaves began to rustle, and then I felt the chill sweep through me again. With renewed hope—from where I didn't know—I looked into the boy's eyes. His eyes searched mine for answers.

I couldn't show him anger. No, rage couldn't heal what was chasing him.

Healing. That was it. I wanted healing for the boy.

Whatever the breeze was, it stirred me and I spoke with conviction I didn't realize I possessed. I met Rafael's searching eyes. "Raf, I...I love you, buddy. It's okay that you want to fix this, and it's okay to see that you can't. Your mom will be sad and feel a little alone sometimes, but listen to me. You can go play. You can swing in the backyard and play with your trucks. When she gets up to go in the house, tell her you love her, tell her you'll be with her for as long as you live, and go play. It's okay."

 I still ached for the boy but didn't feel so angry anymore. When I looked across the street, there was no sign of the wolf.

CHAPTER TWELVE

After bringing Rafael home to Aila, Scott and Wendy had gone back to Alaska. They set up a basecamp in a valley not far from Blueberry Lake. From there, they ventured out in all directions in search of the rock resembling a wolf. Two weeks passed, with Scott becoming more edgy and frustrated by the day. The search and his desperation were taking a toll on him and on their relationship.

"I wonder if there's a chance you're spending your remaining time searching for something you may never find," Wendy said on one of their hikes. "I wonder if it would be better to just enjoy life. We could be going on dates, and you could be seeing Rafael. He really wants time with you. He loves you, and so do I."

Scott spun around to face her. His nerves were already frayed, and this was more than he could bear. "Don't you dare suggest

I stop. I will never stop! I can't stop! I *have* to find it. I don't want to disappear. You could never understand. You don't get it. My father, my grandfather, my great-grandfather. They all disappeared! And generations before them too!" He clenched his jaw, then slowly drew out the words, "Every...Last...One. I don't want my life to end before it's my time. There's so much I want to do and see and be. Don't you get it? I want to explore the world and realize the fullest version of me. I want to find myself and find my potential." He shook his head. "I will never stop searching. Even if no one else is with me at the end. I won't stop. Ever."

She stepped back, stunned. "Scott, can you not hear yourself?" she said, sounding shaken. "If you're alone at the end, isn't that the same as disappearing from everyone else? From me? From Rafael? You didn't mention me or him as a reason to find the talisman. You want to be the best you. I get that, but sometimes I'm not sure your plans for being you include me or Rafael or anyone else. You already disappeared on Aila. Am I next?"

The words hit him squarely in the chest. How could he admit she was right and yet proceed? In his heart he knew he was chasing his dreams apart from the thought of anyone else being in them. His heart felt like it was searing with pain as he remembered the day he drove away from Aila's house while an almost-three-year-old Rafael was napping.

He had carefully avoided that memory and resented Wendy for bringing it back. How dare she judge him! She didn't understand! He had to leave! Aila's and his paths were heading in different directions. She didn't understand him either, and she just wasn't interested in adventure like he was.

"Until you're faced with something like this, you can't possibly understand," he said.

Wendy really had been there for him, but maybe this is what it would take. Maybe he'd have to find it by himself. Having others with him would slow him down. Once he found it, he could fix everything with her and spend more time with Raf. That would at least make it worth it. It made sense, didn't it? He couldn't drag Rafael or Wendy around the world searching for something he might never find.

He'd find it, and find himself in the journey, then connect with Rafael after. He'd understand when he was older. When he became a man, he would understand it's just one of those things a man does...find himself in a way no one else can do for him.

"Wendy...Wendy, I..."

Tears welled up in her eyes. She'd likely guessed what he was about to say.

"Wendy, I think I'll do better on my own for a while. Besides, you don't deserve to have me grumpy with you all the time. I'm just stressed and frustrated, and it comes out at you. You can go back home and have a nice bed and warm showers and I'll keep searching. Maybe our paths will cross again." He hoped his words would take some of the sting away, but in his heart he knew this was a breakup.

Wendy stared at him incredulously. "I've chased all over the map with you, giving you my best. I've been your helper, companion, friend, and lover. Now you're just discarding me?" She didn't wait for an answer. She picked up her pack and put it on. "Good luck at finding whatever it is you're looking for, Scott. I hope you find it, and I hope it's not too late when you do."

What was that supposed to mean? "Too late?"

"Too late for you to not be alone. Scott...Rafael and some perfect woman are not going to wait for you forever. You may find your 'best self' but find out there's no one to share it with. You better really like yourself, because you may be all you'll have." She turned and walked away.

He opened his mouth to call after her and apologize, then stopped. It was better just to let her go. *For her sake and mine.*

He picked up his backpack, consulted a map and compass, and began walking the opposite direction.

That night he tossed and turned, dreaming awful dreams of being surrounded by wolves in some sort of Northern Pacific rainforest. His feet were chained to the ground, and he had no hope of escape. The wolves were circling closer and closer through thick trees and shrubs.

In his dream, he knew what was happening outside of himself. Though he couldn't see the wolves, he knew what they were thinking and where they were moving. They were coming for him, not to attack or hurt him, but to take him away.

"He'll follow," said an enormous gray wolf with a six-inch scar on his hip. "All we have to do is show him the way." The wolf's hair was thick and luxurious save for the spot with the scar, and he stood five inches taller than all the others and walked with an air of inner confidence. He was clearly the alpha of this pack, and though he was terrifying, Scott found him regal and had the urge to follow him.

"Just let me eat him!" hissed a second wolf, holding his head low and leering at Scott through the trees. This one seemed slightly malnourished yet wiry and strong. He was all muscle, with no fat to speak of, and signs of various fights marred his body. He had a missing nail on his right paw and several bald spots. What fur he still possessed was scraggly and tussled.

This wolf scared Scott more than the first. While it was smaller, it seemed more unpredictable and menacing. Though they were separated by the trees, in his dream Scott could see their leering eyes shining in the moonlight, stirring panic in him.

"Patience," the first wolf commanded. "We'll offer him enough of what he thinks he wants and take everything else from him. All in due time."

To his left, a branch broke under a footstep.

He whirled to see Rafael approaching. "Raf! What are you *doing* here? You've got to get out of here!"

"I came to get these chains off you! We've got to go! The wolves are going the wrong way. I've found a better way."

Scott awoke suddenly at the sound of howling. He sat up, his heart pounding. He had gone to sleep under the stars and was out in the open. Now there were actual wolves nearby. Their unmistakable howling was both magnificent and terrible.

He grabbed a pickaxe he'd packed. Though he'd brought it with the hope of finding the wolf-shaped rock and digging near it, he'd never imagined he'd also need it as a weapon. Fear gripped him as he held the pickaxe at his side and strained his eyes, scanning the rocky fields around him for the wolves.

A nearly full moon gleamed silver in the sky above, illuminating everything below it. Another howl pierced the air to his right and he jumped. About a quarter mile away, four wolves gathered near a large rock. Their eyes glowed in the light of the moon and their fur danced in and out of shadow. Two of the wolves stared at him. He set his feet, bent his knees, and gripped the pickaxe. Adrenaline coursed through his veins.

Then Scott forgot about the wolves. He forgot about Wendy and Rafael and loneliness. His mouth hung open in disbelief. There, where the wolves were gathered, was a large boulder sitting on an incline. At one end it was a foot tall, while the other end stood about ten feet high. It was a plainly shaped boulder except for a key defining feature: at the high end, facing the moon, were two gleaming objects. From this distance it looked like the boulder had two glowing eyes like the wolves, both gazing at the moon.

"A rock that *looks* like a wolf!" he yelled.

At the sound of his voice, all four wolves faced him and he shrank back again. Then, in a show of indifference to this intruder in their space, they headed away from him. Just before they walked off, he could have sworn the largest of them used his head to motion him to come.

It couldn't be. But whatever was going on, he needed to search around that rock.

He rummaged through his pack for his head lamp, then pulled it on. When he clicked the button, the battery was dead. He cursed under his breath, threw it back at the pack, and walked tentatively toward the boulder. Feeling more than a little exposed, he walked cautiously across the open, rocky field, carrying nothing but the pickaxe.

When he arrived at the rock, he approached carefully, still nervous about the wolves. He held the pickaxe with white knuckles, mustering the courage to walk the perimeter of the rock to check for any remaining wolves. After three loops around it, he was convinced the wolves had left.

Now he stood in front of the tall end of the boulder where the two gleaming objects had glinted in the silver moonlight. He stared up at the "face" of the boulder.

"Where are you hiding your secrets, old girl?" he asked. "Probably right under your nose where you can keep watch, I guess."

It was as good a spot to start as any. He lifted the ax, but froze at the top of his swing when he noticed a paw print missing one toenail—just as he had dreamed. He shuddered, then brushed it off as crazy coincidence, or perhaps some sort of cosmic understanding in his subconscious. What if there were powers helping him find the talisman? It wasn't impossible to believe.

He lifted the pickaxe again and drove it into the dirt. His heart raced. He lifted the pickaxe and drove down again. As he progressed, it found more than a few rocks. Prying the rocks free of the earth's grip made for back-breaking, sweaty work despite the cool evening air.

Scott barely knew he was working hard. He was in a trance. Rhythmically, he swung the pickaxe, working at rock and dirt. His adrenaline—triggered first by the wolves—now ran high with anticipation, and it seemed he could do this all night.

A little over an hour after he started, a new noise stopped him. The moon moved behind several clouds as he stared down at the dark earth below him. This noise was not the thud of axe on rock. The clanging of metal on metal had frozen him where he stood. His mind almost wouldn't allow him to believe what he'd heard. Slowly, he released his grip on the pickaxe and dropped it to the ground.

Could it be?

He knelt down and peered into the hole he'd dug, brushing dirt around with his hands to feel for what had made the noise. After a minute, his fingers found what felt like a corner of something. The world felt like everything was moving impossibly fast and yet stopped in this moment. It was almost too much. He straightened and tried to let his eyes adjust in the darkness. On cue, the moon peered from behind the clouds to highlight the dig.

There it was, in the midst of the loosened dirt and remaining rocks attempting to hold their purchase after being disturbed for the first time in many years. The corner of a small tin sat in contrast to the rocks and dirt all around it. It didn't belong. To Scott's eyes it looked as if the earth wanted to spit the tin back up. To cast it away from a place it had no business being.

Unbelievable.

He got down on his knees and grabbed for the pickaxe again. This time he held it by the head and scratched around the tin with the point of the ax, turning it into a precision tool as best he could. His heart raced and he was nearly hyperventilating, though he now worked much slower, taking care not to damage the tin. After a few minutes that felt like ages, a final scratch around the edges caused the tin to move a little.

C'mon, baby. C'mon!

Setting the pickaxe aside, he reached down with both hands, which were now shaking from fatigue and anticipation. Carefully he lifted the tin from the earth to examine it, then attempted to pry the lid off. The tin put up a fight of stubborn refusal to reveal its belongings.

"Ow!" Scott cried, pulling a hand away with a jerk.

He'd bent the fingernail on his right index finger so far back, blood started to appear where it had ripped from the skin.

"You think that would stop me?"

His uninjured hand reached into a pocket and pulled out a multi-tool. Taking care to protect his injured finger, he pried out a flathead screwdriver head and set to work prying the lid off.

As if the tin possessed its own will, it struck one last cruel blow. Scott was caught by surprise when the lid popped off and went through the air before careening over several rocks. He winced and searched for the wolves with each clanging bounce, his eyes darting across the horizon. He barely made even the sound of a breath until he was satisfied there were no wolves. Finally, he returned to the open container. The sun was beginning to transform the sky into dawn and was on the edge of rising but not yet visible.

Silence and stillness surrounded him. There were no more pickaxe strikes or heavy breaths. No wolves. Not even a bird could be heard. It seemed the whole earth held its breath for the sun to call everything to a new day.

A small bird flitted above his head just high enough for its feathers to gleam in the sun that still hid from him. The ground was still gray and dark. Frost covered the rocks and wildflowers.

How nice it must feel to be the first to receive the warm embrace of the sun each morning. If only Rafael were here to see this.

The wildflowers clawing their way up between the rocks around him rustled under a light breeze, and he felt a chill run through him. He thought about closing his eyes and embracing the moment. Perhaps he might learn from the moment itself. Learn to be in the present. Learn to find joy and contentment.

Learn to stay and not disappear.

Curiosity returned his attention to the tin. It looked like there was a folded cloth inside. He delicately put his fingers around it and lifted it, careful to avoid spilling anything that might be held inside. The cloth felt light in his hands as he unrolled it.

He had all but stopped breathing. Every muscle in his body tightened with anticipation. The weight of the cloth, and whatever it held, seemed light enough for a small talisman.

Whoever had put this here was so meticulous. There *had* to be something special here.

Painstakingly slow, he unfurled the cloth and revealed its contents. His head dropped in agonized frustration. All the cloth held was some sort of map—and not a very detailed one at that. He slumped over for a full minute before he could bear to look more closely at what he had found.

"Another freaking clue? Really? That's what you have for me!?" His voice began faintly, then steadily climbed with each word until he was yelling. "You damned wolves! Keep your damned clues!" He stood up, now screaming. "You hear me? Do you hear me you stupid, mangy, flea-ridden sorry excuses?"

He dropped the cloth and the little four-inch-by-four-inch map in it, which separated from the cloth and floated a foot away from him to the rocks and dirt.

I'm not doing it. I'm not going after one more clue. Screw it.

He kicked the tin as hard as he could, then threw a rock at it. It felt good to release years of frustration and disappointment in a fit of rage. He kept throwing rocks at the tin and at the boulder, all the while screaming and cursing at the wolves and the talisman.

Finally, nearly out of breath, he dropped to the ground and sat despondently, head in his hands. How had it come to this? Why was he screaming at wolves? All they wanted was their next meal.

He sat perplexed, wondering why he'd dreamed of the wolves and was now yelling at them. None of it made sense.

More than a decade. He'd been traveling and searching for more than a decade. All the other things he could have been doing. And now....now there was a new clue?

He was certain he didn't have another decade to spare.

"Maybe Wendy had it right," he sighed to the map, which still lay on the ground. Maybe it couldn't be done and he should make the best of what years he had left. Maybe just go be with Rafael.

The breeze suddenly picked up, and the little map rustled where it lay against a rock. He watched it, apathetic to its fate. It broke free and took flight, and he felt himself letting it go.

A growl escaped his chest, surprising him and triggering the anger again. "No! I can't give up now! I'd be giving up on me! I deserve this!"

He jumped to his feet and chased the map, which had flown twenty feet from him, skipping up in the air, floating higher and higher in chaotic patterns like a butterfly. He nearly stumbled on the uneven ground and rocks. The map was almost high enough that he couldn't reach it. With desperate focus on the paper, he mis-stepped on an uneven rock, tripped, and scraped a hole in his pants when he landed hard on his knee. Without hesitation he jumped back up again. He was a starving predator, and this prey could not escape. His very life depended on it.

The breeze grew in strength and lifted the map nearly out of reach. It was now or never. He leaped and grabbed the map out of midair. He had saved it.

He stood panting for breath, reeling from pain in his wrists as a result of the fall. Blood dripped down his leg from his knee.

He didn't know if the map would lead him to the crane talisman. Didn't know if he could even decipher what the map would be trying to tell him. Yet a moment ago he'd been prepared to trade everything he owned to secure it.

The bird flapped above him again, drawing his attention.

"Are you okay?" came a voice behind him.

He startled and wheeled around. The man he'd spoken to on the ridge over two months ago—the one who'd told him to build a hill for Rafael—approached. How in the world had the man found him? But he was in too much pain and too tired from an entire night of digging and worrying about wolves to question the man. He stared at him in disbelief, hunched over, as he continued to catch his breath.

"That was quite a spill," the stranger said. "I have some first-aid gear. Would you like me to take a look at your knee there?"

Scott had to be in the early stages of shock. He couldn't process everything—what he held in his hands, what his dreams about the wolves meant, who the man was, and why he was here. His adrenaline had run high all night, and now he was crashing.

A bed. He just wanted a bed right now. He could just close his eyes for a few minutes.

Maybe he could figure out what the map was after a good nap. The fading of the adrenaline increased the throbbing in his knee and wrists, keeping him awake.

He sat down slowly, affording himself a glance at his knee. It was a mix of slowly coagulating blood, dirt, and small rocks. It looked like a tortured mess and it felt worse. "Sure. Maybe we better look at the knee."

The stranger opened his satchel. "It can be dangerous out here. I've found more than a few wanderers over the years. Some have just twisted an ankle. A few have broken a bone and needed help getting back to safety. Others have been lost." The stranger's face grew sad. "A few have gotten too close to the wolves."

Scott pretended he'd missed a tear rolling down the man's face.

"The people who get hurt the worst are the ones who decide the wolves are safe. The wolves out here are different. They're very clever and they can fool you. Be careful with them. Whatever they do, don't trust them."

Anger and defensiveness stirred in Scott. What did this man know about the wolves anyway? Besides, it wasn't the wolves who made him trip on the rocks. It was his own dumb luck. And anyway, he could fend for himself just fine. "I'm not worried about the wolves. Let them do their thing. I'll be ready if they come for me. I don't mess with them. Live and let live, you know? Anyway, I'll be leaving this area now."

The stranger cleaned out the wound, applied some antibiotic ointment, and bandaged it. "There you go. That should do for dressing until you get back to civilization." He pointed to the southwest. "If you make a beeline that direction, keeping your eyes on the largest hill beyond, you'll avoid the wolves. They tend to stay a little north of there. You can do as you like, but I hate seeing people get hurt out here. Makes me sad every time. Please go that direction. It's safer and there'll be plenty of water along your path."

"Thanks." Whatever skepticism Scott felt about the man, he could see the wisdom being offered him. He had helped with the wound and meeting the wolves right now didn't sound like the greatest idea.

"I think you dropped this." The stranger bent down and picked up the little map from between two small rocks. In his shock, Scott had set it down. The man studied it for a moment and his face grew concerned. "The thing about hunting for treasure is there's always more to find. People who search for treasure to fill their hearts are like wolves searching for an animal to satisfy their hunger. They'll always be hungry again. They'll always need the next meal. More often than not, the treasure hunters end up finding the wolves too. It's one of life's big ironies. The hungry end up as prey. There *is* a better way though."

"Let me just stop you there," Scott interrupted with no attempt to hide the annoyance in his voice. "I don't think you and I share the same views on the wolves. Also, you don't know the first thing about what I'm searching for and why, so I don't think I need your opinions about my life."

If the curt reply bothered the stranger, it didn't register on his face or in his voice. He seemingly brushed off the outburst. "Scott, you deserve to be taken care of. Not just physically, but emotionally. You're worth it. I'm sorry you haven't had enough people in your life to tell you that. You're worth it, and you don't have to be alone."

Who was he to say such things? Anger burned in his belly. Nope. Not here. Not now and not him. He wasn't getting in touch with some "inner child" out here in the wild. He'd put all that behind him for good. Forget that. Whoever this guy was, they were done here. "You don't even know me!" he screamed at the man. "Leave me alone!"

The stranger disappeared.

Wait. Had he been a hallucination brought on by the shock?

The bandage on his knee and the satchel left by his side were both very real. He rubbed his eyes. Then he walked back to his camp to collect his things for the hike out.

The satchel would stay there though. *I don't need him or his help.*

After gathering his gear into his pack, he surveyed the land. As much as the stranger had angered him, there was wisdom in avoiding the wolves so long as he was hurt. Southwest it would be. This course took him back by his dig and the satchel before he would hike onward to leave the wilderness.

He stopped at the satchel and sighed. Perhaps he'd been too harsh with the man. After all, he'd bandaged him, offered free advice, and tried to be helpful. Why was it this man angered him so much? How did he strike such a raw nerve? And why was he defending the wolves though they scared him so much?

The satchel did contain supplies that might be useful. It would be reckless to just leave it here. He picked it up to put it in his pack and noticed a little piece of paper in one pouch. Pulling it out, he read aloud to himself, "There are three things remaining that will never disappear. Faith. Hope. Love. Love is the greatest of these and is the treasure they seek."

Tears formed in his eyes and he choked on a lump in his throat. Hurt threatened to come up from hidden places he'd numbed himself to long ago—feelings he wanted no part of.

He crumpled the paper and tossed it, his resolve to find the talisman stronger than ever. Curiously, the little bird flew low, picked up the paper, and flew off with it.

Not my problem. He walked southwest and never turned back.

CHAPTER THIRTEEN

Clickety-clack, clickety-clack.

The train rocked side to side while the beautiful British Columbia landscape passed by outside the windows. Scott had hiked a day and a half out of the wilderness since he'd found the tin and now had a multi-day train trip to dwell in his thoughts.

His eyelids were perpetually heavy from the cradle-like rocking of the train and the mental and physical exhaustion of the search for the talisman. Most of the journey had been spent sleeping off exhaustion and tending to his knee when the pain woke him. The rest of the time he obsessed over the little map he'd found.

It was never ending. He'd finally found something, and in the end it was really nothing. More riddles and clues. Wolves, wilderness, and a crazy man who wouldn't leave him alone—and what for?

He stared at the map trying to make sense of it, feeling he was getting nowhere. Once again his head began to drop and he patted his face to stay awake.

Wake up. Come on, man, you can figure this out.

On the right side of the map was a land mass, then a body of water in the middle and an island toward the west. The island sat diagonally on the map with its upper tip pointing northwest. Just to the right of the northernmost tip of the island was an illustration of a crane's wings. On the left side were words in an unrecognizable language. All he could do was sit and stare at the words he couldn't translate.

It was all but hopeless.

His fingers traced lines traveling southwest from the tip of the island. After the lines was a smaller island with a circle drawn around it and a small sun shining over it.

Where do you go, little lines? Why?

Whatever it all meant, in spite of his frustrated protests, the more he stared at the map, the more his resolve to figure out the language grew. Someone had to know how to read it.

Throughout his hours alternating between obsessing over the map and fitful sleep, the train was moving him closer to the home he'd rented in Eugene, Oregon. It had been too long since he'd seen Rafael. Now, he would be about an hour's drive from Rafael's town of Corvallis, and Rafael would be visiting him in about a week.

"Rafael," he sighed.

He hadn't seen Raf since he'd taken him home to Aila for school. He missed playing games with him. Missed the little boy's laughter and watching him learn new things. Though he could ask so many questions, sometimes it seemed he wouldn't stop.

A smile creased his face and he didn't feel so tired.

He carefully stowed the map in his pack, closed his eyes, leaned his head against the window, and thought about his upcoming time with Rafael and how to make the boy comfortable when he visited.

―〜―

When he finally arrived in Eugene and made his way to his little house, he was spent. He dropped his backpack on the floor near the front door and walked through the kitchen. The red light on his phone's answering machine flashed, but that could wait. He kicked off his right shoe and then his left, leaving them like breadcrumbs on his way to the bedroom. He didn't bother closing the bedroom door. Just flopped onto his bed face first and fell right to sleep.

He'd only been asleep for a short time when he jolted awake. His eyes searched the room in confusion. Entirely disoriented, and with even the recesses of his mind having obsessed so long on the map and his experience with the wolves and the stranger, he yelled, "Go away! Can't you see I *can't* stop?"

His loud voice startled him to his senses, and he realized the phone was ringing in the kitchen.

"Stupid phone. Shut up," he groaned and dropped his head to the pillow again.

They could leave him a message.

The machine picked up. A familiar voice reopened his eyes.

"Scott, it's Aila."

She didn't sound well.

Bleary-eyed, he turned his head toward the open bedroom door to listen.

"Scott, I hope you're home. I'm in the hospital."

"Hospital?" he muttered. What was going on? And where was Rafael if Aila was in the hospital?

"Rafael is okay," she continued. "He's at some friends' house. Friends from my church. Scott, they say I might be in the hospital a while. I hope you can come get Rafael. If you can call me at Good Samaritan Hospital in Corvallis, I can explain. Or maybe you can just come. They'll let you up to my room. Okay. Goodbye. Call, please. Soon."

She sounded concerned. He and Aila had their differences, and he had decided to pursue life without her, but part of him still cared for her. They did have some good memories. Hearing the frailty and fear in her voice now shook him. He went to the bathroom, splashed his face with cold water, and headed back out to drive to Corvallis.

The map would have to wait.

At the hospital, a receptionist looked up Aila's room. "Let's see. She's in room 516, sir. You can go to the nurses' station there, and they can tell you if she's able to have visitors."

"Thanks." He headed for the elevators.

Multiple knots grabbed at his stomach. What would he find when he got to Aila? Just how sick was she? And how was Rafael taking this?

At the nurses' station, a kind-looking nurse with long gray hair pulled into braids sat looking over a chart. She looked up. "May I help you?" Her voice was gentle.

"I'm here to visit the woman in room 516," Scott said.

"Sure. I'll go check if she's able to receive visitors right now. Who may I tell her is here?"

"My name is Scott. I'm her ex-husband."

The nurse stood and walked down the hall. She had some stiffness in her back and an uneven gait. How many hundreds of thousands of steps must she have taken up and down these halls? He wondered what that felt like. To spend one's life walking up and down the halls of the sick.

His chest tightened. The walls felt closer. Someone coughed in a room near him, and he took a step farther away. He wanted to get back to the wilderness as quickly as he could—with a beer or a nice wildflower tea.

"She can see you now," came the nurse's voice, shaking him from his thoughts. "Right this way."

She had a soothing smile and her eyes sparkled. Though she looked to be in her mid-sixties, there was a brightness in her eyes making her appear younger. Like some kind of joy deep within. He didn't feel joy inside and was sure his eyes showed something other than that. Seriousness, maybe. Possibly pain and pensiveness. Not joy.

As she turned to lead him down the hall, a little cross hanging from a silver chain around her neck glinted in the pale lights of the hospital. It seemed she had her talisman. Maybe that's what helped her work in this hard place and not lose the light in her eyes.

How badly he wanted to be out of this hospital and looking for his own talisman again.

The nurse opened the door to Aila's room and motioned for him to enter.

"Thank you," he said as he passed by.

"I'll give you two some privacy and be back in a few minutes." She disappeared behind the door she pulled closed.

"Scott, you're here." A voice, barely louder than a whisper, came from the bed. "I didn't know if you'd get my message, or if you were even home."

"I'm here."

She looked worse than he'd feared. She had an IV in her arm and several monitors attached to her. Forgotten love crept into his heart as he looked at the hurting woman he'd once shared life with. He fought a grimace, and tried to keep his face from betraying the tension inside. He had one thing to do—find the talisman. He didn't have time for love. He brushed it aside, leaving enough room in his heart for concern.

He sat on the edge of her bed. "What's wrong, Aila?" He swept a bit of hair from her forehead. "Your message worried me."

"I have a bad infection in my leg. If they don't take care of it quickly enough, I could lose the leg. It can get worse from there too." She drew back the bedding.

Her leg was exposed from the knee down, and he put his hand to his mouth. Her lower leg was swollen badly. The skin looked impossibly tight and bright red. The sight nauseated him.

"It's giving me a fever too. Kind of feels like having the flu on top of a broken leg. My leg throbs and keeps me up, but the fever keeps putting me back to sleep. And it burns."

"Lose your leg? I'm sure they can help you, right?" He wasn't sure what he was more worried about. That Aila could lose her leg and "worse," as she had said, or that Rafael could lose Aila. He swallowed. He couln't take care of Raf by himself right now, and what if he disappeared? Rafael couldn't lose both his dad and his mom. "Aila, tell me they can fix this."

She had closed her eyes, but opened them slowly and spoke softly, barely awake. "They have me on strong antibiotics, and they'll remove some fluid if it swells too bad. Scott..." She looked into his eyes, hers now sharply focused. "Scott, I think I'll be okay, but it might be more than a month before I can take care of Raf. Even when they get me home, I'm not sure how much I can be on the leg. I may have to keep it elevated for a while. And they don't know yet if I might need surgery, or how long I'll need to be on the IV. I need you to take Raf for a while. You know how badly he just wants time with you. He gets so filled up when he's with you. Please watch him until I'm well. He needs you right now, Scott. Be his father. Be there for him."

He could feel her conviction. She spoke with authority he didn't know she had. When they were together, he'd found her to be a bit of a pushover. There were times when he'd used this to his advantage, to his remorse. Now she was speaking with power he didn't dare say no to. "Of course he'll stay with me. I'll go get him today if you can tell me where he is. I'll make sure he has a comfortable bed, and we'll go to the store and get the snacks he likes. You just rest and get better. He needs you."

Whatever feelings he did or didn't have for Aila now, he knew one thing beyond any doubt: she was a great mother. She provided comfort, care, and nurturing, balanced with challenge, conviction, and training. Rafael was already demonstrating wisdom beyond his years, and kindness unusual for a child who was not quite eight.

Her hand felt soft as he clasped it. "Aila. Listen to me. You're a wonderful mother. You're doing a great job with Raf. He's so lucky to have you. Seriously. You're doing a fantastic job. You should be proud. Get better. The boy needs you."

Tears streamed down her face, but the fever's fatigue was winning. She closed her eyes and ignored the streaks on her cheeks. Scott brushed them dry with the back of a finger.

"Thank you," she whispered. "Take care of him. He needs you too." Her hand slipped open, letting go of Scott's as she fell asleep.

He still didn't know where Rafael was. He was about to awaken her when he noticed a little note on the bedside table. It read "Adams," then a dash and a phone number followed by another dash and "Rafael." That had to be where he was. He'd call and find out. He spied a pen and notepad on the same table and copied down the number, then stuffed it in his pocket.

He bent down and gave her a light kiss on her forehead, then quietly left and closed the door.

Twenty minutes later he arrived at the Adamses' house, where a kind man with salt-and-pepper hair and a silver beard answered the door. His beard belied his age, which appeared to be mid-forties. Several young children could be heard in various rooms throughout the house.

"Hi, Scott. My name is Gaelen. Please come in," he said with a smile. The man looked like a good father. What was it? Perhaps the gentleness in his eyes.

It would be so reassuring to not worry about disappearing. Maybe that was it.

"Thank you, and thank you for watching Rafael. By the sounds of it, you have a full house already." Scott motioned to the rest of the house.

"We do. My wife, Carys, and I have four children. She's getting Rafael's things together. We were so glad to get your call."

"Aila told me you go to church together. It's so kind of you to take him in."

"That's true. In fact, I'm a pastor at the church."

There was something disarming about Gaelen. Perhaps it was his smile. It was subtle, like the twinkle in his eyes. It should have put Scott at ease. But mistrust and frustration built in him, and he hoped he was hiding it well.

Gaelen must have sensed it. "Is everything ok, Scott?"

"Forgive me, Pastor, but I'll admit, I haven't had great experiences with 'church people.' In any case, I'm just glad you and your wife are so generous."

Gaelen took no offense that Scott could see. "I'm sorry, Scott. That's a shame. And please, call me Gaelen. It's something we talk about at church, caring about our community and people outside our homes and, well, I guess it's good to not just talk about caring. I'm a simple, small-town guy, and where I'm from we'd say, 'Talk never filled anyone's belly or put clothes on their back.' I guess you could say I want to be someone who notices people and helps them when I can. Whatever the reason, you have a wonderful little boy there. He's a joy to have in our house, and my kids like playing with him."

Carys ushered Rafael into the room with a loving hand on his shoulder. She had that same twinkle in her eyes. Why did Scott feel both warmed by the love and kindness in the Adamses' eyes and yet unnerved by it? Something seemed too good to be true, and he didn't trust it all. But that didn't matter now, did it? The boy was here.

"Dad!" Rafael leaped into his arms.

Scott twirled the two of them around the entryway, and Rafael's grin lit the room. Scott set him back down on the ground and took a quick look at him. "Those are cool pajamas, Raf! I didn't know you were into the Arizona Cardinals. I didn't even know you like football. But pajamas at four in the afternoon? Wasn't it a school day today?"

Rafael beamed with excitement. "Mr. Adams came home from work a few days ago with these. I didn't have any pajamas. I mean, I like pajamas and all. It's just Mama hasn't had much money or time to get new ones lately. So I just sleep in T-shirts and underwear. Mr. Adams came home with them one day and gave them to me. They're a cool team, don't you think?"

"He doesn't want to take them off, and I didn't have the heart to not let him wear them to school today," Carys said, a little sheepish but also smiling at Rafael's joy.

Scott looked at Rafael with a small chuckle. "I guess maybe there are some church people who don't just talk, eh, Pastor?"

Gaelen smiled at Rafael. "Scott, do you mind if we speak outside for just a moment? Raf, can you go play with Dan and Beth for a minute?"

Rafael obliged, and the two stepped out to the front porch, where Gaelen closed the door behind him. "Scott," Gaelen began.

Here would come the preaching and the 'hell' talk and telling Scott what's wrong with him. Probably even an ask for money.

"Scott, you have a sweet boy there. Like I said, he's a joy to have around. I'm a little concerned for Aila's health. I spoke with her doctor, and he said this kind of infection can get very serious. I don't mean to scare you—and I'm believing the best for Aila and praying hard for her—but it's just..." He looked back at the door. "Look, I'm going to just shoot straight with you. Small-town guy, you know? I know you've been traveling a lot and haven't been available for Rafael. It's not my place to tell you what to do, and you won't get any preaching from me."

Ha! Well, I'm sure you won't be able to help but preach a little, Preacher.

"Scott, that boy loves you. It's so clear. Every memory he has with you gets talked about constantly. The tape player he has with your rendition of *The Night Before Christmas* gets played until the batteries run out. I know. I already had to buy him new batteries. I just want to encourage you. Whatever place you're in, whatever is going on in your life—know that you matter to him and you have good things to offer him."

He sighed. The eyes weren't twinkly now. They looked mournful, like he was carrying a heavy weight. "Look, I've seen bad fathers and the hurt they cause. You're not a bad father. You're just not present. The thing is that can be even worse, because it's a choice. Now's your chance. I'm confident Rafael will benefit from time with you. Heck, if you ever want to talk about it, you have my phone number. Give me a call. You might be surprised how much us preachers spend time listening and not talking. The good ones do anyway, not that I'm a good one."

There was that smile again. It was disarming, and Scott didn't like that. What's more, something in that line about not being a bad father hit home. He'd convinced himself his search for his identity and for the talisman would ultimately benefit Rafael.

In his heart of hearts, he wanted to be a good father. He just had no idea how. His father and his father's father, and as many generations as he'd heard about before that, didn't teach their kids and disappeared to boot.

However meddling he was, the preacher meant well. "Thanks, Gaelen. I'm sure you're right. About him wanting time with me, I mean. I always enjoy time with him too. He is a good kid. He must get that from Aila. You're right, I haven't been around much."

"*Yet*," Gaelen said, winking this time. "Haven't been around *yet*."

He really does ooze positivity.

The door cracked open and Rafael poked his head out, his two hands holding a duffle bag. "Mrs. Adams gave me some coloring books, crayons, and snacks for our drive!" His arms fought to hold the bag up high enough to keep it from scraping on the ground as he beelined straight for Scott's car. Before getting in, he turned to thank Gaelen and Carys, who was now crying but trying not to show it for Rafael's sake.

He looked down at his shirt again, then looked back up to them. "Thanks again for my pajamas. I love them! And thanks, Mrs. Adams, for not putting mayonnaise on my sandwiches!"

"Mayonnaise?" Scott asked.

Gaelen laughed and explained. Apparently Carys had heard from Rafael's teacher the first day he was with them that he'd spent a good part of lunchtime wiping mayonnaise off his sandwich. She'd made him sandwiches just the way he liked them the rest of the time he was with them. "I asked if we weren't babying the boy a bit, but when a mom like Carys or Aila looks in your eyes and says 'the boy gets whatever food makes him happy,' well, what are us guys to do but say 'yes, dear'? I don't make a habit of arguing with a mother's love."

Scott thanked them both, then got in the car with Rafael.

"Can we play on the swings in Eugene, Dad? I want to jump from them! I always feel like I'm flying when I do."

"Sounds good, Raf," Scott said as he pulled the car out of the driveway.

Gaelen and Carys watched from their porch as the car disappeared around a corner. Carys was now crying openly.

A man in a fishing hat walked with a beautiful orange dog along the sidewalk. "You two were very kind to him."

"Thanks," Gaelen replied, wondering how the man knew about the boy.

The man and the dog stopped in front of the Adamses' house, and he peered down the street where the car had once been. "Sometimes little things for a little one are not little things. In fact, you might say they're *the* thing."

Gaelen squinted, but he wouldn't shoo the man on his way.

"I overheard what the boy was saying to you," the man said, perhaps sensing their curiosity at his knowledge of their situation. "Little things like warm beds and pajamas are the things that change the trajectory of lives. Even change whole communities." He looked up and winked at them as they stood with their arms around each other. "Come on, girl." He and the dog both resumed walking.

When he'd gotten a few houses away, Carys asked, "Who was that?"

"I don't know," Gaelen said. "But he was at the store when I bought the pajamas. I was there for some new shoes for myself, and he pointed the pajamas out to me. Said something about how some kids he knew liked them. I thought it was kind of strange, but now I have to say, that was the moment I had the idea to buy the pajamas for Raf. You could almost say it was his idea."

CHAPTER FOURTEEN

Rafael's face felt the warmth of the sun peeking through the windows in Dad's little farmhouse. On a foam mattress on the living room floor, he contorted and stretched away any remaining sleepiness with a grunt. How long had it been since he'd come here? His little fingers counted it out.

Three sleeps so far. Today was the fourth day.

He smiled at the sun, recounting a great three days. He'd been to the indoor swimming pool, gone for a hike nearby, watched a movie, eaten his favorite snacks, and kicked a soccer ball around a field. And Dad was there for all of it. If only every day was like those.

It should have been perfect, but Mama was still in the hospital. His thoughts kept reaching for her. He hoped he'd hear from her soon. Yesterday there wasn't even so much as a "good night" phone call. The nurse had told Dad her fever was spiking most of the day and she was too weak to speak on the phone.

Footsteps came through the kitchen into the living room. "Good morning, Raf. Time to get dressed, buddy."

The scent of hot oats, peanut butter, and raisins wafted from the kitchen. He took a deep breath and remembered mornings in the little hut at Blueberry Lake.

Sheba and Cinnamon. Wonder how they are?

He looked out the window. What fun it would be to play with them here! Dad lived on some land just outside of town—a great place for dogs to run around. Would Rafael ever even see the dogs again?

"Come on, Raf. We've got to go soon."

He got up. "Where are we going, Dad?"

"I need to do some research. We're going to meet a professor. That's a kind of teacher for adults. She's going to help me, I hope. I'm meeting her at the library. I thought if we meet there, you can look at some books while she and I talk."

"What does she teach?"

"She teaches languages and cultures. A culture is kind of like a group of people. I need her help to figure out something about a language I found. I can't find anyone who knows it, and I need help to understand some words. So we're going to the library."

Rafael thought of trips to the library in Alaska. He loved those drives from the lake, up over the pass. He still thought about sitting at the top of the pass with Dad's arm around him, looking at the lake below, the eagle above, and the sun nearly setting. It was a moment he would always remember, and it made him hope for more of those moments of togetherness. Now he could ask

Dad to check out some books for him and read them to him at home to make memories in this place.

The morning passed quickly. Dad took him to the children's area of the library and gave instructions to stay there while he met with the professor. He enjoyed reading some children's books he found and selected a few he hoped to take home.

Then he found a spot where a woman was reading a book to kids gathered around her on a carpet. He sat and listened to a story about a little boy who could speak with animals and all the adventures he had. He pictured sharing those kinds of adventures with Sheba and Cinnamon and Benjamin.

Benjamin! I should show him my dad's house. I bet he would play with me too.

Yes. It was time to try summoning him. He would do it tomorrow when there was more time and if Dad was too busy to play.

Dad reappeared. "Hi, son. I see you have some books there. Sorry, but I need you to put them back. We're leaving tomorrow, and you won't be able to take them with you."

The smile that had curled Rafael's lips when he was claimed as "son" now disappeared. "Leaving?" Was Mama home? Or were they going somewhere else?

A nearby mother shushed them.

"Come on over this way," Dad whispered.

He had Rafael hand him the books, then he set them on a cart and ushered Rafael outside. Rafael was confused and a little disappointed about putting the books back, but feeling his dad's hand on his shoulder made him happy enough to let it go.

Outside on the library steps, Dad got on one knee and looked into Rafael's eyes. "Raf, I'm looking for something. Something really important."

"Can I help you? That could be fun!"

He sighed. "No." He looked off in the distance a moment. "Raf, I have to go to another city for a little while. I'm hoping to find someone who can help me."

"Didn't the professor help you?"

"Well, yeah, she helped me in a way, but it's like a puzzle I'm putting together. She had one tiny piece, but she pointed me to someone else who can maybe help me with the next piece. It's hard to explain, Raf. I just need you to understand. This is really important. Just something I have to do."

Rafael felt like Dad seemed to retreat. It was hard for his father to keep eye contact. There was some kind of tension covering his face, but from what he wasn't certain. How could he understand things so profound that even adults barely comprehended them? "Can't I please come with you?" he pleaded. "Or can't you at least wait a few more days?"

"Raf, it's something I have to do. I hope I can explain when you're older. Your mom is going to be okay, but she's not going to be able to take care of you for some time and I have to be gone for a while," Dad explained. "I'm going to take you to your grandmother's house."

Rafael barely remembered his grandmother. She lived nearly a thousand miles away on the Southern California coastline. With Dad's travels and Mama's lack of money, there hadn't been opportunities to see her. He knew Mama regularly sent her pictures of him, and he got letters and money from her for his birthdays and Christmas. But that was about it. "How long will I be with her?"

"I'm not sure yet. I'd say it'll be at least a week and maybe a few weeks. Raf, she has a nice house and lives near the beach. And the town she's in is so fun. You're going to love it."

Rafael pursed his lips and stared at his feet. How could driving nearly a thousand miles, then leaving his father, and staying with a near-stranger sound as exciting as splashing in creeks, running with dogs, or going home to a healthy Mama?

IN THE SILENCE OF the fifteen-hour drive over the next two days, Rafael spent most of the time silently staring out the backseat window, clutching Benji while disappearing into his imagination, away from the trucks and cars around them. He wandered around Blueberry Lake, played with Sheba and Cinnamon, talked to Benjamin, revisited the kind stranger, and raced cars down the hill with Dad. When he wasn't thinking about all that, he was walking into Mama's room on early mornings and snuggling his head onto her arm.

Long into the second day's drive, he was woken from a nap by Dad's voice. "Wake up, Raf. We're pulling into Santa Barbara. Look at how beautiful it is here!"

He opened his eyes and wiped the sleep from his face. The ocean was to his right, mountains were to his left, and palm trees grew here and there as the car sped down the freeway. A few minutes later they were driving up a hill, rising above the ocean behind them and into neighborhoods. Eventually they pulled into a steep driveway that took them to the top of the hill.

"Raf, your grandma is kind of old school. She was a little tough when I was a kid. Make sure you say please and thank you. She likes when people are respectful. And don't go breaking things around the house, okay?"

It sounded so ominous. Rafael nodded back, clutching Benji tighter. He didn't follow Dad out of the car.

His door opened and Dad's hand appeared, beckoning him. "Come on out with me. It'll be okay, buddy. You'll like it here."

He barely felt he could make his feet hit the ground outside the car. When they did, it was as though the whole world had gone sunny and fresh. Above, the sky was uninterrupted blue. The air smelled light, and a slight breeze brought hints of the ocean spray from far below. A sweet, crisp aroma woke him up from the lethargy of the many hours in the car. As they neared the front door, the smell became stronger and he noticed, just past the front patio and near the corner of the house, was a large lemon tree with too many lemons on it to count.

Dad opened the front door. "Hello!? We're here!"

"Come on in. I'm just chopping up some vegetables." A woman's voice came from the kitchen on the other side of a partial wall that kept her from view.

Rafael looked around at the entryway and what he could see of the living room beyond. Everything looked like it was carefully arranged. He saw no toys or children's books and noticed a great many things he was liable to break if he touched them.

It was doubtful she had any trucks or swings. It did smell nice here though.

"Come on, son." Dad placed his hand on Rafael's back to move him forward.

Rafael swallowed hard. The air was closing in on him. Exactly who and what would he see around the corner in the kitchen? The sound of the knife chopping vegetables didn't help. A passing thought flashed. Would Benjamin come settle his nerves in this place? He'd only seen Benjamin in Alaska and at home with Mama. He couldn't process the thought before they moved forward and the kitchen and the woman came into full view.

"Rafael, you remember your Grandma Mariel, right?" Dad introduced them.

She looked up from the broccoli and cauliflower she was cutting. Was that sadness in her eyes? Rafael had expected to see meanness or at least grumpiness. Sadness took him by surprise. Sadness wasn't a hard emotion. There was something soft about sadness, and all of Dad's preparation since they'd started the drive had indicated this was a hard woman.

She looked down at Rafael, who quickly averted his eyes when he realized he was staring at her. She set the knife down and wiped her hands on her apron. "Every time I see you, Scott, I swear you look more like him. And now you're off like he was too, aren't you?"

Her eyes changed, and now they made sense. Rafael could see frustration, hurt, and bitterness.

She continued looking at Dad, and her eyes became even harder than before. The veneer of calm was starting to crack. Now felt like a good time to disappear. If only that were possible.

"I just could never understand why he left. If he didn't want me, fine, but to leave the four of you little children? For the life of me, I can't fathom why you're following in his footsteps either. Just what are you thinking? Why would you follow him in this?"

"Not now, Mom," Dad said. "Not around the boy, at least. Look, I found new information. I have to do this. You're not a man. You wouldn't understand."

"You're right. I don't understand," she said, now staring him down.

She turned away from his dad, back to the broccoli and cauliflower. Rafael couldn't see her face. She swept vegetables into a colander, walked to the sink, and began to rinse them. "Well, if you're going to do it, then just do it. I don't have any more goodbyes in me. You know I hate goodbyes."

Dad got down on one knee and put his hands on Rafael's shoulders. "I'm sorry, son. I love you. It's just something I have to do. There's a person in Los Angeles who I think can help me. When I'm done, we'll go to the cabin, okay? I'll teach you to jump off the rocks into the water. I know how much you love to fly through the air." He lowered his voice. "Remember, do as your grandmother says. Just respect her orders and you'll be okay."

Why couldn't Rafael stop his tears? He would learn not to cry someday. This was terrible. Benji hung from his right hand by a carefully clutched ear.

Dad put his arms around him, and Rafael soaked in comfort and warmth, forgetting his fears for a moment. He nearly fell forward when his dad released him to stand and walk to the door.

"Goodbye, Mom. Thanks for taking Raf," he called and closed the door behind him.

Grandma Mariel put her hands on the counter, one of them still holding the knife, and stared out the window above the sink before moving back to the food preparation. "Well, Rafael, you'd better get settled, then. You can put your things in the back bedroom, down the hall. I'm going to finish dinner here." She didn't look at him as she added cheese and cream to the pot with the vegetables.

He should obey right away. So why was he still studying her? She looked hard, yes, but there was something soft there too. Tenderness that wanted to come out but couldn't find its way. Like a flower trying to find the sun from underneath a cement patio. "Okay, Grandma Mariel."

Through the back windows near the kitchen, the early evening sun was shining over the deck outside, which looked down the hill at the valley below. The view would have to wait. He gathered his duffel from the entry.

For a moment the house grew silent. Loneliness bit at his chest and stomach. He missed Mama and Dad. What would these next days or weeks hold? Nervously he carried his bag down the hall. The lights of the hallway were off, and everything was cast in gray shadow as he approached a closed bedroom door at its end. Just before the bedroom, to his right was an open door to a bathroom. The room was painted a bright, happy aqua color and had cheery yellow towels on the towel racks.

The contrast of the bright colors of the room against the gray of the hallway gave a sliver of hope. Maybe he could ask her to get him some bubble bath? That would mean braving the question to a woman who was so serious.

Maybe later.

As his hand reached for the bedroom door, his heart beat in his throat. What was so sad on the other side of the door that it must be closed, and how dark would it be in there? The door creaked on old hinges, heightening his anxiety.

The room came into view, and he sighed, releasing the tension from his shoulders. *This room isn't scary at all!*

There was a small fuzzy area rug that would feel wonderful to bare feet in the morning. Just past the rug was a bed with white linens and a colorful patchwork quilt on it. This couldn't be so bad. Quilts were so cozy!

He approached the bed to drop off the duffel and smelled the freshness of hand-ironed, starched linens. The pillowcase smelled so sweet and clean that he wanted to lay his head down on it right away.

Next to the bed was a little nightstand with a nightlight on it. It was a statuette of a little boy next to a dog. The boy held three balloons—one red, one green, and one yellow. He flicked the switch on, and the brightly colored balloons lit up along with the dog and the boy. He smiled for the first time since he'd arrived at his grandmother's house.

"Benji, look!" he said to his faithful companion. "We have a night light. You won't have to be afraid of the dark. I'll keep the nightlight on for you and we can tell stories. I wonder if Benjamin likes night lights too." He set the dog down on the bed, laying its head on the pillow. "It smells good, doesn't it, boy?"

The nightstand had a drawer. He really shouldn't look, but what was in it? If he was quick, Grandma Mariel wouldn't have to know. He peered through the doorway and back up the hallway.

Still in the kitchen, probably.

He held his breath and pulled the drawer barely open, just enough to look inside. The colorful lights of the balloons cast a glow into the drawer like sunlight through stained glass. Something was in the far corner but it was too dark to make out.

He looked up the hallway once more, and its emptiness offered a chance to catch his breath.

Just a little bit farther.

As delicately as possible, he edged the drawer open. There was a picture frame face down in the drawer. When he picked it up and turned it over, he saw a little boy holding a rope strung up with fish. There were six fish on it, and the boy held the rope up with both hands, using all his muscles to keep the fish from falling to the ground. Next to the boy stood a man with his hand on the boy's shoulder. Both were smiling, but it was the boy's grin that jumped out of the picture and lit up the whole room. He was proud. Proud of his fish, proud of his muscles, proud to be loved by the man with his hand on the boy's shoulder. Rafael smiled back at the boy and the man.

"What are you doing? What do you have there?" a curt voice asked.

He startled and dropped the frame, then watched in horror as it crashed onto the floor, shattering the glass. How had he been so stupid? How had he not heard her coming?

"Don't you know not to go digging around in people's things?" she scolded. "You can't just go looking in everything in this house, Rafael! These are my things, and I'll thank you to leave them alone. Look at that. You've broken it too."

"I'm sorry! I didn't mean it! I'll clean it all up."

She sighed. "Step back. No sense in you cutting yourself on the glass now. What's done is done. Let me go get a broom."

She left him staring at the mess he'd made. If only he could go back five minutes!

She returned with a broom and dustpan and set them down to

pick up the frame. "What is it you were looking at anyway?" she said as she turned the frame over in her hand.

Rafael watched her face closely. Who were the people in the picture? What was the story of the boy, the man, and the fish? There was no way she would tell him now that he'd frustrated her. He saw her cheeks drop and her eyes looked softer again. Maybe it was an opening?

He braved the question. "Who is that little boy?"

Her softening eyes flamed. "Never you mind! This is something I forgot was here, and it should've stayed forgotten. I'm not interested in remembering it." She stormed away, picture in hand.

When she'd passed from sight, he began to tiptoe down the hall. What was he doing? If he was caught now, she might *really* be mad. He heard her pass through the living room to the other end of the house where her suite was. He reached the entry, where he hid behind a wall, then he dared to peek around the wall. In her bedroom, she opened a little box on her dresser and started to place the picture in it.

She paused a moment. It seemed she was thinking about something while she kept the picture in her hand. Then she pulled back and set the picture down on her dresser before replacing the lid to the box. Turning to the window, she looked out and raised a hand to her mouth. Was she crying?

As if against his own will, he stepped from behind the wall and began to walk across the living room.

What was he doing? She'd take away the night light or Benji or something! If she was mad at him for looking at the picture, she'd go crazy if he went to her bedroom without asking! Why couldn't he be walking to his mom's room?

Despite his fears, he couldn't stop his feet from padding across the living room floor. Couldn't get himself to turn around.

He walked right up to her. She was staring out the window at the ocean below, hand still to her mouth, and a tear dropped from her face and landed at her feet. Before she realized he was present he reached her side and put his two little arms out wide. She turned and looked down at him.

This was it. She was going to really yell at him now. What had he done?

She looked at him with soft eyes. Without saying a word, she knelt down and patted his shoulder. It wasn't a hug, but it wasn't yelling either. "Rafael, don't ask me about that picture, okay?"

"Okay."

"Come on. Let's go have dinner." She stood and left the room.

That was it? Just don't ask about the picture? No yelling? He followed close behind, not touching anything. With her back to him, he snuck a quick glance at a small desk on the way out. There, on the desk, was a letter. He couldn't read it well—and didn't have the time to read it without getting caught—but he could see it was signed by Mama. The letter sat in front of a little shoe box with the lid mostly hanging off it. On the front of the shoebox was a label: "Rafael Pictures."

A single picture sat just to the side of the letter. It was nearly identical to the one he'd found. Rafael held a line of fish, struggling with his arms to keep them from dropping to the ground as Dad, grinning widely, had his hand on Rafael's shoulder. They'd just caught rainbow trout in a lake near Blueberry Lake this last summer. Rafael remembered how proud he felt. Proud of his muscles and of catching fish and of being called "son."

Mama must have gotten a copy of the picture from his dad. Or maybe Wendy had been nice enough to send it to her. Then Mama must have sent it to Grandma Mariel. Rafael knew she regularly sent updates and pictures to give her a window into his life.

She'd always told him, "Your grandmother has hurts, but she's a good woman. She's a strong woman. I want her to be in your life and get to watch you, so I send her the letters and the pictures." Mama especially reminded him of this when he didn't feel like smiling for pictures.

Fearful of being caught again, he hurried to the dining table. She brought a plate full of broccoli and cauliflower smothered in cheese sauce with a little bit of meat on the side, set it on the table, and placed a roll beside the plate.

He sat down at the place setting and smiled. "Thank you, Grandma Mariel. I love cheese sauce!"

"You're welcome, Rafael." Her voice sounded warm. But maybe he was just hearing what he wanted to hear? "Your mom told me you like cheese sauce in one of her letters. Your mom is a strong woman, Rafael. She's going to be okay. She's come through so much. Far more than you know. To go through what she's gone through, even since childhood, and to have the strength she's shown to not pass her pain forward to you. She's a strong woman. She'll be okay."

They ate mostly in silence. She seemed to be in thought, and he was unsure what to say. After they both finished, she collected the dishes, washed them, and left them to dry.

"It's almost seven," she said. "Rafael, let's move to the living room for a bit."

She settled into her favorite chair, an old leather armchair with an ottoman, and wrapped a blanket over her legs before turning on the television. "I like to watch my game shows," she said as she watched the TV light up.

Rafael found a spot on the couch near her chair. The couch looked like something from the 1940s. It was covered with tasteful upholstery and seemed like one more thing he might damage, though it was comfortable to sit in. Behind him, a large window revealed the hillside and, a couple miles away, the ocean below. In front of him another room expanded with many windows looking down the hills to the valley and the city of Santa Barbara. It was a beautiful place and, though he was nervous just how hard she might be on him, something about the place set him at ease. "Is it okay if I walk around outside for a minute?" he asked.

"Hmmm," she answered. "So long as you stay right by the house. Don't wander down the driveway to the street. And don't—"

"Touch anything," Rafael finished. "I won't." He thought he saw a wry smile on her face, but that couldn't have been. He went outside before he got in trouble for mouthing off.

After stepping out the front door, he walked down some steps to a flagstone patio with some small palm trees around it. The hilltop ocean air was still as invigorating as when he'd arrived, and there was that fragrant smell again. The lemon tree. As he approached it, the smell of the citrus and the leaves washed over him. He knew the lemons would be bitter to the taste, but their smell was so refreshing and lovely. He gently touched one before remembering he was not to touch anything, and then pulled his hand back.

He left the tree, opened a little gate to the backyard, and walked around the house until he reached the deck off the back where the sun had been shining before Dad left. He sat down on a chair and looked down at the city of Santa Barbara far below and the mountains to the north. The sun had been sinking slowly and now glowed orange against the mountains. The city was embracing the oncoming night, with lights beginning to dot the landscape here and there. He hugged his legs to his chest, thinking of Mama, and hummed one of his favorite songs from church.

He prayed a little prayer that the doctors would fix her quickly and that she might even call him this night. He daydreamed about her surprising him here as he watched the sun slowly set and the city glow more with each passing minute.

A breeze began to rustle the oak and eucalyptus trees covering the hills just beneath him. He didn't know why, but he didn't feel alone anymore. Like someone was with him. The hairs on the back of his neck stood up, and he felt like someone, or something, was there to comfort him.

The door to the deck slid open, bringing his thoughts back. "Do you like ice cream, Rafael?" Grandma Mariel asked.

He looked at her. "It's okay. I don't need ice cream." That was the opposite of what he wanted to say. Ice cream sounded amazing in this unknown place, but he didn't want to make anyone give him anything. It was easier to hide inside his own thoughts if he didn't ask things of people.

"Don't be silly." She waved her hand. "I'll get us each a bowl."

A moment later she returned with two bowls of vanilla ice cream with some chocolate sauce drizzled on it. She handed him a bowl and a spoon and sat in the chair next to him. They sat together as the sun cast its final light over the city and the mountains. The sky to the west seemed lit on fire, and all around was orange. Comforted by the creamy, sweet bites, he looked over at his grandmother.

She sat, staring to the southeast. By now, Dad would be nearing Los Angeles. There was still sadness on her face, but in the orange evening glow, something about her looked inviting and beautiful.

"Grandma Mariel?"

Her cheeks moved, nearly imperceptibly. Had her face softened?

"Yes, dear?" She still stared at the mountains.

"Thank you for letting me stay with you. I like the lemon tree. It smells nice."

"Mmmm. Yes, I like the lemon tree too. It does smell nice, and I like the way lemons can be bitter and still useful. Still refreshing. Maybe we can make some homemade lemonade together tomorrow, dear."

There was that word, "dear." He wanted to be dear to someone right now. Maybe even needed it. He looked at her amid the orange glow and thought that might be what angels look like.

Maybe some angels could be hard on the outside.

CHAPTER FIFTEEN

Night set in as Scott drove Highway 101 toward LA. Stars appeared in the sky above, and he drew a deep breath and sighed slowly. Santa Barbara was one of his favorite places. In spite of their terse interaction today, he and Mariel had a fairly close relationship. He knew she was hurting and frustrated, and tried not to take it too personally.

The road led him away from the ocean, where he wished he could spend the days swimming in the waves, and up into the hills away from Mariel and Rafael.

He sighed again and let his mind wander to childhood memories at the beach. Memories from before his father left his family and disappeared. There had been wonderful times splashing in the ocean with him and feeling so secure. They'd shared a connection to the ocean, he and his father.

The last day he'd seen his father, they'd gone fishing together. He'd clutched the rope that held their abundant catch with his two arms while his father's hand rested on his shoulder. That might have been the best he'd felt his entire life. It was also the day his father left. Emptiness and anger now shrouded those memories.

He turned on the van's radio to distract himself. It wouldn't do to watch his father drive away in that boat again, only to disappear forever. He'd replayed that day far too many times and refused to let it touch him any longer. He found a rock station playing an angry song, turned up the volume, rolled down the windows, sped up the car, and let the wind and the music help him forget.

Still, his heart pulled at him. Couldn't he just turn around, go back, and spend his remaining days with Rafael playing in the ocean and lying on sun-soaked beaches?

No. Whatever it took. It had to be done.

It wouldn't be his heart that led him. Will and determination drove him and would now carry him away from Rafael, Mariel, and the sunny sands. Whatever it took, whatever the cost, he was willing to pay it to ward off the disappearing and buy himself more time.

The anger fueled him. He stared out the windshield, narrowing his focus to the San Fernando Valley far below. The day he and Rafael had been at the library in Eugene, a local linguist had suggested the language on the map might be from a Native tribe in British Columbia and told him of an expert on the peoples of that area who had moved to the LA area. Hopefully he was there, and hopefully he could decipher the map.

Without him, all might be lost.

A week later, Scott awoke on the couch in his friend's apartment in Los Angeles. The cool morning air outside was fresh, and water droplets dotted the windows from a light rain that had passed through.

Through the window, he saw the mountains beyond the city, shrouded by the smog of the valley around him. It had begun to feel like he might be on a fool's errand. He'd scoured the city and met multiple dead ends. Yesterday evening, he'd finally met someone who knew of an anthropologist who had studied the people groups of Vancouver Island.

Hopefully he could help.

Scott showered and dressed and set off on a new day's search. He approached an old university office room in a hallway full of them. The nameplate on the door read "Dr. Driskell Silas, PhD, Professor Emeritus." The creaky office door whined as Scott cautiously stepped in to see an older man with silver hair, small round gold-rimmed glasses, and a scraggly white beard hanging from only his chin. He looked like he hadn't kept up with the times and had never cared to.

"Come in and have a seat," the old man greeted him.

"Thank you so much for meeting me, Professor Silas."

"It's no problem, no problem. You said you might have an old document for me to look at?"

Scott procured the map and set it on the desk.

To his delight and excitement, the anthropologist's face lit up. He obviously recognized the language right away. "This is interesting!" the man said with a look of wonder. "Where did you get this?"

"That's a pretty long story, but I found it up in Alaska."

The man adjusted his glasses at the end of his nose and squinted at the map, then smiled at Scott. "I'll confess I'm mighty curious how you came across it, but never mind that. I couldn't be happier you brought this to me!"

Scott slid to the edge of his seat to listen, hardly able to contain himself.

"I've been studying the people of Vancouver Island most of my life." He paused a moment, intently examining the map. "Firstly, this incomplete piece of land on the right is assuredly mainland Canada. This diagonal-facing island is Vancouver Island."

He adjusted his spectacles and made a twisting shape with his closed mouth and a funny droning sound between thoughts. Scott was so pleased to be getting new information that he was ready to tolerate any number of quirks and eccentricities.

"These words to the left of the island are fascinating. Mmmmm," he droned again in a voice a little more excited than before. "Mmmmm, Nnnnnn, yes. Very interesting, yes." He adjusted his glasses and twisted his mouth again. "'The crane cannot be caught. The wolves guard the way to the remaining island. It can only be reached alone.' Very curious indeed."

"It almost makes sense to me, to be honest," Scott interrupted the man's droning noises. "Like I said, it's a long story, but you could say I've been doing my own research on this topic. I'm confused, though. What is the 'remaining island'? Does that mean anything to you?"

"Ah! Aha! Yes, aha, aha, aha!" The man's eyes never left the map. "Of course, that's it, that's it, that's it. Yes, yes, yes. It's my fault, you see. No, no, no, not the remaining island. I've transposed the order. It's been some time since I've thought about the grammar in this language. Not the remaining island. It's the 'Island of Remaining.' It's the name of an island."

Remaining. Scott ached. To remain was all he wanted in life. To remain and not disappear. Someone in this tribe, long ago, must have known of the curse. He'd never felt so close.

His heart raced, and it took everything he had in him to be patient enough to listen to the man rather than run to the spot on the tip of the island where the crane's wings were drawn.

"Mmmmmm, but...ehhhhh...what is this here? See? See? See? Look at the little island to the southwest. These lines from Vancouver Island lead right to it, and the circle around it. That's very interesting. Very interesting indeed. And the sun shining over it."

"What is it?" Scott asked, trying not to sound impatient.

Get to it, old man. Spit it out!

The old professor adjusted his spectacles again. "Mmmmm...I met a family once. They were part of a long line of people descended from one of the oldest Native nations on the island. The oldest man in the family shared with me a tradition I'd never heard of but which I've always found fascinating. Their family believed the circle had magical powers to ward off death. And they believed people didn't die, rather their spirits disappeared. This family believed the circle could ward off evil powers seeking to disappear the spirit. I wonder...mmmmm."

"What? What is it?"

"This family also believed spirits traveled to a sacred island. The map says 'The crane cannot be caught. The wolves guard the way to the Island of Remaining. It can only be reached alone.' Then the lines lead from this location here." He pointed to the extreme northwest point of Vancouver Island, known as a forbidding and uninhabitable place. "They lead southwest to an island with a circle drawn around it and a sun shining over it. If I had to guess, they may have had a legend about a tropical, sun-soaked island far to the southwest where the spirits could remain."

Scott could hardly believe what he was hearing. A way to remain. It sounded better than he'd even imagined with the talisman. What if it were true? What if, instead of a couple years of stalling the inevitable disappearing, he could find a sunny island to live out his days? His full days. Could there be such a place?

"Of course...of course, this is all just the stuff of legends," the man said, twisting his mouth again. "Mostly tales used to pass long nights trying to keep warm against the rain and snow, and often used for teaching lessons. Thank you for sharing this with me. It's such a fascinating piece." He handed the map back to Scott.

Scott thanked him and excused himself. With the office door closed behind him, he leaned back against the wall, closed his eyes, and clutched the map to his chest.

The Island of Remaining. It sounded amazing.

CHAPTER SIXTEEN

For the next few days, Grandma Mariel and Rafael existed more beside each other than with each other. He learned to stay out of her way and not interfere in her home too much. She grew to tolerate him and give him enough comforts to create some sense of home.

The best part of his days involved walking down the driveway, then up the road to a little park at the end of the street. He would play on the swings and go down the slide for hours. She let him go, as it meant a little quiet time for herself.

Rafael mostly let go of the idea that Grandma Mariel possessed hidden warmth. After the lovely evening on the back deck eating ice cream and watching the sunset, he'd woken up the next day to find she had pulled back from him. She'd transformed from the woman who called him "dear" to one who alternated between silent indifference and harsh chastisement. She ensured he was fed, bathed, and clothed, and that he brushed his teeth, but there were no other warm moments or ice cream and certainly no homemade lemonade. He'd come to generally avoid her, other than when he needed something or when she addressed him.

He'd tried once to get her to talk with him about Mama, but she'd dodged that too, saying it was better not to discuss her while she was still in the hospital. Another time he asked her about his grandfather and quickly decided not to do that again.

"He left me and four children. He disappeared and hasn't been seen since. That's all I have to say about him, and there's no value in your learning about him," she'd said.

Rafael thought back to hearing bits and pieces of a story about disappearing when Dad had explained it to Wendy, though at the time, he'd slipped into sleep and missed most of it. He remembered thinking he'd seen his dad's hand become partly transparent for a moment when he was fixing the van in Alaska.

What was this disappearing they all kept talking about? He didn't want to ask her and have her coldly shut him down again.

Today was the fourth day of playing at the park by himself, and while he enjoyed the park and dwelling in his imagination, it was getting a little monotonous.

"Come, Rafael. We're going to town." Grandma Mariel's voice came from the edge of the playground.

He hadn't noticed her arrival at the park and was caught by surprise. She sounded demanding, and he moved quickly before it might escalate to almost shouting at him. He wasn't sure where they would be going, but he was sure it was something different, so he didn't ask.

They walked silently back to the driveway and up to the car. The only time either of them spoke was when she called to him, "Come on, Rafael! Keep up! Don't dawdle."

She walked quickly, and his little legs were working hard to keep pace. He found himself panting up the steep driveway but didn't dare slow. At this point he was more than a little scared of her and wasn't thinking of glowing angels with soft insides any longer. He kept quiet and did his best to catch up.

They drove down the hill, and to his surprise, she gave him the agenda for the day. "I need to go to drop off some mail, then we'll go get you some new clothes. After that, we'll head to the bank."

None of those sounded fun, but at least she was talking, and the plan promised a change of scenery.

The day passed by quietly and strangely, with his grandmother barely uttering a word to him. He spent the day watching the Spanish roof tiles painting nearly every rooftop red, and the landscaping around the city. When he grew bored, he turned the day into a sort of game. He decided to try to read what she was doing and anticipate, so he could do what she wanted before she asked. If the car stopped in a parking spot, he hurried out. At the post office he found chairs to wait in before she could say, "Go sit over there," and he did the same at the bank. Each time, he Imagined her politely asking him to do whatever it was he was doing and, while the day was boring by the standards of a little boy, Rafael found joy in the bit of togetherness it brought the two of them.

As they left the bank, he decided she wanted him to open the door. He remembered once hearing someone say something about taking time in life to do little things for people, like opening doors or picking up things they'd dropped. He struggled with the door which was just a little heavier than his small arms could manage, and managed to get it open with some effort. Was that a hint of surprise and a smile on her face?

They got back in the car to drive home, or so he thought. On the way home, Grandma Mariel drove near the ocean. She pulled into a parking lot at the marina. Rafael hadn't heard anything on the agenda about the ocean or a marina and sat confused. Should he get out of the car? Should he stay and wait? His chest tightened. He didn't want to be yelled at for not knowing what she wanted.

"We have just one more thing to do, Rafael," she said without looking at him. She reached for her purse and put it over her shoulder as she got out. Rafael felt the stress rising further, not knowing whether to follow.

His door clicked open. "Come on, then," she said, her voice rising a bit. "We don't have all day. Get going, will you?"

He fought back a frown, disappointed with himself for not guessing correctly this time. He stepped out and followed her as she walked at a brisk pace. He scanned and saw a few dozen boats in the marina and a jetty blocking the ocean's waves to create a safe harbor. They passed the boats on their left and a few restaurants and shops on their right as they walked toward the ocean and the jetty.

He tried looking at the boats as they walked but could only half glance at them since he had to look forward to avoid tripping, or bumping into other people. A man and a boy who looked twelve or thirteen were cleaning fish together on the back of their fishing boat. It was a big boat, with a cabin they could sit in and a deck in the back to fish from.

"That would be really cool to fish in the ocean," he said. He shuddered. Why had he said that out loud?

"It's not that great, and you'd probably just get sick anyway and throw up the whole time," she replied. "Come on, let's get this over with. I don't want to be here one more second than I have to. Whole place smells of fish guts, men who haven't showered, and sadness. It's really just awful."

Rafael didn't think it smelled awful at all. The ocean air was fresh. Nearby, the smell of fried, breaded fish wafted out from a restaurant. Even the smell of the bay behind the jetty and of the kelp floating in it didn't bother him. He turned to watch the man and the boy again and found himself bumping into Grandma Mariel and falling to the ground, reaching a hand out just in time to keep his face from hitting the sidewalk.

Now laying on the sidewalk, he turned up his hand to survey the damage. Tiny pebbles stuck into the skin like shot, and there was a little bit of blood on his palm.

If she felt any pity, she didn't show it. "Get up, and for goodness' sake, don't cry. You're fine. Tough it out and get up."

Tears were welling up in his eyes. He looked up at her. She might judge him all the more if he couldn't fight the tears. He sighed with relief that she stood staring away from him down the jetty and didn't see. He stood quickly and wiped his eyes and nose with the sleeves of his T-shirt.

Grandma Mariel stood motionless, still staring at the other end of the jetty roughly a quarter mile away. Rafael looked down the jetty but couldn't see anything of note other than a wave splashing now and then, sending spray onto the walkway.

She clutched her purse, looking down at it, contemplating its contents. Rafael became aware of a shift in their surroundings. The wind changed direction. Her body visibly tensed. The change in the air brought Rafael some new, unknown, invisible fear. What had been invigorating, refreshing crisp sea air was now replaced with foul odors and heaviness. Thoughts of gulls gliding on the breeze were replaced with dark imaginations.

What was going on? He took a half step toward Grandma Mariel. He didn't feel comfortable and safe with her, but she felt infinitely safer than whatever was brooding.

She appeared to be wrestling within herself. Eager to begin walking out on the jetty for the mission she had before her yet desiring never to set a foot on it. The clouds had been gathering and now covered what had been a lovely, brilliant sun. Rafael was nearing panic and decided to run back to the car.

Maybe she'll follow me, and we can leave.

He turned around to take his first step and froze. If he had been panicked about an unknown fear before, he now stood face-to-face with something much more real and far worse than he had even imagined. Just ten feet in front of him, in the middle of the walkway, stood two wolves. Grandma Mariel still stood with her back to the wolves, clutching her purse and gazing down the jetty pensively. She was locked in a debate of competing wills and was entirely unaware of the danger Rafael now faced.

He pictured himself flying up in the air over the wolves and not stopping until he reached the safety of Mama's arms. In her arms he found a strong, safe place where wolves and storms could be forgotten. He remembered nice spring mornings and walking into her bedroom to sleep on her arm. He felt something stirring in him. The thought of Mama and her strength brought newfound courage. He considered sprinting directly past the wolves until he could reach the safety of the car.

The larger of the two wolves looked at Grandma Mariel, then at the other wolf. The smaller wolf looked wiry-thin and mangy, with several bald spots from fights it had been in. To Rafael's astonishment, the larger wolf gave direction to the wiry one. The large wolf nodded toward Grandma Mariel, while maintaining eye contact with the second wolf, who then complied and began walking toward Rafael. But that couldn't be, could it? No, he was sure he'd seen it.

The wiry wolf looked straight into Rafael's eyes and bared his teeth as he took two slow, menacing steps, slinking toward him. He didn't growl, but only stared with piercing eyes which was somehow worse than if he made any sort of noise. Why was he so quiet? A growl, a sniff, something, *anything*, would be better than the silent stalking.

Whatever courage had been gathering in Rafael vanished. He forgot about Mama and spring mornings and didn't even remember Grandma Mariel was standing by him, still deciding whether she would walk out on the jetty or not. He didn't think of the car or flying, or really of anything. As the wolf stared at him now, ice washed through his veins and nausea gripped his stomach. He nearly vomited. He had the sensation his head was empty and he could fall over faint any moment.

A knowing look spread across the wolf's face. He took one more stealthy step toward Rafael. Not even his paw padding on the sidewalk could be heard.

In the midst of wondering how the wolf could be so silent,

Rafael noticed a curious thing. The wolf was missing one nail on his right paw. He could take no more. He broke and gave himself fully to panic. Turning away from the wolves, he sprinted down the jetty. Surely the wolves would chase him, but he couldn't bear to look at them any longer.

The sight of the little boy hurtling himself forward on the jetty's sidewalk must have startled Grandma Mariel, breaking her trance. "Rafael! Stop! Come back here now! *Rafael!*" she screamed.

It was no good. There was no way he was going to turn around toward the wolves. He could hear from the sound of her voice, she had released her indecision and reticence to step a foot on the jetty and was propelling herself forward in pursuit of him.

He reached the end of the jetty, and unless he were to swim, he could go no farther. He feared the wolves had followed him and couldn't bear to turn around. He was sure this would be his end. He wouldn't see Mama, Dad, or Benjamin again. As much as he feared knowing what was behind him, not knowing was even worse. He forced himself to turn, his heart throbbing all the way up in his neck.

It seemed like the act of turning around took agonizing years. When he did finally reach the point where he could see behind him, he saw the speed-walking, perturbed figure of Grandma Mariel approaching out of a mist that now shrouded the rest of the bay and hung over the jetty. He braced for being yelled at and scolded. To his surprise, she walked just past him. He was so shocked he nearly forgot about the wolves.

She made her way to the wall at the end of the jetty where she stopped. She briefly looked out at the ocean and a tear slid from one eye. She wiped it away. Rafael watched her steel herself. To him it looked like any emotion she felt was driven away by her own strength of will.

She pulled a small envelope out of her purse.

What was in there?

She held out the envelope and looked out at the ocean. She looked so strong to him.

Maybe not an angel after all. She was more like the jetty wall.

He was filled with new reverence for her. He wanted to learn how to be as steadfast as a wall that could fight against the sea for ages and not yield. To be hard. So hard, nothing could get in. Not panic, or fear, or hurt.

"I haven't stood here for a long time," she said to Rafael without removing her gaze from the ocean. "The waves. They never stop. They're always reaching their fingers and will never quit until they grasp what they want. No amount of frustration or coming up empty will make them yield. They will always keep seeking, keep trying to grasp and take."

She reached out her arm with the envelope in her hand. He understood now.

She'd come here to give it to the sea. Maybe she wasn't supposed to have it.

He looked at the waves. They kept reaching for the wall, one after the other. There was no end in sight. What were they reaching for? It made him sad. She was right. The ocean kept reaching, over and over, yet never seemed to grasp whatever it was looking for.

The wind shifted again. The misty fog that had covered the jetty behind them slid aside. Rafael looked back where they had come from and could see the larger wolf nodding to the smaller one. Was he giving his approval? Then they walked away. *Were they really ever going to attack me, or did they just want us to come here?*

Maybe they weren't as dangerous as he'd feared? He had an impulse to follow them, but they had disappeared from view. And it would be crazy to follow them.

A single ray of sun pierced through a tiny hole in the clouds above, making its way to Grandma Mariel's face. It drew his eyes back to her illuminated figure. He knew things about her without knowing why he knew, and heard his own words as if they came from some other place or person. "I feel sad for the ocean. To reach for something, or someone, and never to find a hand reaching back."

A tear dripped from her cheek. Her outstretched arm held the envelope past the jetty wall over the water. At any moment, if a wave were big enough, it would grab the envelope and its contents and pull them into the sea.

Rafael persisted. "I don't know what's worse. Reaching for someone who doesn't reach back or reaching for someone who isn't even there."

Steady tears dripped from her face. He felt his mouth pouring out words his heart hadn't found before and which he sensed were for both him and her. Where these words came from he didn't know. Were they really his words at all? It felt like they were given to him. He was channeling wisdom from some unseen source.

"I think reaching for emptiness is worse. At least if someone is there who doesn't reach back, you can hope they'll change their mind. You can reach your hand out again and hope this will be the time they take it and hold it...and you. But when they're just gone...when they leave and aren't even there to be reached, then it's too hurtful to hope." He stared at the ocean's horizon with her. "I know why the waves keep reaching, and I know why people stop."

He watched her steel her face to stop the tears. Her extended hand was now shaking.

She was going to drop the envelope.

"It must be done," she said. Her eyes were unmoving, though her arm continued to shake. What was happening in her, and why couldn't she even give one sideways glance at him?

"Sometimes in life you have to have walls."

Was she talking to him, the envelope, or the sea?

"I don't know how you poked a finger through. Call it a wave splashing. Time to build the wall higher. It won't happen again. It can't happen again."

Still no idea. Was she talking to him or not?

"Rafael, what on earth possessed you to run out here in the first place?" she demanded. "This is *not* a place I want to be, and I definitely don't want to chase little boys around out here."

So she was talking to him. Now he wished it weren't so. If only all those words hadn't spilled out from him. Her hand was still extended over the ocean and shook with what looked like anger. But why did she still hold onto the envelope? "Why are you holding that so long?" he asked, ignoring her question. "What's in it?"

"Never you mind. It's none of your business. Now answer my question! Why did you run out here!" Her voice exploded with impatience and frustration.

This was beyond anything he'd seen from her. But did she really have to ask? Wasn't it obvious? "The wolves scared me, and I wanted to get away from them!"

Her face grew pale. "Wolves?" she asked, looking at him with fear, not anger.

"Didn't you run from them too?" Rafael asked.

"I didn't see them," she said.

How could she not see them?

"Rafael, it's important you tell me exactly what you saw. Please tell me carefully." She sounded concerned, afraid even.

It was unnerving and he spit out unfiltered thoughts. "The big one kind of told the littler one to come get me, and the little one really scared me. I thought he might eat me. I wanted to leave really, really bad and go to the car, but they were in my way. When he showed me his teeth and looked right at me, it scared me so bad, I just ran away. I'm sorry. I was worried they would get me. And, well, it doesn't make sense, but now I kinda feel like they wanted you to come out here and they maybe weren't going to get me."

"Rafael...Rafael, the big one. What did he look like?" She didn't sound as shocked as she should have.

She must know something.

"Ummm. I didn't look at him much. It was the other one that was coming for me. But I did see he had a line on his back-left hip. Like he had a big owie or something before."

"A scar?" she asked.

"Yeah. A scar."

Grandma Mariel's face was usually unreadable and unmoving.

Not now. She looked fearful and broken.

Her outstretched arm lowered slowly back away from the water. She paused, looking at the ocean one more time, raised her arm slightly to reach over the wall again, then slumped her shoulders, dropped her head, and brought the envelope down to her side. She stood silently, and the waiting for her next move was unbearable.

When she finally looked at him again, she had changed. There was understanding and compassion on her face. "Rafael, I'm sorry I was so cross with you the first day when the picture broke. And all the times I've been short with you since then."

What was happening? Wasn't she going to yell at him? He could hardly believe what he was hearing.

"It's not your fault. There's something about that picture you found the first day you were here." She looked back at the ocean. "The last time I stood in this spot…" She bit her lip and drew in a breath of the sea air. "The last time I stood in this spot, your grandfather was leaving me, your dad, and your aunts. I watched him leave in a boat out the mouth of the bay and off into the ocean where he disappeared. That was a terrible day and one you could say I've never recovered from. That picture was taken of him and your dad earlier that same day."

Something big was happening. Something like awe overcame Rafael. He was hearing things long ago buried away.

He nearly startled when he heard a voice like it was inside his head. "Pour out old, bitter water. Make room for fresh new water." He didn't have time to think about it.

"I haven't come here in years. I'm not sure how that picture got in the nightstand, but something has been happening to me since you found it. I...well, I..." She was struggling to get the words out. Would she close herself off again? He reached up a hand.

She looked down at it, then slowly put the envelope in her purse. Rafael's hand hung in the air.

She's wasn't going to take it. She'd put that envelope away to go back to the car, and he'd have to follow behind. He lowered his head to the ground, but kept his arm out with his open hand.

Warmth surrounded his little fingers. His hand was enveloped within hers. He looked up at her and saw softness on her face again. The tiny hole in the clouds had grown. The sun cast its warm glow directly onto the back of her head, making the ocean mist form a halo around her.

"No one has reached a hand to me in years," she said.

A wave broke on the jetty and splashed up over the wall. A spray of water enveloped the two of them and splashed on the sidewalk all around them. Rafael stood shocked and held his free arm out wide in a futile attempt to keep his cold, wet shirt off his skin.

Grandma Mariel looked at him and laughed loudly.

It was the first time he'd seen her laugh and it was contagious. He noticed how wet she was too and began laughing with her. They stood soaked and laughing for almost a full minute. The entire time, they never let go of each other's hand.

When the laughter calmed, she finally said, "Oh my, that's the most laughing I've done in a long time! I was just going to say earlier, I don't know why I've waited this long to remember what it feels like to care about someone. Rafael, I haven't felt some things for a very long time. It can be scary for someone like me to feel certain ways. To let someone past the wall and to take a risk.

But sometimes there are things worth the risk." She smiled at him.

He couldn't quite follow her, but he knew it meant something was better between the two of them.

～

For the remainder of his stay with Grandma Mariel, the two of them came to the jetty every day to walk down to the end and watch the sun set while holding hands. Rafael never grew tired of seeing the evening's glow cover her, nor did he tire of feeling the warmth of her hand on his.

He had been with her nine days. Each of the last three, he'd received calls from Mama, who was recovering, though it would be two weeks before he could return home to her.

The evening of the ninth day, as he watched Grandma Mariel glow, she told him, "This is the last day here, Rafael. Tomorrow we'll go up to the cabin."

The cabin!

He had four favorite places. Mama's bed on Saturday mornings when she wasn't going to work, here on the jetty with Grandma Mariel, the rustic cabin she owned on the American River, near Lake Tahoe, and anywhere Dad was.

"Your dad is joining us part of the time too. He's coming for the first few days, then he has to leave. We'll stay there until I can send you on the bus from Placerville back to your mom."

Amazing! He was getting to go to one of his favorite places, with Dad *and* Grandma Mariel, then go home to Mama. It sounded like a fairy tale. Something about the part where his dad would have to leave felt ominous, but that could be pushed aside for the moment. He was getting so much of what his heart desired. He thought about sitting on granite boulders at the river's side with his grandmother watching the sun set in the river canyon. It sounded perfect.

"Rafael, promise me one thing," she interrupted his thoughts.

"What is it?"

"Whatever you do, don't follow the wolves and don't trust them. The last time a little boy saw those wolves and followed them, his father disappeared." She grew silent.

If only she would go back to laughing and talking about the cabin. Why had she grown serious again?

She held his hand with both of hers and looked at him in the eyes. She didn't look angry, and that at least was good, but something was clearly important. "Then the little boy began disappearing too. Never, *never,* follow those wolves, Rafael. There's something special about you. You don't belong to the wolves."

More disappearing talk? This time a boy? "Who was that boy, Grandma Mariel?"

She sighed. "Your father, Rafael."

CHAPTER SEVENTEEN

Four weeks had passed since I'd seen Rafael. I'd been so busy, I hadn't thought much about him, but as time passed, I began to miss him. Now, with frustrations at work building, and growing malaise at home, I was irritated.

I was tossing fitfully at night, trying to fall asleep. *So the kid just calls me when he wants, and that's that? Well, what about what I want? He's not going to just use me like that!* Why was I thinking about a character in my dreams as someone I was annoyed with in real life? It made me all the more upset with myself and my situation. "Hmph," I growled.

"What's wrong, baby?" Krynn asked.

I didn't feel like explaining, so I offered her a misdirect. "I'm just annoyed with some of the decisions people are making at work and how a few leaders are making my life miserable."

There was enough truth in it that I felt she wouldn't suspect any thoughts of my dream world.

"Sorry, baby. You know we all think you're awesome, and maybe you can get a different job someday. I'm so sorry they don't treat you like you deserve. For now, let me give you a scalp rub."

"You know I'll never say no to that." She began running her fingers through my hair as I lay silent beside her. I could feel tension being let go and my body and mind relaxing.

We'd been married over twenty years, and I could read her. I knew she'd begun to feel a little uneasy about me lately. As far as I could tell, she wasn't yet to the point of fear or worry, but she sensed something seemed to be growing. Like a gathering thunderstorm, where the sky begins growing dark and the air changes pressure and temperature. She could feel the gray gathering over and around me.

"I wish I could fix whatever is going on for you. I love you so much. How can I help?"

"I'm fine. I'll be fine. I just have to keep plowing through and get to the other side of all this. Sorry, I know I'm not happy as often these days. I just don't love my work. I'll get better. I'm still the guy who loves you."

With my back turned to her as she scratched my head, I didn't see her face, but a sudden silence warned me she was probably crying. I knew her well enough to know I'd just found a nerve.

"There's no one who knows me like you do, Krynnie. You're still the girl I love and you're beautiful. You've never stopped being beautiful to me." My heart grew in love for her as I said the words. I meant them, and while they felt good to her to hear, they felt good to me to say too. A reminder of the woman who had walked through years with me and journeyed through good and hard things together at my side.

"I needed to hear that," she said, now more than a little teary.

I rolled over in the bed to face her, as I held her head in my hands. "You are so beautiful." I stared into her eyes.

"I don't feel beautiful. I don't know why you're pulling away, but I doubt myself and wonder if I'm part of whatever is causing it. Part of the problem."

"You are the answers in my life, not the problems!" I embraced her and we expressed love for one another more deeply than either of us could remember for a long time.

Afterward, we fell asleep in each other's arms, her head resting on my chest. We drifted into the deep sleep of confident lovers, having been reminded we still carried a flame for each other.

Shortly after falling asleep, I felt warm air covering me and noticed it was growing bright behind my closed eyelids. The sound of water rushing over boulders and rocks swelled in my ears. A sweet smell entered my nostrils and was so fragrant, it carried joy into me. A wave of relaxation and peace rolled throughout my body, and I slowly opened my eyes and had to squint and shade them with one hand.

As my eyes adjusted, I first noticed I was sitting on a sunbaked boulder with the clear water of a river running by. I turned to find a rock-and-mortar sea wall a few feet behind me, and beyond that, a small dirt footpath in front of a rustic cabin. Towering pines stood over the path. That's where the smell was coming from! I knew I could sit with the sounds of the river and the smell of the trees and be content not to move. Here in this place, I felt complete. There was no desire for entertainment or distractions from grayness. Just sun and water and sugar pines, and those were life-affirming.

A sound caused me to swivel my head back to the right. After the boulders around me, some river sand led down to a small pool, barely more than ankle deep, where the river spilled a little water to the side and made a calm wading area. There in the water, a little boy stood trying to skip rocks.

I cleared my throat. "Ahem."

"Do you know how to skip rocks, Benjamin? I think I need some help." He didn't even look at me.

Annoyance returned. How quickly I had transitioned from contentment to frustration! If only I knew how to hold onto peace. I'd have to spend more time on sunbaked rocks by rivers and keep working on my mental state. But that would have to come another day.

So why *was* I so grumpy? First, I didn't like that Rafael was continuing to act as though I was at the whim of his beck and call, and second, that he didn't even acknowledge me or say hello but just asked about skipping rocks. How could he ask me nonchalantly, as if nothing extraordinary was happening? As though I hadn't just been plucked from my bed to appear on a warm boulder by the river.

"I'm not the greatest at skipping rocks. For some reason I can't quite get my elbow right and the dumb things just keep going *sploosh* into the water."

I closed my eyes and took in a deep, calming breath of the sugar-pine and river air to let my frustrations melt away for a moment. I sighed, stood, and walked down to the little pool, where I removed my shoes and socks and rolled up my pants.

Here I was stepping into water with this little boy again. He really did have some kind of magic over me.

I laughed as I waded into the water. "Well, Raf, first off, you need smoother rocks. Try to find little round ones that are circle or oval shaped and that are smooth on both sides if you can."

He held up a misshapen rock. "Is this one smooth, Benjamin?"

"Not really, buddy. Hang on a sec and I'll help you find some."

I stooped over and peered through the water for good rocks. Little golden flecks that our feet had disturbed shimmered and sparkled in the sunlight.

"Is this stuff gold, Benjamin? Should we collect it? I could buy some really cool toys!"

"No, buddy, this is fool's gold. It's called pyrite. It's really cool looking but it's not gold." I plunged my hand down into the river and picked up a few rocks. "Here, buddy. See these?" I held four smooth skipping stones in my outstretched hand. "That's step one—find good rocks. Now let me show you how to throw them. First, you stand sideways to where you want to throw."

I demonstrated how to stand, throw, and release the rock. He stood enrapt, soaking it all in. After explaining all the mechanics, I told him to watch me.

I crouched down, brought my arm back, and snapped with power from my elbow to my wrist. My forefinger released the stone, sending it spinning before it skipped across the river, then careened off a boulder sticking its head above the water, finally splashing down into the river again and disappearing.

"Wow!" Rafael exclaimed.

"If you practice a lot, you can do it too, buddy. Here, you can have the rest of these rocks."

Rafael took one of the stones and tried his best to copy what he'd seen. The rock skipped once and he leaped into the air, squealing. "I did it! I did it! Benjamin, did you see that? I did it!"

"That was great, Raf!" I smiled at him. Seeing the expressions of pure joy from the boy gave me comfort. *I really do care about this little boy. Who is he?*

He threw a few more, getting some of them to skip.

"You're doing great! If the water was calmer, like a lake or a pond, we could skip these even better."

"I know a place where the water is calm, Benjamin. Want to go there? It's one of my favorite places and it's just down the river. We can walk down the path to get there. Actually, can we hop on rocks down the river to get there instead of taking the path? I love hopping rocks. I like looking ahead and figuring out where I'm going to step before I get there. I'm really good at it!"

I grinned. He was like a little puppy. How could I say no? "Sure, bud, we can do that. Lead the way."

"Okay! First we have to go down the path a little bit. Follow me." He was walking up toward the path, past where I had sat on the boulders, before he finished.

Together, we walked down toward a bridge allowing entrance from the highway to this side of the river. After a bit, we got to an area where the river ran wider and shallower with some boulders peering up above the water at the sun. He turned from the trail, picking his way back to the river, where he hopped on and off seemingly every boulder, gracefully shifting direction, winding down the river.

I followed suit. It felt therapeutic. The focus of anticipating each foot-strike and next hop pushed all thoughts of my world and the disappointments of life away. The monotony of landing and leaping, landing and leaping, was meditative. I paused on a larger rock and watched Rafael. He looked like a small forest sprite leaping about in the sun, with the gurgling water all around.

"Come on, Benjamin!" he called. "It's not much farther!"

I just smiled and watched. It wasn't really him I was frustrated with, was it? I was disappointed I didn't feel joy more often, and didn't feel the power to fix that. How could I blame him for that? I couldn't stay in that thought. The boy was getting farther away and I needed to catch up. "I'm coming!"

After a few minutes we came to where the river became faster and deeper with larger rapids. I could see there was one final rapid ahead, where the river was pinched between two gigantic boulders standing like sentries. I imagined they'd been placed there to guard something special. A little past the rapid, I saw the river ran quickly but gently. A rock the size of a house blocked me from seeing what lay beyond.

Rafael had hopped to the far side of the river and was now moving about on rocks at its edge. I followed until we got to the house-sized boulder. He scampered up its diagonally laying face up to the peak, which was shaped a little like the bough of a great ship. I caught up to him at the peak and could now see why he loved it here.

Below and to my left, I could see the quickly running river flowed over massive, flat-topped boulders, then dropped off into a twenty-foot-deep pool. Like a great amphitheater, all the boulders and rock walls spread out, creating a large swimming hole. It was at least sixty feet across and ninety feet from beginning to end. At the end, the pool gently spilled over a shallow, natural damn before heading down in small rapids again. There were little beaches of pebbles and river sand to get to at one end, and across the water from the rock I stood on, a twenty-foot cliff face rose above the water to a steep hillside covered in plant life.

Maybe I could absorb some peace from this place. I had just closed my eyes when a screaming Rafael went airborne next to me. "Woohoo!"

He was all arms and legs, flailing through the air in joyful movement. He disappeared into the water with a splash, then quickly resurfaced and swam back to shore. "Try it, Benjamin! The water feels great, and when you're flying through the air, it feels amazing!"

Flying. He had told me about a curse and men needing to learn to fly. Of course, I didn't believe. What a silly idea! But I'd entertained the boy enough to listen without challenging him. So why did I feel sadness overcome me like a great emptiness? I missed Scott on Rafael's behalf. But there was something else. My dad too. He had left when I was young.

Something was filling my chest, and it was so deep it haunted me. I froze. What was happening? Tears began to form. I couldn't start openly weeping here in front of this boy.

Across the river, up on the cliffside, something stirred. Had a wolf passed from shadow to sunlight and back into shadow again between the bushes and trees? There weren't wolves in these parts. My eyes were just playing tricks on me.

Though I convinced myself of these truths, my blood ran cold and I became fearful. I was scared of the wolf, or my imagination. Scared of the height I was now very aware of, and the drop to the water. Scared of losing control over my emotions. Scared for

Rafael, who I worried might soon be fatherless if the curse were true. Even scared the water might be cold. I would turn and walk back down the rock. I could give Rafael an excuse and maybe just go back to skipping rocks.

Across the river, wind blew through the underbrush where I'd seen or imagined the wolf. It swirled, picking up dead leaves, pine needles, and dirt, creating a mini tornado. Through the debris, I couldn't clearly make out what I saw. Had something run away?

No. Just my imagination.

The wind moved all the swirling debris off the cliffside into the air above the river, still spinning around, then whisked it down the river until it was out of sight.

Above me, the pines bent and bowed in the wind. I thought of the boulder sentries standing guard at the river. It was as if the boulders and the bowing trees were greeting someone or something special today.

Then I heard a whisper so quiet it seemed it came from inside me: "Take the leap. I'll catch you."

A chill rushed through me, but I wasn't giving in. *I'm not going to jump. I don't want to jump, and I don't need to jump. I'm fine. I just need to relax. I don't need this. I'm sure I'll wake up soon. I'll just walk down and keep Rafael company until I wake up.*

I steeled my will, summoning what stubbornness I could find.

I ducked at a whooshing noise, just before a crane flew right by me. It glided with wings spread wide, floating silently and swiftly to the cliff across the river, where it spread its wings impossibly wide and alighted. It looked at me and I at it. I couldn't look away, unable to break the gaze of the crane. Then I heard the whisper again. "Leap. Let go."

"Come on, Benjamin!" Rafael yelled again. "It's so—"

Before he finished his sentence, a surge of power rose within me. I pressed my feet down onto the rock, bent my knees, and leaped forward, reaching one leg far out while exploding off the other.

I felt like a damn broke and a mountainous rush of water released from within me. I let go of sadness, let go of frustration. I said goodbye to doubt and fear. I set down baggage and pain. I floated, as if everything hard and sad and dark I carried was cast away from me.

A grin spread across my face, making Rafael giggle. I spread my arms wide and everything around me slowed. A breeze pushed under my outstretched arms like nothing I'd ever felt. My lungs filled deeply with the sugar-pine and river air. I was completely weightless.

I closed my eyes, stretched out my arms, and turned my face and palms up to the sun. I might as well have been flying.

The next thing I knew, with eyes still closed and arms out, I was enveloped by water. It turned out to be cold, but even this was good. It refreshed me and awakened my senses. I swam upward, and as my head broke through the surface, I felt new, clean, and fresh. I felt lighter.

"Benjamin! You looked like you know how to fly!" Rafael yelled as I swam up to him. "Doesn't it feel great?" The little boy's face beamed.

I beamed right back at him and tussled his wet hair. "It's like nothing I could even explain, Raf. It's amazing! I see why you love this place."

We stood, chilled a bit by the air evaporating the water on

us. I now realized I'd jumped in the water fully clothed, but I didn't care.

We each found ourselves a smooth boulder and laid stomach down, arms spread to warm ourselves with the heat the rocks had absorbed from the sun.

I lay embracing a warm round boulder, drying myself with the sun on my back and still feeling the freshness the river had given me. I smiled with my eyes closed. A peace I hadn't known in a long time covered me. We lay there long enough that I had nearly dozed off when I heard Rafael collecting rocks.

"Whatcha doing, Raf?" I called sleepily.

"Just getting some rocks for later." His pockets were nearly overflowing with rocks and the elastic of his swim shorts was barely winning the fight against their weight.

In spite of the peace I felt, my mind returned to the creature I'd seen. It couldn't have been a wolf, right? There weren't any around here. Still, it had me unsettled. "Raf, should we walk back to your cabin soon?"

"Sure! I'm getting pretty hungry anyway."

We walked back up the path rather than hopping rocks again, passing a few other cabins spread out now and then. When we passed the point where the bridge crossed over from the main road to this peaceful oasis, Rafael turned and crossed a small field of dried boulders serving as markers for the high waters of last spring's snowmelt. I followed him to the edge of the river, which flowed deeper under the bridge.

"Sometimes I like to come fish at this spot with my dad."

I looked down at the boy who was staring up at the far side of the bridge where sporadic traffic went by on the road. I had watched his face fall when he spoke of Scott. As it had been for me, the peace of the river was proving hard for him to hold. "He's not here right now, is he?"

He stared at the entrance to the bridge. "No. Just me and my grandma." To my surprise, he spilled out the rocks from his pockets into the river.

Why would he simply dump them out after he'd spent time collecting them for skipping? I noticed a smooth stone near his feet, and old habits took over. I picked it up, curled my right index finger around it, bent my knees, and released it perfectly. The stone spun through the air, then kissed the river gently as it glided again and again before reaching the far side of the river.

Bending over, I ran my fingers over the rocks around my feet, now and then finding one I kept in my left hand while my right hand kept probing. Rafael mimicked me. We were both bent at the waist, searching among the rocks like two people looking for a lost item. A diamond ring, a gold earring, or a family heirloom. Something small and valuable. Hard to find, but worth the effort—the type of thing someone would search for even into the dark of the evening. Without a word, we each took turns standing and skipping rocks we found, then continuing the search for more.

Rafael got one stone to skip four times, a new record for him. Without pausing to celebrate, he bent down to look for the next one again. I felt the heaviness of this place and this moment and continued along in silence.

"He won't find what it is he's looking for today. But he *is* getting pretty good at skipping stones now, isn't he?" The voice behind me broke the silence, startling me.

It was a voice I'd longed to hear. I whipped around to see the stranger standing a few feet behind us on the rocks. "I've been wondering if I'd see you again."

Rafael continued looking for rocks.

"Raf, look who's here!"

"He can't hear me right now, only you can. In fact, he can't hear *you* right now either," the stranger explained.

What? I waved at Rafael, but there was no response. "Wait, he doesn't know I'm here? We were just talking!"

"He's in a place of deep sadness. He knows you're with him, and that helps, but he can only see one thing right now."

Crushing sadness grabbed my chest, and I didn't want to know more. *Don't ask, don't ask, don't ask.* But I knew it was no use. I sighed and braced myself. "What's that?"

The stranger reached two fingers toward my face.

I jerked back. "What are you doing?"

"Trust me."

Warmth passed through me and I felt the goosebumps again. I stepped toward him. "Okay."

He touched my eyelids. My head swirled. Why was he here? Why was I letting him do this? I could barely process what was happening before he pulled his hand back.

When I opened my eyes, I was facing away from the river, back across the field of boulders, and toward the dirt road leading up to the bridge. The sound of skipping rocks told me Rafael was still behind me. In front of me, I saw another little boy with his arm reached out and his little hand clasped in a man's hand. *Wait, that's Rafael and that must be Scott!* I turned and saw Rafael still behind me. But how could there be two?

"It's a mirage, isn't it? A vision."

"This place is wonderful," the man answered. "It's beautiful and it fills the soul to be here. There's peace here. Unfortunately, even a place as lovely as this can't keep sadness away sometimes. You're watching the way his day ended yesterday."

I blinked several times and did another double take of the two boys before focusing on the figures walking slowly up the road. Rafael seemed to take the smallest steps he could. He looked a little ahead to where a car was parked, waiting for its driver. Then I realized I could feel the boy's feelings and hear his thoughts. "Scott is leaving," I said, with a painful lump in my throat and stinging in my chest.

The two figures walked quietly down the road toward the car while I continued feeling Rafael's heart and thoughts. I knew everything.

It was unbearable.

Scott had said his goodbyes to Mariel, but the boy wasn't ready to let go. He'd walked the path with Scott a quarter mile from the cabin, holding his hand the whole way. A few more steps together. A clinging to connection, to togetherness, to stalling a dreaded goodbye.

A paved driveway rose up from the dirt road toward the bridge where the car was parked, and here they paused. Behind them was a simple dirt parking lot and then a path to peace. Next to them a beautiful, clear river babbling over rocks. Ahead of them the bridge to the other side. To the highway and leaving.

They hugged and the boy cried. Scott had to go. He let go of Rafael and walked up to the car waiting for him on the bridge. He opened the gate used to keep this side private, then stepped into the car to drive it through the gate, before closing it again.

Slowly he drove across the bridge, before turning onto the highway, disappearing from view, and leaving this magical place and Rafael behind.

The Rafael on the road stared at the river a while, then walked toward me and the rock-skipping boy. He stood right next to today's Rafael and began picking up rocks to skip but failed every attempt.

I could feel every heart-wrenching feeling. The sadness and longing for Scott to return. It felt like reaching a hand toward emptiness. *Make it stop!*

I looked up the river in the direction of the cabin and listened to the sounds of the water over the rocks. Yesterday's Rafael and I both took a deep breath of the sugar-pine air at the same time. It was still lovely, and it helped, but something wasn't complete anymore.

"Scott is leaving. Rafael doesn't know when he'll see him again, and he'll go home to Aila soon. This could be goodbye for a very long time," the stranger explained.

I felt a sense of déjà vu. Like I'd experienced this before. I was more upset than ever. I was cracking. Now there were dreams I remembered as though they were real experiences, hallucinations of wolves, whispers in my head, visions of past events, and feeling someone else's feelings and thoughts. Was I slipping into a mental breakdown? I could no longer take it.

"Is any of this real?"

The irony that I was asking a man in a dream if anything I was experiencing was real was not lost on me. Yet I felt like I might trust this man. Maybe trust him from the depths of my being. Maybe even trust him with my life.

"What do you say, Benjamin?"

It all came spilling out. "I'm not sure of too much right now. I don't know who this little boy is, why he keeps calling on me, or what my connection is to him. I don't know why I care about him and think about him even when I'm with my family. I don't know why I feel so heavy in my real life all the time. I don't know how long Krynn will put up with me being this way. I don't know if I can keep working in that soul-sucking place. I don't know..." I paused and looked at him, my face surely betraying uncertainty and fear.

"It's okay, Benjamin," he said gently. "You can say it. I've heard it before."

"I don't know if you're real."

I thought it would feel good to say, but instead sadness plunged even deeper within. Then I turned and saw a wolf on the other side of the river, walking near the entrance to the bridge. This time there was no mistaking it. An oversized wolf with a large scar on its left hip glared at me as it paced back and forth, its head low and shoulders hunched up. The sun had sunk behind the trees down the river and the rocks were all growing cool and gray in the dim light of dusk.

The boys! What would happen if darkness set in before they were back at the cabin, with the wolf prowling nearby?

"Everyone I meet has to decide at some point whether they think I'm real or not. Not just whether I exist."

Did he not see the wolf?

"Deciding if I exist is the easy part. When the wind moves the trees, you see it, you feel it, and you accept it's there. That's different from harnessing the power of the wind or following its direction. You can see me here, before you. Some part of you knows already. The bigger decision is whether you believe what I have to offer you is real."

I wasn't sure what to think. So far, I'd thought what the man had to offer was safety and comfort for Rafael. I'd seen it as my job to convince both the man and Scott to help Rafael. Maybe even get the man to help Scott stop leaving. It hit me. I'd looked forward to seeing the man as much or maybe more than Rafael. Why?

I remembered the first time I sat on the big boulder at Blueberry Lake and the way everything around the lake, even the lake itself, had shivered when the man appeared. I'd felt it myself. I remembered how, each time the man had showed up, I'd found myself feeling joy and wanting to learn more about this mysterious stranger.

I'd wanted some kind of help and support from this man, and I *hated* wanting. In my life, wanting things from others usually meant being let down. I should just tell him to go away. To end this whole charade. I could just say "I don't believe in you. I don't want you. I don't need you" and be done with it.

Instead I spoke a truth, surprising even myself. "Yes. Yes, I believe you're real. And yes, I believe you have good things. Real things to offer. Real for Rafael, and for Scott, and...and for me."

"But?"

"But I'm not sure how much I trust you—yet, anyway. I'm not saying I won't. It's just that I don't really know you." It wasn't like me to be so vulnerable, but the way he could seemingly read my thoughts was disarming

"It's okay, Benjamin. First, know this. No matter what you believe about me, I'm here and I will always want to help him."

He pointed at Rafael and smiled at the oblivious boy, then he looked into my eyes. "And you."

I felt so cared for. It was foreign—something I wasn't prepared for. It was the feeling of a father's love—of being loved by a good father. I wanted to accept it with abandon. To pry my heart wide open and let this feeling of love fill me. To reach my hand out to the stranger. So why was I afraid and unable to do so. I grew angry at myself and my fears.

"I know you don't understand yet, but you will. You are valuable to me. You—and he—are priceless treasures, and I'm the type of person who would search the rocks all day and through the night if I lost something of value to me. How about this one simple request? Will you trust me right now, this one time, in this moment? Count on me to deal with that wolf up there?"

So he *did* see it.

"Trust me to keep you two safe. Can you do that?"

I remembered the moment on the boulder before I jumped, when I heard the whisper. "Leap. Let go," it had said. I remembered the feeling of flying through the air. The feeling of release and of soaring. I closed my eyes again. "Yes. Okay."

When I opened my eyes, he was gone. Yesterday's Rafael took a step toward his current self and the two formed together into one. He looked up at me. *He can see me again.* I knew the look on his face. It was one of heaviness.

Evening was setting in and it was getting darker. I looked across the bridge and the wolf was still there, perhaps biding his time until the darkness covered everything. I thought of running with Rafael back to the cabin, then remembered the man asking me to trust. "Raf." I put a hand on one of his shoulders. "I'm sorry your dad had to leave. I understand. I didn't have my dad around either. It's hard. I'd like to tell you the pain goes away, but it doesn't. At least not that easily. But I can tell you, the best thing you can do is let it go as much as you can. Just let it go."

The words rang hollow. I'd never figured out how to let it go, yet I was telling him to do so. Until the moment on the boulder earlier, I'd felt the weight of pain my whole life. I knew what it was to reach and to find no hand reaching back. Even that moment of release, flying over the river, now felt like it wasn't lasting. I wished I could go jump off the boulder to feel the lightness again.

Rafael bent down and picked up another rock.

Worry closed in around me. "Raf, what are you doing? Don't you see the wolf up there?" I pointed.

"What wolf?" He looked right at it but seemed to not see it.

I stood perplexed. *He doesn't even see it! This little boy doesn't even know danger is all around him!* "Never mind, buddy. It's okay." I hoped I sounded reassuring, though I didn't believe my own words.

He shrugged. "Benjamin, do you know why I throw all these rocks?"

"I just figured you liked it and maybe it was relaxing and fun, I guess."

"Whenever I throw one of these,"—he released a rock that skipped twice before dropping into the water, then picked up another—"I picture things I'm sad or mad about." Another rock was sent skipping and he bent to search for more. As he spoke, he kept repeating the process. "And when it goes into the water, I picture the river takes the sad things away. And when they go away, I also picture forgiving anyone that gave me the sadness. That's why I put all those rocks in my pockets. I needed a lot of rocks today. I don't want to keep the sad stuff and the mad stuff in me. I would be too heavy to run or to jump in the air and fly if I had all those rocks with me."

The little boy never ceased to amaze. "You are wise beyond your years, little man. In fact..." I walked a few steps back and grabbed the biggest rock I felt I could carry, wobbling a little under the weight. "Should we do it?"

Rafael looked at the big rock I held. He figured it out quickly. "That's gonna splash *really* big! We'll get all wet. Do it! Do it!"

"Okay!" I pictured all the times my own father had missed birthdays, sports events, homework, illnesses, bullies, and learning how to shave.

With a loud grunt I pushed the great rock as high into the air as I could, releasing it like a shot-put throw. As the rock plunged into the river, a massive wall of water appeared more than ten feet tall, moving toward us both and masking all behind it. The water fell over our heads and we both laughed deep-throated, loud, body-shaking, belly laughs. I grinned nearly as widely as I had when I'd leaped from the rock.

After a moment of great laughter, I remembered the wolf and looked one more time up to the entrance of the bridge. There, standing between the wolf and the bridge, was a crane. Maybe the same one I'd seen earlier in the day. The wolf seemed crazed. It growled, snarled, and bit at the air toward the crane. But for all its fury, the wolf didn't take so much as a step toward the crane, which stood immovable and unruffled. After a moment of wasted energy, the wolf slunk away into the shadows of the approaching evening and could no longer be seen.

"Do you like graham crackers dipped in milk, Benjamin?"

Clearly he missed all that. "That sounds yummy, buddy!"

"We can go back to the cabin and eat some crackers and rock on the rocking chairs on the porch. It's close to the river where we can watch it and listen to it. You're going to like my grandma. She's going to like you too."

"That sounds great, buddy."

"Benjamin?"

"Yeah?"

"Thanks for teaching me to skip rocks today."

"Sure thing, bud."

"Benjamin?"

"Yeah?"

He smiled at me. "You really looked like you could fly today. That's the best smile I've ever seen you make too. You looked really happy."

CHAPTER EIGHTEEN

Scott had driven through the night and into the next morning. Over the long drive he alternated between obsessing about the talisman and warding off the disappearing, and thinking about Rafael, wishing he could spend more time with the boy. It had been awful to say goodbye to a tear-filled Rafael, but he was closer to the talisman than he'd ever been.

If he found it, Rafael would win too and he'd be able to explain.

He sped up the freeway on his way to a ferry and Vancouver Island beyond that, and was jolted from his thoughts when a sign announced he was thirty miles from Corvallis.

Aila. Was she okay? He hadn't heard from her in a while and couldn't shake a nagging worry. If she didn't recover and he disappeared, it'd be disastrous for Raf.

In his sleep-deprived state, his walls were down, and he found himself taking an exit off the freeway to drive the few miles to Corvallis to see Aila.

It might be the last time he would see her. The thought was sobering and a little shocking. Feelings he still carried for her, and memories of their time together, flooded his heart. He was too tired to push them away. He would give her one last hug and end things on a good note. She deserved that.

When he entered her hospital room, he breathed a sigh of relief. She was standing up, walking around her room. She had gone from possibly losing a leg and slipping in and out of fever-sleep to walking. This was very encouraging.

She was visibly shocked to see him. "What are you doing here?"

"I'm passing through and wanted to see how you're doing. You're up out of bed! That's so good."

"Yes. They want me to move around to help the blood flow and to keep the leg from atrophying. The swelling has gone down considerably, and the antibiotics seem to be working. They say I'll be here another week or so, but I think I'll be okay. I hope to send for Rafael in a week and a half to two weeks. How is he, Scott? Is he okay? Is he worried? Is he with you? He can come say hi to me. I'm sure he'd like a hug and I *know* I'd love one."

So many questions, so quickly—and Scott wasn't sure which one to begin with. Aila would be frustrated with him for passing Rafael off to Mariel, and he didn't want what could be his last interaction with her to be an argument. He knew from experience he usually got the upper hand in their arguments and she ended up being hurt. He wasn't going to hurt her today.

It dawned on him more clearly than even before. He'd come to say goodbye and make peace, hadn't he? He might never return to Corvallis. Why had he had such a dark thought? Whatever the reason, he decided to tread delicately. "Aila, I'll tell you everything, but first, let me share something."

She sat down on the bed gingerly, wincing a little. "The leg still hurts. It's not as swollen, but it's still pretty painful. Go ahead, I can tell you have some things to say. I don't want to argue today. I don't have it in me."

Good, she gets it. "Aila, look. You know I love Rafael, and there's something I have to do. I don't see it as a choice. It's not an option. I...Aila, I...". He was tired and sad, but the words needed to be spoken. Then his hand briefly looked like a hologram.

She gasped. "Oh my God! Scott, your hand!"

"It's real, Aila. And it's started. Now you see why I *have* to find the talisman."

She stared at his hand in disbelief. She'd always entertained his tale about the curse, but never took it seriously. Now that was changing.

"Rafael is with Mariel, and you're off to search down some new clue." He was surprised to hear pity, not anger in her voice.

He nodded. "I'm sorry, Aila. I know it's not ideal and I know the boy needs me. It's just something I have to do." He stared at the floor, feeling the fatigue of all his worries and driving through the night. A spot on the hospital bed in the room, even ten minutes of sleep, sounded incredible. All the anger he'd fed on through the night, all the fear of disappearing, all his regrets about hurting Aila and Wendy, all the emptiness of watching his father leave him and his family, and all his sadness over leaving Rafael behind overwhelmed him. He was too tired to hide it from Aila.

He dropped into a chair by her bed. "I still miss my father. I'm broken, Aila. I've been angry so long, I don't know another way anymore. It's like I'm stuck. I'm still seven years old, and I'm watching my father ride away in that damn boat and I can't stop him." His voice became barely more than a whisper as he stared ahead, looking past his surroundings into an imaginary scene. "It's like watching a nightmare over and over. I reach for him and he disappears. I can't relive it anymore. I can't. Aila...I have to find peace, even if that's by myself. I don't know how to stop missing him."

He stood as if to leave, and looked at Aila with pleading eyes. "I don't want to hurt anymore, and Raf just brings it all back. I'm sorry. Tell Raf I'm sorry. I can't do it. I'm not strong enough." He hung his head, not knowing what else to say.

Aila watched as his hand become translucent again. He wondered if she saw a man defeated—a man who would soon reach a point there was no coming back from. She stood, wincing again from the pain.

She walked to him without words. None were needed. She hugged Scott, who melted into her arms, his shoulders slumping into the embrace of grace. Forgiveness, strength, and hope surged from her to him in a kind of divine gift. He was being loved—a love reaching beyond hurt—by the woman he'd rejected. He melted, he wept, and, for a moment, began to find his footing.

Electricity surged through him. Suddenly, his hand felt completely solid. It was empowering, though confusing and scary. He felt vulnerable, exposed, and afraid.

The anger came back. How could he even consider stopping? He should be racing there right now! There were many more miles to drive, and he should be putting them behind him. "Aila."

He stepped back from the hug. "I'm sorry I've hurt you and Raf. Look, if...I mean when...*when* I find the talisman and slow my disappearing, I'll come back to him. Tell him I love him. It will be hard to understand."

He gave her a look that told her he could not be dissuaded, kissed her on the forehead, and left the room without turning back.

CHAPTER NINETEEN

I woke up in my bed feeling depressed. The joy I'd felt in last night's dream—when I'd jumped from the rock—was drowned out by anguish for Rafael and for myself. I'd spent much of the night tossing and turning after I'd woken sometime around two a.m.

Each time I'd closed my eyes, hoping to reenter the dream and the magic of the river, all I could see was the image of a sad little boy watching his father drive away. It had shaken me and kept me awake until I finally fell asleep only minutes before being roused by the alarm again.

It's not real. I repeated an internal mantra in an effort to convince myself. *It's not real. It's...not...real!*

I forced myself from my bed and all but stumbled to the bathroom. I regretted having what I now realized was too many beers the night before and felt a little sideways. Between the beers and the lack of sleep, today was going to be a struggle.

I flipped the light switch and squinted from the sudden brightness throwing the darkness outside into stark contrast. As I stepped into the shower, I thought of Krynn still lying warm and comfortable in the bed. If only I could go back to bed.

My thoughts turned to the workday ahead of me. Nine meetings today. *Oof.* This wasn't even unusual—just a normal day—and every one of the meetings would require me to be "on" and fully present. I wanted to be far away. In places where peace smelled like pines and sounded like rivers. It was overwhelming. I tried to melt away the night, the beers, and the dream with the shower's hot water running over my head.

It didn't work. With my eyes closed in the water, all I could see was Rafael saying goodbye to Scott. Maybe I didn't want to see the boy anymore. *No, don't think that.* I busied myself getting ready for the day. At least that offered some distraction.

When I arrived at the office, I had an email telling me the first meeting of the day was canceled. For the third time this week I'd come to the office early, in the dark, only to have my boss cancel a meeting at the last minute.

Thanks for waking me up early again. It was still dark outside. Inside, only half the usual fluorescent lights were on since not many people had come in yet. All was cast in a dim, pale glow.

I spent the recovered time obsessing over how much longer I'd have to work before I could secure my financial freedom. Unfortunately, I'd have to put my dreams on hold and keep the paychecks coming. I'd been burying dreams of doing work I could be passionate about for years. Too many more years remained. I slumped in my chair.

My phone buzzed with a reminder the next meeting would take place in five minutes. I took a deep breath and willed forward the energy needed for the daily race ahead of me.

Aside from the usual nonstop meetings, texts, phone calls, and impromptu hallway conversations, it was not a particularly eventful day. In general, the company I worked for was a good place to work and I felt fortunate to have a job I knew others would want. Yet it all felt empty. My heart was no longer there.

I walked out the doors to see rain pelting the sidewalk. Mist hung in the air and even the covered walkways struggled to keep me dry. Of course, I didn't have my umbrella. I'd been inside for nine hours without stepping a foot outside.

When I arrived home, Krynn, Abigail, Lucas, and our dog all enthusiastically greeted me. I walked in the door to shouts of "Dada!" The dog rushed to me, then jumped up to lick my face and receive so much as even one pat on the head. In spite of whatever cloud I was under, they all wanted time with me more than anything else. It should have felt sweet. So why was it all overwhelming?

"Hi, babe!" Krynn greeted me.

For a moment I felt the gray lifting. I loved this family and found peace with them. Lucas gave me an extra-long hug, patting his little hands on my back, and I soaked it in. The overwhelmed feeling was giving way to joy.

"Dada, can you play with me?" Lucas asked.

"Yeah, Dada! Can you play with us?" Abigail added.

I made the mistake of looking at an email from work on my phone. My blood pressure rose. Some new stressor and the ever-present call to solve a never-ending stream of problems.

"Uh, not now guys. I have some work to do," I answered without looking at them.

I walked by Krynn, who was preparing dinner in the kitchen, failing to look up at her. I grabbed a cold beer from the refrigerator and went into the living room. The skies had paused the rain, and the kids went outside to play without me.

Krynn washed her hands and sat by me on the couch. She stared through me, waiting for me to sense she wanted my attention. Feeling awkward silence and tension surrounding me, I looked up at her.

When I finally met her gaze, acknowledging her presence, I knew she wasn't happy with how long it had taken me to look at her. Her face could never lie to me.

"They want time with you so bad, honey. They love when you play with them. You don't even have to do anything special. They just want you. To them, time with you is like food for empty stomachs." She may as well have been speaking for herself and not just the kids.

I'd spent the day meeting external demands. Frustration rose within. "That's just it, Krynn. Everyone wants a piece of me. Sometimes I need some me time. It can't always be about them and you." I didn't like the tone of my own voice.

I'd been under a gray cloud for months, and Krynn had found the limits of her patience in this moment.

She scowled. "Benji, if you think it's been all about you, you need to do some thinking about how life has been with you in this house. It's not been a picnic, let me tell you."

The words were hard to hear, but it was her eyes that set me off.

Sure, I'd been fighting a general malaise, growing discontentment toward my employers, and a feeling of aimlessness, but I still loved her and the kids. The level of concern and disappointment on her face felt unwarranted and unfair. I wanted to defuse the situation, yet as I spoke, frustration moved toward anger.

"Well, I'm *sorry* life with me isn't the picnic you dreamed of in your fairy-tale world of imagination and unicorns. It must be so tough being married to a man who has provided food on the table and clothes on everyone's backs. And those poor, poor kids. What a bummer they have a dad and not a playmate instead."

Everything I said was unfair and I knew it. In my heart I knew Krynn only wanted to invite the joyful parts of me forward. Parts of me I'd been burying under the gray. The parts of me that fed the hungry stomachs.

It was too late. I'd pressed all the right buttons to hurt her. She stood and walked silently back to the kitchen to prepare dinner, her head down. I couldn't see but I knew there would be tears on her cheeks.

She wanted desperately to find the answers to whatever was going on with the man who, for years, had been wonderful. That man was slipping into a cave she couldn't figure out how to pull him back from. The worst part was, against all reason, I knew she blamed herself. Feelings of inadequacy were growing in her by the day, seizing her heart, preying on her fears. I knew from past discussions that she lay awake at night wondering if she wasn't good enough. Questioning her worth, skills, and beauty.

Why did I keep making us both feel awful? I set my phone down and walked to the kitchen, where I gently rested a hand on her hip with just enough pressure to invite her toward me. She turned and stepped into my arms, which wrapped around her and held her tight to me. She cried on my chest, mascara running onto my shirt. *At least she still turns toward me and not away.*

"I'm sorry, Krynnie. I don't know what's wrong with me. I'm just sad and frustrated all the time now. I need to tell you something." I put my hands on her shoulders and looked her in the eyes, which met mine with fear. She had no idea what she'd hear next, and it looked like she wasn't sure she was ready for whatever might blindside her. I needed to get to the point quickly to allay her worries.

"I've been having more dreams about the little boy and the man I told you about once. I...I don't really know how to explain it. Part of me thinks I'm having a breakdown. Like they're some sort of hallucination or something. Krynn...it's...I...I feel more and more like they aren't dreams. They're real. And they're messing me up."

Krynn looked at me with a blank stare. This wasn't at all what she'd feared she was going to hear. It was confusing and different and hard to understand.

"Whether they're dreams or real, there's something I think I'm trying to figure out. This little boy, Krynn, he needs my help. Maybe he's real, maybe it's just my dreams working something out. Whatever it is, it's got me stressed and sad and frustrated. Add to that how hard things are at work, and how my life isn't what I wanted it to be. Krynn, please be patient with me. Please don't leave me."

Her face shifted from the blank stare to extreme hurt. "How could you *ever* wonder if I would leave you, Benjamin? I *love* you! I've been worried *you're* drifting away from *me*! It seems less and less of you is here with us, but I will *never* leave you!"

"I'm sorry, Krynn. I know. I know." I hugged her tightly again.

Out the window, I could see the kids playing. I wanted to be better for them. Wanted to give them what I hadn't received from my own father. I had an idea. "I think I need to clear my head. How about I call in sick tomorrow and go hike my favorite trails." As I had fought the beginnings of depression or a breakdown or whatever this was, I'd grown less and less active and stopped doing things I used to enjoy.

Her face lifted a little. "Maybe a day in the forest will do you good. Maybe that'll be the refreshment you need."

Secretly she probably wished I'd have wanted to hike with her and not go off alone, but she was glad it was at least something other than sitting on the couch. We agreed I'd do it, and, with that, I went outside to play with Lucas and Abigail.

Unaware of the hard conversation in the house, they were thrilled when I played tag and pushed them on swings. It was exactly what they wanted from me. We played until dinnertime, and afterward I read them books and tucked them into bed. I thought of Rafael when I made the kids each "burrito babies" in their covers and pretended to eat their necks. Their giggles lightened Krynn's and my spirits.

I caught her standing in the doorway smiling at the three of us. When I walked by her on my way out of the room, she spoke softly in my ear, "You're a good father, and I love watching you play with them. Not just for them, but for you."

THE NEXT MORNING I awoke before the sun had risen, to beat the local traffic and was soon on the road to make the hour-and-a-half drive to one of my favorite hiking trails. I headed to Silver Falls State Park, a little west of Salem. The trails that wound behind multiple waterfalls and over and by creeks always refreshed me. On this rainy weekday, I knew I'd almost have the area to myself to be lost in my own thoughts.

As soon as I parked, I stepped from the car and drew a deep breath of the fresh, wet air of the Pacific Northwest forest. Leaves that had fallen from the deciduous trees blanketed some areas of the ground below, while mighty firs stood regally above everything with their green needles. Within ten minutes of starting the hike, I was behind one of the largest waterfalls in the park. The river, swollen from fall rains, rushed loudly and violently in front of me as I stood in a cleft where the path passed through, carved out by thousands of years of persistent water, weather, and wind.

I'd come to do an eight-mile hike and take my time to let the sounds and spray of the waterfalls fill me up and renew me. I wanted to recenter and refocus, and it would begin here at this first waterfall. I closed my eyes and allowed the roar of the falls to overtake my senses. Slowly, opening my eyes, I focused on the wall of water before me. Its speed and volume played tricks on my eyes and made me feel as though the cleft I stood on was on rockets, racing skyward, and it was me, not the water, that was moving now.

I began to feel just a little dizzy and I closed my eyes again, attempting to push any conscious thoughts away and just be present.

Then came the whisper again. The same one I'd heard at the cabin the last time I'd seen Rafael. "Leap. Let go."

I thought about the way stress, tension, and sadness had been released then. What would it be like to become fully content? A light breeze picked up, blowing through the cleft, and I had a moment of inspiration.

With my eyes still closed, I saw Lucas's, Abigail's, and Krynn's faces. *What if I stopped caring so much about not failing near-strangers at work and I focused on loving my kids and Krynn? What if my legacy was...*

A loud noise down the path to my left jolted me. It sounded like the breaking of a tree branch on the ground. The breeze ceased and I lost my train of thought.

"What was that?" I wondered aloud.

I took several steps in the direction of the noise.

What? I stopped at seeing one leg and the tail of a wolf disappear as it rounded the corner of the trail below. Right before it disappeared, I saw the scar on its hip. This could be no hallucination. I recognized the wolf from the cabin.

But how was it both here and in that reality?

A shiver of fear coursed through me only to be met with intense curiosity. The wolf really was a beautiful creature. Why did I have the feeling it had some sort of wisdom about life to offer? It seemed crafty and intelligent, but I could be on alert and make sure it wasn't aggressive. Anyway, I'd have to hike that direction if I was going to do my loop.

I grabbed a sharp looking rock that looked like it could have been an arrowhead in bygone times and headed in the direction of the wolf. *This is crazy! What am I doing?*

Despite my trepidation, I found my feet kept moving. Curiosity carried me forward as an almost unwilling bystander. When I neared the corner where the wolf had disappeared, there was a broken branch across the middle of the path. Must have been the sound I'd heard.

Rounding the corner, I stopped to see if there might be any ambush planned. Oddly, the wolf's prints stopped here. Most of the trail had grown muddy from the rains, and the tracks until now were easy to spot. Ahead of me on the path, there were no marks. It was confusing. How could they just vanish? Perhaps I should abandon curiosity and continue with the hike.

Snap!

Another loud noise echoed from the hillside above me. I looked up to find a small tuft of fur snagged on a branch.

So he'd gone up the hill here. What was he up to? What old wisdom would he be teaching today?

Deciding that the wolf meant me no harm and had something for me, I dropped the rock and proceeded off the path and into the brush. It was thick and slow going. For an hour, I picked my way up the hill, pausing now and again to look for tracks and listen for sounds. I was led deeper and deeper until I could no longer see the path, the waterfall, or anything I was familiar with.

I paused to catch my breath while looking myself over. It had been rough terrain and I'd ripped my pants and shirt multiple times. Blood came from several cuts on my legs and arms. My stomach rumbled, reminding me I hadn't brought any food for the hike. I'd planned on eating when I got back to the car.

I turned and looked back down through the thick, nearly jungle-like terrain I'd fought through, and grew hungrier at the thought of battling back through it. *Just a few steps deeper, then I'll turn around.*

I took a step forward and crumpled to the ground in pain. Instinctively, I reached for my ankle, which had lodged between two rocks I hadn't seen underneath the thick underbrush. In pain and anger, I cursed loudly at the wolf and myself.

When I had my fill of cursing to the trees and bushes around me, I got up to attempt a return to the path. I'd never get the hike in now. Better just go back to the car. The moment I put a little weight on the foot, pain shot through me, and before I could process it, my body reflexively removed all weight from the ankle, now adding injury to my wrist, which I'd landed on to catch myself.

My anger at myself and the wolf turned to fear. If it hurt this bad, I didn't know if I could make it to the path before dark. And then how much longer might it be before I reached the car? What if this had been part of the wolf's plan and I would be out here at night, alone and injured? But that was impossible. Wolves might be cunning, but that was a diabolical thought. Panic swelled and I dry heaved, barely managing to keep from throwing up.

A tear rolled down my cheek. *What have I done? Why did I follow this wolf?*

The feelings of malaise I'd had at home now paled in comparison to the resignation I was experiencing. I was about to give up. As I looked down at my injured wrist, fear gripped my heart and blood drained from my face. It was undeniable. My hand momentarily went partly see-through. "Disappearing," I said, staring with dread at my hand. *Like Scott. This is it. It's going to hit me too.*

I lay down and closed my eyes. I'd allow myself just one moment to catch my breath. But fatigue overtook me and I fell asleep.

I dreamed that Lucas and Rafael met. I watched them hopping in my footsteps on the beach, feeling warmth in my heart and a smile across my face as I took in the scene. The two little boys approached me, holding hands and looking angelic in the light of the setting sun behind the sea at my back.

"Will you fly with us, Dada?" Lucas asked.

"Yeah! Let's fly!" Rafael echoed.

A remnant of the rain dripped from a branch overhead, landing on my face. Some kind of freak windstorm had gathered suddenly and violently. Branches crashed down with loud cracks, leaves whipped in the air, and the trees above bent so far, I feared one might snap and land on me.

I thought of the two boys in the dream and of Abigail and Krynn. I imagined them discovering I'd disappeared. "No!"

The loud sound of my own voice rising above the storm rekindled passion. I screamed at the storm, "That's not happening to my family! Not to Krynn! Not to Abigail! Not to Lucas!" The angelic boys in that dream deserved better. "We'll find a way, boys. I swear it."

With newfound determination, I grabbed a branch that had landed feet from me and was perfectly shaped to work as a crutch. I rested my armpit in a fork in the limb, pressed the end of the branch into the ground and gingerly stood up.

While it had taken me a little more than an hour to hike in, it took me a painful, plodding three hours to find my way to the path and back to the car just before darkness set in. I pulled a bottle of ibuprofen from the glove compartment and popped several pills into the back of my throat before devouring all the food I'd left in the car.

Embarrassed at having made such poor decisions, and abundantly thankful I'd made it out okay, I pressed my right foot on the gas, thankful that wasn't the ankle I'd hurt. What would I say to Krynn? She'd wonder how I'd gotten hurt. How could I tell her I'd followed a wolf in unknown territory?

This was not going to sit well with her. I could already hear all the objections and anger from her. I'd risked not returning home to my family to chase after curiosity. This was going to hurt her feelings at a time when I was doing that too much.

I'd been out of cell phone reception for the day. The car crossed an invisible border, and the phone picked up reception and began buzzing. It rang out so many buzzes and beeps, I pulled to the side of the road to check what was happening. *I don't know this number. Why did they leave me a message?*

"Hi, Benjamin, my name is Sandra, with St. Vincent's Hospital. We're here with your wife, Krynn, and I think you'd better come quickly."

Hospital?! Quickly?! Tires squealed loudly as I raced away without checking any more texts or voicemails. The entire journey to the hospital was a blur until I was led into Krynn's hospital room in the intensive care unit.

"We're not sure what's wrong with her. Her organs seem to be shutting down, and we're acting as fast as we can to figure out why," a young doctor said as I entered.

The room spun around me as she lifted the bedcovers off an

unconscious Krynn to listen to her breathing with a stethoscope. I fell into the chair behind me, clasping my hand to my mouth.

"Sir, are you okay?" the doctor asked. "Do you need attention? We're helping her as best we can, okay? We're going to do everything we can for her."

"Why haven't you bandaged her up?" I asked, incredulous.

The doctor furrowed her brow. "I'm sorry? Bandaged what?"

"Can't you see she's wounded!"

The doctor's face moved from confusion to pity. "We're using every bit of advanced medicine we have at our disposal, sir. She has some sort of internal problem, and we'll do everything we can to identify it and help her."

"It's right there!" I said, nearly yelling.

My commotion must have drawn attention, as the nurse came back into the room. "Sir, I'm going to have to ask you to calm down."

"Surely you see it, right?"

It was unfathomable. How could they not see what I saw? Krynn had a bite mark next to a large claw wound across her stomach. It looked like a wolf had bit into her, then ripped its claws across her, leaving a bleeding wound with streaks of blood dragged across her by its nails. There was an untouched gap between the streaks, where the wolf must have been missing one nail.

"He may need a sedative," the doctor said to the nurse.

I couldn't let that happen. I put my hands up to defuse the situation. "No, no, I'm okay. I've had a hard day and was probably just in shock. I understand. You're going to help her. Please, Doctor. She's my world. Please help her."

I kept looking right at the wound but now understood only I could see it. It defied all sense of logic and reason, but it was there, it was real, and I knew they couldn't see it.

Thankfully both the doctor and the nurse accepted my contrition. "Let's get you something for that ankle," the nurse said. "I saw how you hobbled in here. Let's take a look, shall we?"

"Thank you, but please just help her," I insisted. "I'll be fine. Help her, please. She's my world. I can't lose her."

Both of them left to confer outside, and I made a call to Krynn's mother, who was watching Lucas and Abigail.

"Don't you worry, honey," she reassured me. "I'll take care of them. You just watch our Krynnie." My mother-in-law was a caring woman. I knew the children would be loved, and the worst of their troubles would be they'd be given too many treats.

I moved my chair near to Krynn, placing one hand near her wounds and holding her hand with the other. With tears dripping from my face, I looked at her. She looked peaceful. With her gentle curves and sweet face, even in her frail state, she looked beautiful. "I'm sorry, Krynnie. I'm so sorry. It's my fault. It's all my fault. I don't know why I followed the wolf. I'm so sorry."

I rested my head on the corner of the bed next to her and fell asleep holding her hand, glad I could feel her warmth in my fully solid hand.

CHAPTER TWENTY

Not long after dozing off by Krynn in the hospital room, I was jolted awake by the loud hum of an engine and a hint of diesel exhaust in the air. I opened my eyes to find myself sitting next to Rafael on a Greyhound bus as we sped along a country highway.

He sat by the window, staring at the scenery going by. By the sun's position in the sky, it was about midday. I decided not to even bother asking how I'd gotten here, or why.

Okay, we'll just see what the Pan wants this time.

"What's wrong with your ankle, Benjamin?"

I looked at the ankle I'd twisted. My pants covered it, keeping the ugliness of the black and blue swelling hidden. "How do you know about my ankle, Raf?"

His gaze still fixed outside the window, he just shrugged his shoulders as if to say, "I don't know how I know, I just do."

I could see enough of his profile to see there was something like joy or contentment on his face. The passing landscape looked like we were driving through the Oregon countryside. The last time we'd been together, I'd witnessed him saying a heart-wrenching goodbye to Scott in California. Since he was on this bus headed north, he would have said goodbye to Mariel as well. So why did he look content?

I couldn't reconcile his face with his situation. He should look sad. Loneliness should shroud him. How could he look so nonchalant, so peaceful? Where did he get that from? It bothered me and I grew annoyed with him again.

I pushed it aside. If I didn't answer his question, he'd likely ask it again. "Well, Raf, I'll be honest with you. I followed a wolf into the forest. I left a trail I was familiar with and went bushwhacking. I nearly got lost and I got really hurt. The worst part is, while I was busy wandering through the woods, my wife, Krynn, got attacked by another wolf. I think that was my fault too. I don't know how to explain it, but I believe my following the first wolf allowed the second one to attack her."

"Benjamin?"

"Yeah, Raf?"

"I didn't tell you before, when you saw the wolf at the bridge. I saw one a few days before that. In Santa Barbara. I almost followed it even after it really scared me. I don't know why, but I just want to know more about where it goes and what it does. It's like something is pulling me toward it. Does that make sense?"

A shiver of goose bumps ran over my skin. It was terrifying to hear the boy wanted to follow the wolves. And more terrifying still was the fact I understood. "It makes perfect sense, buddy. I get it. That's what happened to me. I didn't really want to follow it, but I didn't stop myself. It was so strange. It was like he had some power over me. There was this feeling he had something to offer me, and I wanted to follow and find out what it was."

The boy turned and looked out the window again. "I'm sorry your wife got hurt. Benjamin?"

"Yeah, Raf."

"Is she nice? Your wife? Is she sweet and nice, and does she give good hugs?"

I smiled and walked through sweet memories. Thinking of Krynn always helped ward off the gray clouds covering me. "Yeah, buddy. She's all those things and she gives great hugs."

"Will she be okay?" Rafael asked, searching my eyes for a clue.

I tried to put a good spin on the situation to avoid scaring him. "I'm a little worried, but she'll be okay. The doctors are helping her. I don't know how long it'll take before she's better. It might take some time, but one thing about her is, she's nice, yes, but she's also strong. She'll make it if she gets the right help."

Rafael watched the rolling hills far beyond the fields. Between them, a gently winding river found its way through a valley. He reached into a backpack probing for something, then stopped suddenly. "My grandma told me about the wolves. I just remembered. 'There's something special about you. You don't belong to the wolves,' she told me."

I watched him resume rummaging in his bag as he explained to me, "I don't know why anyone would follow a wolf. They're scary. Sometimes I can't sleep at night when I think of them. Anyway, wolves can't fly and that's what I like best. I won't follow the wolf." He spoke with such conviction it was clear he'd reached a final decision.

"What's that?" I asked, looking at a booklet he pulled from his pack.

"A math workbook," he replied, as though a seven-year-old doing math on a long bus ride alone were a normal thing.

I blinked hard. "Math? Don't you have any storybooks or comics or toys in there?"

"I like doing it. It's for kids a whole grade above me. It makes me feel good to get the problems right."

The bus pulled to a stop and the driver announced, "We'll stop here for a few minutes. You can all stretch your legs."

We followed the shuffling crowd out the bus. As we stepped out the door, we were hit with a strong aroma. It made me feel awake and energized. We looked out across vast fields of mint next to the winding river. The sun above glinted off the peaceful water.

"What's that smell, Benjamin?" Rafael asked, pointing his nose to the air and sniffing.

"That's mint, Raf. These fields are full of mint."

"Thought you might like that," the bus driver interjected into our conversation. "It's a nice spot, isn't it? On these long journeys, I like to find a spot where everyone can stop and stretch for a minute. I love how the hills and the river roll along and the mint offers up a sweet fragrance. It's good to have little moments and places in life to refresh the spirit."

Had I seen this man before? I could swear I had but couldn't place him. My brain was in a bit of a haze from the day's drama, and the driver kept a conductor's hat pulled low, his face slightly tilted downward, so I couldn't clearly see him.

"I couldn't help but hear your conversation," the driver

continued. "If I may, I know a thing or two about the wolves. Had some experiences with them myself. They do have things they'll offer you, but they'll always take more than they give. They'll make you make trade-offs you never meant to make."

Rafael had picked a leaf of mint and was sniffing it so deeply, he was nearly sucking it completely into his nose.

Under the driver's cap, a broad grin formed at the sight. "As for you, little boy, I happen to have a couple comic books and some activity books with stickers in them too. You can have them. It's great you're doing math. Take some time to play too. There'll be plenty of time for studies." Then he announced to the mingling crowd, "Back on the bus, please, everyone!"

Rafael enjoyed the activity and sticker book the driver gave him until he became sleepy and put his little stuffed dog like a pillow on my shoulder to take a nap.

Until now, I'd focused on him. I became suddenly aware of the sounds, sights, and smells on the bus. A man toward the rear of the bus could be heard loudly using profane language. He'd clearly been drinking too much, and the women he was talking to were crude and loud. Several people nearby had neither showered nor worn any deodorant in days. One person was listening to violent-sounding music loudly enough it could be heard from their headphones. Two rows behind, a mother struggled to stop two children from bickering with each other while her baby cried.

I knew each one had a story, and I didn't pass judgment. It was just a skill I'd picked up. I knew Rafael had the skill too. He had learned how to read people. He'd had to get good at it to know who he could trust in life. That was what came of being hurt at a young age. He'd learned to read people to decide who could be let into close places, and the list of those people was kept at a minimum. He'd adopted a façade, a poker face. In front was an evenness, not too high or too low. Behind were all the real thoughts and feelings, and not many people would be let in behind. He was already learning his own ways to be hard, though he didn't understand that yet.

But the cacophony swirling around me was making me claustrophobic and I wanted off. I hadn't always been afforded peace in my own childhood and had come to seek it out wherever I could find it.

Rafael had been joyful all day and now slept blissfully within this bus full of sounds and smells. How did the boy do it?

He shifted and I spied a little mint leaf held in his hand. I had my answer. The mint leaf, his backpack of personal items, his stuffed dog, even staring out the window at the landscape. He'd made a bubble for himself. He had created an oasis of peace in this sea of humanity.

The bus pulled to a stop and the air brakes hissed loudly. "Corvallis. This stop is Corvallis," the driver announced. "8:01. Right on time."

Rafael's face transformed from sleep to a beaming smile.

Aila would be here to pick him up.

He hopped from the large steps of the bus, his backpack slung loosely on his back jostling with each step. He took off in a sprint toward Aila, who held her arms wide. His backpack fell off one arm and barely clung to the other just before he flung himself into her arms and nearly knocked her over.

I forgot all the smells from the bus and the people I wasn't sure were safe for a little boy. All I could see was Raf being wrapped in his mother's arms. If it was him being held, why did it feel like some kind of healing for myself? And shouldn't that have made me happy?

Their joyful embrace should have lifted my spirits—and to some degree it did—yet something was missing. I wished Scott was here to hug him too. I wasn't just sad for Rafael. I was aware of a gaping hole in my heart that needed filling. It was too uncomfortable to think about, and I immediately chased those thoughts away.

"I've missed you, *liebchen!*" Aila exclaimed with a broad smile. She stepped back, rubbing his head with one hand.

Rafael grinned with contentment.

I SHIFTED IN MY chair, and barely squinted my eyes open. I was disoriented and confused. What was this dark room and where was the bus station? Slowly the clouds of sleep lifted and I remembered I was in the hospital. My hip and neck ached from an awkward sleeping position. I let go of Krynn's hand and reclined my chair, kicking up an ottoman for my feet. She was still unconscious but resting peacefully. Thankful she was breathing and alive, I closed my eyes again.

Almost immediately, I found I was at Rafael's house in Corvallis. "Hi, Raf!" I called.

He stood in the driveway near the house, looking intently at the mailbox at the end of the driveway. He didn't answer me.

"How's it going, Raf?"

He still didn't respond and walked toward the mailbox.

"He can't hear you again," a familiar voice said.

Calm came over me. I was glad to hear that voice. I turned to find the man standing in Rafael's yard just in front of the willow tree whose long branches swayed in a sweet breeze.

If the boy was the one with the power to bring me, then why couldn't he see me? And why was the man the one I was talking with? "I thought I come here when he brings me," I said. "Isn't that how it works?"

"He did bring you today. He wants friendship with you and doesn't always know how to explain who he is and what he thinks."

I remembered the first two times I met Rafael. The first had been when I'd been on the boulder and knew in my gut we shared a deep connection. It was one of the most inspiring moments I'd had in my life when the lake rippled, the grasses bowed, the eagle dove, and I locked eyes with the little boy across the lake. I was sure I'd never find the words to explain what that moment meant to me.

The second time, we'd played with the cars on the hill and Rafael had asked if I might be a good friend. That was the first time I knew I wanted for all the world to protect the little boy. Somehow through the graying of my life since that moment, I'd begun to forget how I wanted to shield him.

I'd been too wrapped up in myself. It felt good to recall feelings of care and love for him.

"To be friends with you, he needed you to appreciate something," the man said. "To see and to feel so he could share understanding with someone. Sometimes the deep parts of us can't be put to words. He wants someone who feels what he feels so the knowing can go where words can't."

The willow swayed much harder, and wind swirled around the man.

Rafael walked to the end of the driveway with a look of anticipation. He opened the mailbox, pulled out the contents, and rifled through them. After shuffling through each envelope, he hung his head and slowly trudged back to the house.

Sadness poked at my heart and a lump grew in my throat.

The winds behind me shifted around the man and the willow tree. Had time rushed forward? The mildly cloudy day turned to a bright sunny day, but not as a normal weather change. It was sudden, like all around us had rolled forward some amount of time as we stood still.

Rafael reappeared on the driveway in different clothes. He repeated the walk to the mailbox, the shuffling through the day's mail, and the slow, sad march back to the house.

"What's happening?" I asked the man.

"You'll know what he wants to show you soon enough," he replied.

I wanted to demand answers, but while his voice was kind and comforting, it was also serious, and I sensed he would be immovable.

Once more, the weather, the clothes, and the skies shifted. Once more, Rafael repeated the mailbox ritual and returned to the house dejected. I'd now seen the ritual three times, and heaviness threatened to envelop me. I fought to keep an invisible wall up, wrestling to maintain control over my feelings for fear I would lose an unseen battle with sadness. I looked at the man who kept watching Rafael and didn't appear likely to save me from whatever was happening.

Again and again, the events unfolded the same. There were rainy days, sunny days, mornings, afternoons, days with Aila near, days where the boy was alone. None of it made a difference. The same thing kept happening, and each time the heaviness claimed more of my heart until I was openly weeping. I couldn't bear the heartbreak.

"Please. No more of this," I begged.

Then something changed. After seeing dozens, maybe even hundreds of trips to the mailbox in rapid succession, something finally seemed different. There was no look of silent defeat on Rafael's face. *He's smiling!* On instinct, I walked down the driveway to see what he had in his hands.

He had put everything back in the mailbox except a small, tan envelope that appeared to be from some sort of government agency. He opened it and pulled out what looked like a check.

I walked back to the man, but not before a tear-filled look at the little boy's shining face. "It's child support. It's not even a big check. It's nowhere near enough to cover his needs, especially not with Aila's means," I said to the man who nodded. But it was more, wasn't it? It wasn't a check to the boy. It was a hug. It was Scott saying, "I see you. I care about you. I love you," all wrapped in that drab government envelope.

"Today it wasn't a check that came," I told the man. "Today a hug came. Today he isn't without a father." I didn't want to say the rest. Somehow the words needed to be spoken, though. "There are too many months when the check doesn't come, and he's going to stop looking for it one of these days."

"Benjamin!" Rafael called cheerily, still holding the check in his hand.

I quickly wiped the tears on my sleeve and turned around. "Hi, Raf. It's a good day today, huh?"

"Yup! My dad sent some money to help me and my mom. She was worried we wouldn't have enough money for food and gas for the car this month, and the check came just in time! Isn't that great?"

I didn't think it was great. I wanted to find Scott and explain to him how hard things were for Aila and Rafael and to make him understand what the boy really needed from him. I was angry and extremely uncomfortable with all the feelings of sadness and frustration within me. And didn't it all come from the boy?

Why does he use me like this? I know he needs help, but he needs to understand I have my own problems, and he needs to find someone like a therapist or something—or maybe start magically summoning someone better equipped to deal with all of this than me.

"Benjamin, can you push me on the swings today? Let's do something fun!" he called out as he ran to the house to put the check in the kitchen before bursting out the door and running around to the backyard. "C'mon, Benjamin! Let's play!"

I don't want to play! It was great that this was a good day for Rafael—a day where the check came—but I'd just witnessed so many days when the mailbox didn't deliver hugs and knew there would be many more. I did love and care for this boy, but didn't I end up feeling empty every time I was around him? Why?

My mind filled with fears for Rafael that Scott would disappear and there would be no checks in the mailbox or twirling-through-the-air hugs after that. What if I couldn't bear that?

I approached the man. "I don't think I can take this anymore. I told you that day at the cabin, I'm already having a hard time in my life. Adding his sadness on top of it all is a burden I can't bear. He's going to break me. I need you to stop this. I think you have the power. Can you please get him another friend? I'm not the right one for him. Besides, I'm almost certain you can fix things for him. Why don't you *do* something and help him?"

That was it, wasn't it? A fire kindled in my chest, and I was sure I could stoke it further if I wanted. After all, Rafael's dilemma wasn't my fault and it certainly wasn't his fault. If this man was powerful and didn't do anything to solve it, well then...

"Remember when I asked you to trust me, Benjamin?" His steady voice calmed me again. "I help people in ways that aren't always seen in the moment and are understood only later. Keep trusting me. I'm helping him...and you."

Though I was annoyed, there was no denying there was care and compassion in his eyes.

"C'mon, Benjamin! Let's play!" Rafael yelled from the backyard.

I sighed and walked to the backyard.

"Can you give me a push now, please?" he asked.

"Sure." He didn't deserve coldness, but it was all I could summon. I pushed him on the swing a few minutes, then decided to try and reason with him. "Raf, I don't know how much I can play today. I feel like I might need to take a break and get some rest. I hope you understand. Maybe we can play another day."

"We should race cars down the slide!" He jumped from the swing and ran to the house, appearing a few moments later with a basket full of cars.

The fire in my chest stoked hotter. I hated being ignored and was tired of feeling used by a boy who wouldn't listen to reason. "Rafael," I said slowly in an attempt to convey seriousness. "I don't know if you heard me. I don't think I can do this today. I don't feel much like playing. I think I need some time to relax. Raf, I wonder if you might be better off with another friend. Someone happier and more fun than me." That was it. I was actually thinking of his best interests, wasn't I? "I'm sorry buddy, but I—"

"I know! We can play big trucks instead!"

The fire was ready to rage and I fought against it, forcing my voice to sound calm. "Not today, Rafael."

"Okay, Benjamin. Then let's go throw stuff in the creek! I'll go get my sandals!"

The dam broke. "You're not listening! Don't you get it? I'm not well, Raf! I have my own problems! I can't keep being dropped into your world on a whim, and you can't keep giving me all your hurts and fears! I can't take them! Don't you get, it little boy? You're breaking me! Leave me alone!"

THE MOMENT I YELLED at Rafael, I woke up in the hospital as a nurse entered the room. I rubbed sleep from my face, hoping the nurse couldn't see remorse covering me from yelling at a boy in a dream.

"Sorry to wake you, sir," the nurse apologized. "We're going to take your wife for a few tests. She'll be back in an hour or so."

"Of course. Thanks for helping her. Whatever she needs."

I sat up in the recliner and checked a nearby clock. It was now four a.m. and I was exhausted from a long, uncomfortable night, filled with fitful dreams that I couldn't stop believing were real. I felt awful for yelling at Rafael but was certain I had done what was necessary.

The man would find him a better friend who could really help him, and I could work on my problems and on getting Krynn better.

Wait. What was I saying? He wasn't even real!

My eyes grew heavy, and I hoped I could get just a little more sleep before what would be a long day trying to find out what treatments Krynn needed to recover. I pulled a blanket over me, tried to get comfortable, and closed my eyes once more.

A cold drip of water shook me from sleep. I opened my eyes only to be filled with anger again. "I told you to stop doing this!" I yelled out, though I saw no one who would hear me.

I stood on the road in front of a farmhouse. Rafael had described Scott's house to me, and I was sure I was looking at it. It was a dark night, and a hard, driving rain was quickly soaking me. All the lights in the house were out, and I didn't have a clear sense what time or even what year it was. I didn't even want to know. I just wanted out.

I was about to walk to the house and knock, or even kick the door down if I had to, and tell the boy to leave me alone once and for all.

"You should wait a moment."

I turned to see the stranger with me again. There was still something in me that was glad to see him and wanted to learn from him, but the anger raging in my chest was my driving force now. "Listen, I appreciate what you're trying to do here. I know that boy deserves love and needs it. I'm just not the guy. I have all the same hurts and brokenness he does, and I can't help him. I'm telling you, find someone else. And as for him, I'm going to set him straight. I told him not to bring me here again, and he needs to know I meant it! I'm not a dumping ground for all his hurt. I'm not equipped for that, and if I go deeper into darkness, I might lose my own family. I just can't deal with this right now!"

I'm not waiting this time. I took a determined step toward the house.

"He didn't bring you here. I did."

I balled my hands into fists and let out a sigh of exasperation. "You *what*?"

I'd have no hope of stopping both the boy *and* the man. There was something magical about the boy in a sweet way, even if he was frustrating me. But the man had power and authority I wasn't sure could be overcome.

My voice quieted, and was barely audible above the rain. Maybe a calm approach could summon his pity. "Why? Why did you bring me? Please. Please, I can't take all this. Just find someone else. Please."

A car came speeding into view, its bright headlights shining through the heavy rain. The car jerked suddenly, jumped a ditch, narrowly missed an electric pole, and careened across the front yard. Mud flew everywhere before a deafening crash shook me to my core. The awful crunch of the car and house roused several neighbors, whose houses started lighting up one by one.

I stared at the corner of the house where the car sat mangled. The wall was punched in and the roof was partially collapsing around it. Glass and wood debris were everywhere. I couldn't move. Didn't know what to do or how to help. I was too afraid to go near and survey the scene, knowing I wouldn't be able to cope if I found out the boy was sleeping in the room the car had hit. Lacking the courage to step forward, I stood frozen.

Sirens rang out from a distance. They grew louder until all around me was a blur of red and white ambulance and fire truck lights. Women and men sprang into frenzied action all around the house and still I stood paralyzed. Two paramedics tended to the car's driver and passenger. One of them yelled through the rain, "By the smell of it, they were driving drunk. We'll need to see if they need their stomachs pumped."

The stranger put a gentle hand on my shoulder. "Come," he said with comforting kindness and deep sadness. "Walk with me a moment."

I couldn't move. I wanted to go back and hide from it all. Pretend it wasn't real. Maybe I could just go home to my house with Krynn and sleep it off, in the safety of my bed. If I could just wake up to my life before Krynn had been hurt, I'd be okay.

Somehow I was walking and we neared the house as paramedics loaded a bed with a little boy into a second ambulance. "The boy was sleeping near the wall!" one of them said. "Get him in fast!"

Hopelessness overtook me. I closed my eyes like a child hiding from danger. Maybe I could run away.

"Come," the man said, his kind hand still on my shoulder.

I sensed we'd moved. I opened my eyes and found myself in a hospital room for the second time today, only this one wasn't Krynn's. I looked at the man, then at the frail, little boy in the bed.

All manner of tubes, cords, and monitors were attached to him. Without thinking, I went to him and took his little hand into my own. *He reminds me of Lucas.* Tears streamed from my face and I turned back to the man, who I now suspected had supernatural powers. "You have to help him," I said through blinding tears. "You have to save him!"

I had no more strength left to filter my feelings. It was all going to come out. "Why didn't you stop this? Why haven't you *done* anything for him? You could fix it! You could make Scott stay and you could have prevented all this, couldn't you? *Couldn't* you?"

Had I wanted him to fix Rafael or me?

He opened his arms, while his eyes invited me forward. I wanted to step toward him and receive a hug—to melt into those arms and find healing for myself—but anger and fear wouldn't let me.

"Will you trust me?"

I wasn't sure how to answer. I looked at Rafael. Whatever frustrations and anger I harbored toward him didn't matter anymore. Closing my eyes I felt that melt away. My shoulders dropped forgotten tension and my chest heaved a sigh of relief. My eyes still closed, I remembered laughing with Rafael at the cabin and the feeling of lightness as I soared off the rock. I remembered the crane and the wolf and the moments I'd felt great hope around the boy. I realized the love I felt for him was the love I'd missed from my own absent father.

I'd been proud and blind. And I'd been doing everything by myself. Without Krynn and—

It sounded too weird. But it was right too, wasn't it?

And without the man.

I dropped to my knees and clutched at him. "I'm ready to trust! I know I need your help too. It's not just for him, it's for me. I have this brokenness inside me. I don't know how to stop it from hurting the people in my life. I know now, you can help me. But please, *please*, save him! Please! You can't let him die!" Then I surprised myself uttering words which sprang from a place beyond my comprehension—a place my mind didn't understand but my heart knew. "I need him as much as he needs me!"

I woke up again in Krynn's room and felt her squeezing my hand. "Are you okay, honey?"

"You're awake!" I sat up to hug her. The sight of Krynn no longer comatose was enough to help me briefly forget the intense scene I'd just left.

"She turned a corner just a few moments ago," the nurse said. "We aren't sure why, to be honest."

The color had returned to her face, and she looked beautiful and strong.

"You seemed to be having a bad dream," she said to me as the nurse exited the room.

"You're here, Krynnie. You're awake, and you're okay. That's all I need. Don't worry about the dream. I'm here with you!" I leaned forward and gave her a kiss.

"Rafael, wake up." In the recesses of his mind, Rafael heard the kind stranger calling him, then felt him gently lift his hand.

All the tubes and monitors fell from him and he opened his eyes. "Where am I?"

"You're in the hospital, but it's okay, son. It's time to go, Raf."

"Go where?"

"It's time for you to go to Benjamin's world. He needs you, Rafael."

"Needs me for what?"

"You're going to teach him and his children to fly."

CHAPTER TWENTY-ONE

It had been a week since Krynn had come home from the hospital. The doctors never found a reason for the deterioration in her health, but she was much better now. Whenever she changed near me, I could see she still had a scar on her stomach and continued to believe this was my fault—that somehow my following the wolf had something to do with her being attacked.

I entered our bedroom on the fifth morning with a bowl of oatmeal I'd prepared for her, having lovingly stirred in peanut butter and added a spiral swirl of honey on top just as she liked.

"It's been so nice to have you home with us these past few days," she said. "Thank you for taking time off from work to take care of me. I feel so loved."

Taking care of her felt good to me too. It spoke the words I couldn't find to tell her how much she meant to me, and I was glad to see she was nearing complete recovery other than the scar. "I just wish I didn't have to go back today, but we'll have to keep paying the bills and life keeps going, you know?"

Though things had seemed a little better since we'd come home from the hospital, her face told me she still worried melancholy was hanging over me. She knew going back to a work environment I didn't relish wasn't going to help. "Promise me one thing, baby," she said.

"What's that?"

"Remember we love you. While you're at work, I mean. Think of us and think of good times."

I bent over and gave her a kiss on the forehead. "You're with me every day, Krynnie," I said, holding her hand and looking into her eyes. "You're the only reason I've been able to keep working as long as I have. You and the kids. You're worth it."

"Thank you," she said, fighting tears and giving me a sweet smile. "And thank you for my oatmeal."

I gave her one more kiss before going downstairs to hug Abigail and Lucas followed by the trudge to the car. They had the day off school for a teacher in-service, and I wished I wasn't leaving them. The walk to the car felt like fighting a gravity source coming from within the house pulling me backward.

It was a routine day at work, and it felt nothing had changed. All that had seemingly happened while I was away was a piling up of tasks and requests people had for me. They had waited for my return and now bombarded me. I knew that when I got home, I'd have to let Krynn know I'd be working most of the evening.

I pulled up in the driveway and gathered my things. After just one day back at work, the feeling of having more to do than one person could accomplish weighed on me, and I was already tired again. I stood in the driveway, holding the bag with my computer in it, and stared at the front door. Abigail, Lucas, and Krynn would be on the other side. A smile formed on my face, I took a deep breath, and sighed out the stress of the day. I really loved them.

A breeze blew through the yard, rustling the leaves of a poplar in front of the house. A wave of goose bumps covered me—a feeling like a presence other than my own was near. Would I see the man again? High above, a circling hawk used the updrafts to soar effortlessly.

Weird. I hadn't thought about the wind and flying in this world. It had always been in the dreams about the man and about Rafael.

For what seemed like the hundredth time, I was surprised at the confidence with which I felt the dreams were, in fact, another existence. Something real. "One day back at work and I'm already going mental again," I said and laughed at myself, then proceeded toward the front door.

As I reached for the knob, the breeze turned into a gust. Pine needles and stray leaves swirled and were carried away like my yard was being swept clean. I looked up again and, though the day had been entirely gray, the sun was now breaking, and the wind had pushed all the clouds away.

My hand turned the knob, and I heard giggles. It wasn't uncommon to hear Lucas and Abigail playing and laughing in the house. They loved each other and enjoyed each other's company. But did I hear *three* small voices?

Looking through the entryway into the kitchen, I caught a glimpse of Krynn preparing dinner for the family. She had music on and hadn't heard me come in. Attraction and affection swelled in me and I smiled. *We need a date and some alone time.*

But what was that third giggle I heard? She would know. "I'm home, Krynnie! Whatcha making there?" I moved in for a hug.

"Oh, just some skewers. It seemed like a nice enough day today to eat in the backyard, and I wanted to have something nice for when you got home from going back to work."

"What are the kids doing? Did I hear another voice upstairs or am I crazy?"

"They're up there playing games. Right now, I think they're playing hide and go seek. As for our guest...well, maybe you can just go see for yourself, sweetie." She gave me a little kiss and went back to preparing dinner, taking a large plate of skewers out the sliding door to the grill on the backyard patio.

I walked to the stairs, feeling entirely suspicious. If Krynn acted coy, it meant she had a fun surprise in the works, or she knew there was something that would displease me. What was I about to walk into? But the sound of children's laughter was so sweet, I decided whatever she was hiding couldn't be all that bad. I let my guard down. "Hi, guys! I'm home!" I called through the upstairs hallway.

Our dog came running, spilling joy from its every movement.

"I see you, girl. I see you," I said, stooping down to pet her before moving on to the playroom at the end of the hall.

"Dada!" came two voices in unison. "Come play with us!"

More giggles broke out. I entered the room and wished right away that I'd kept my guard up. At one end of the room were three children on all fours each playing like they were animals. Lucas whinnied like a horse and Abigail reared up like an unbroken thoroughbred.

Between them, another little boy was also behaving like a horse. It seemed the boy was the leader of the three. Lucas and Abigail mimicked his movements and behaviors, watching him for cues. I stood, mouth agape, unable to say a word.

It couldn't be!

The boy finally noticed me and jumped into a run toward me, throwing himself at my legs, wrapping his little arms around me. "Benjamin! Your family is so fun! Your wife is even nicer than you said, and your kids are already my best friends!"

I peeled the little boy's arms off myself. "I'll be back in a minute, guys," I said to Lucas and Abigail.

Surely this wasn't real. I stole a sideways glance at the boy, which confirmed I still saw him. In a state of shell-shocked confusion, I made my way down the stairs and into the kitchen. Through the window I saw Krynn grilling outside. She at least could ground me. I walked with purpose to the sliding door and the backyard. "How did he...? When did he...?" I stammered, unable to complete a sentence. "What is he doing here? Why is he in my *house*? *How* is he in my house?"

"He said he came to play with the kids." Tears formed in her eyes. "And..." She choked the words out. "And he said he came to play with me, and that I'm pretty and nice." She looked at me, holding barbecue tongs to her side while a tear slid down her cheek.

I couldn't hide my disturbance at the presence of the boy. I was about to object, which she must have sensed.

She pointed the tongs at me. "Benji, I don't know what to tell you. From the moment I saw him, I knew he belonged. He stays. I love him, so you be nice to him. He deserves your kindness."

She didn't wait for me to reply, just turned away to tend to the food on the grill. "Can you please round up the kids for dinner?" she said without looking my way. "*All* of them." She smiled and winked but her voice was tinged with fire I dared not touch.

So it was done then. The boy was welcomed by Krynn, and there would be no undoing it. How could she frustrate me and make me feel so in love with her all at once? It was like a new puppy had been let in the house without my permission, and the family had fallen in love before I could stop it. What had been done now could not be undone. The Pan had struck again.

I walked up the stairs, my mind racing with questions. How was this boy in my house? How was it possible? Was I going crazy? But Krynn and the kids could see him too? Entering the room once more, I called for the kids in the most positive tone I could muster. "All right, horsies! It's time for dinner. Come on down, guys."

Lucas and Abigail stood up and headed for the stairs. Rafael looked up at me looking like a boy seeking approval and reassurance that the invitation was for him too. I saw hurt and rejection in his face and knew where it came from. I knew the emptiness chasing after this boy, seeking to claim him and pull him into the void.

He kept looking for reassurance he hadn't yet received and might always seek. He reached a hand up and dropped his eyes to the floor.

I could walk away before this got worse. I could let him disappear.

It was no use. Even I wanted the puppy to stay now. Even if this did irritate me a little. All the walls I'd constructed so carefully were being dismantled by one look.

I can't even be mad at him. I just love him too. The boy has more power over me than I think I'll ever understand.

I took the little hand into my own, and we walked out into the hallway and down the stairs together. "It's nice to see you again, Raf," I said as normally as I could, though the entire situation was absurd. I wondered if I might be having a psychotic episode. After all, a boy from my dreams—and from another time and another town—was now in my home. Not only was his physical appearance completely irrational, but the fact that Krynn was acting like this was perfectly normal and that the boy would stay with us defied all reason.

I'd always felt somewhere in my gut, the dreams were real.

A hopeful thought took hold as I sat Rafael at our backyard table and looked up at sunny, blue skies. Would the man come visit us too?

Actually, I might *need* a visit from the man, and wished I could talk to him. Not just talk for a moment or two, but really sit and spend time together. The trees swayed in the breeze again, and I closed my eyes, allowing myself to really feel it. I nearly put my arms out.

"You look so peaceful, honey," Krynn said, bringing me back to them.

"Just seems like a good day."

"Where'd you go that time?" She smiled at a fidgeting Rafael who was playing with his silverware and kicking his legs back and forth.

Look at the way she looks at him. She already loves him. Just like the first time I met him too. It was easy to understand. At the tender age of seven, the boy had more experience with grief and loss than most adults. It wasn't right. The injustice of it felt like a rock in my gut.

I remembered the first time I met Rafael and how I'd wanted to shield him from ever feeling the gray. How I'd wanted to ensure he never felt the sting of loss or rejection. Over the few months I'd been entering his world, I'd found myself completely powerless to protect him. It seemed all I could do was witness hurt after hurt. The powerlessness was almost too much to handle, and I felt the walls coming up again. *He can stay, but he can't be in here.* I put a hand to my chest and steeled my face.

"Benji," Krynn called. "Come back to us. Here are your skewers, baby. Just like you like them."

Those eyes and that smile of hers. "Sorry, Krynnie. I'm here. Thanks for the barbecue. It's always so good!"

We all ate together and shared small talk about our days. Krynn gently rubbed her foot up against mine, and I smiled at her. We exchanged the knowing look of two people who knew, in spite of any current troubles, we still wanted to be with each other.

Both Lucas and Rafael grew more restless as time went on. Each barely picked at their food and had to be reminded to eat many times.

Finally, Krynn gave up the struggle. "Okay, boys. Go ahead and play if you want. You may be excused."

Both boys pushed their chairs back and ran into the grass. Sharing the kind of telepathic understanding only young children have with each other, they simultaneously began acting like two little dogs. They barked and woofed at each other, pretended to pant joyfully, jumped on each other, and rolled around together.

Krynn watched with her chin on her hand and a warm smile on her face. Abigail giggled at them from the table, then joined in.

The three of them moved around the grass in spontaneous, unbridled expressions of joy. Their joy was like a salve to my troubled heart as I watched the three laughing and rolling over each other.

The leaves on the poplar trees rustled again. The hairs on the back of my neck stood up and a shiver traveled out from there until electric current ran through every part of me. The hawk circled overhead, and I heard what was becoming a familiar voice from within. The whisper had returned.

"Leap. Let Go."

I knew now, it was the stranger's voice. Krynn had no idea what was happening right by her. As had happened at the river and the willow tree, I knew he and I were sharing a conversation hidden from all around us. Whether through my imagination or by some magic, he had appeared to only me.

"I'm scared," I confessed.

"I know. And I know why. But do *you* understand yet?"

My heart raced and felt it might come out my throat. My stomach filled with acid and my face wrinkled in discomfort. This would usually be the moment I would put walls up with anyone who threatened to get too close. It had become my way. So why was I prepared to spill everything inside me?

"Part of me still wants you to leave me alone, you know. Part of me wants to scream at you to leave and to take him with you."

"You know why, right? You feel it. Will you trust me enough to share it with me?"

His eyes confused me. There was love in them, but also hurt.

It's compassion. I realized these eyes told me he knew every hurt I had ever felt. That he felt—not just knew or understood, but *felt*—my most intimate and fragile places. This man's heart had gone to the places in me where words couldn't go, and he'd taken my hurts as his own.

"Do you understand why you want the boy and me to leave?" he repeated softly.

My mind flashed to the picture of me and my father on a hike, when I'd been a little boy with peanut butter on my face. My heart and my mouth ran ahead of my brain as I heard myself utter things I'd never known myself. "Because *he* left me! Because it hurts like hell and I'm still not over it! Because I *never* want to feel that way again, and I won't let you, or Rafael, or even Krynn ever make me hurt like that again! No one gets to do that to me. *No one*! So get the hell away from me and never come back! You won't have the chance to leave me, and that dumb kid reminds me of how it felt, and I can't take it! He has to leave too!"

My mind raced and flashed memories. I was back at the cabin the day I jumped from the rock, and hearing the words he'd spoken to me: *I know you don't understand yet, but you will. You are valuable to me. You—and he—are priceless treasures, and I'm the type of person who would search the rocks all day and through the night if I lost something of value to me.*

His voice brought me back to the patio. "I love you, Benjamin, and I love Rafael. I will never leave you."

I slumped and nearly fell to my knees. I didn't have the strength to push back or build walls anymore. I had broken that moment in the hospital and knew that now. The man and the boy had been reaching my heart, and I couldn't fight them back any longer.

"Benjamin, when something is damaging and hurts people, it's okay for it to break and even good to break it. I will never break people. I will only break what stops them from finding what they seek."

My voice was weary and my head hung low. "I don't know what people seek. All I want is some peace. I'm so sick of being angry and hurt and gray all the time. All I want is something besides the gray."

"Benjamin, Love is the treasure people seek. Some don't know it yet, but I am that love."

This was getting ridiculous. "*You* are?"

"I am."

The electricity ran through me again. How could he keep doing that? "Just *who* are you?" I asked, still tempted to send the man away and rebuild the walls around myself.

"I have a few names people call me. To you, I am The Good Father." As he spoke, a breath came from his mouth and surrounded me with what seemed like a hurricane. It wasn't terrifying or chaotic; it felt like being wrapped up and protected. A great wind swirled all around me, then filled me within. I'd never felt so safe, so secure, so loved in all my life.

The man stood before me with his arms held out. "I'm here for you, son."

The word washed over me and felt like the thing I most wanted in all the world. I felt wanted, loved, and affirmed. It was the first time I had felt true belonging and not a sense that to belong required finding something "out there."

"All you have to do is decide I'm real, what I have for you is real, and that you don't want the walls anymore. Instead of hiding your heart, if you give it to me, I'll start the process of making it new and whole. You can trade your walls for my love."

I felt ready to step into the man's arms. To receive a hug I realized I'd been wanting since I was little, when my father had left my mother, my home, and my state. I felt like a little boy who wanted to run into safe arms and be twirled through the air. To fly in safe arms and soar over and away from anything that could trouble or hurt me.

I thought of stepping into the arms, but fear, anger, and hurt overcame my will. "I'm not ready," I said.

The man disappeared.

In the yard, the three children were still imitating dogs. Through some trick of time, all had happened in an instant, and they were blissfully unaware.

They looked so sweet and so happy. I was relieved they had no idea the heaviness and wrestling I felt inside. Why couldn't I just trust the man? Why couldn't I have just received the hug I knew I wanted desperately? Whatever this exhausting season of my life was, it needed to end. I didn't want to need so much. It made me feel exposed. I needed some quiet for a few minutes to try and relax.

I excused myself from the patio table, "Sorry, Krynn, I have some work I better get done. It should only take an hour, then I can help tuck the kids in for bed."

"Can't you play with us, Dada?" Abigail asked.

Rafael looked up with hopeful eyes.

"Sorry, guys, but I have some work I have to do." I grabbed a few plates to help clear the table and went inside.

CHAPTER TWENTY-TWO

For several weeks, I did as much as I could to keep space between Rafael and me. I had the feeling of being torn into two people. I was a man who wanted to shield himself from hurt and was growing more and more resentful of the boy who was making the family fall in love with him, as he provided one joyful moment after the next. I was also a man who felt my own heart still longing to comfort and nurture the little boy. What was more, with each day around Rafael, my mind blurred memories of myself as a child with the boy now in my house, which was unnerving. Each day I became wearier from the battle within.

It was all coming to a breaking point. Krynn had been trying hard to get me to embrace Rafael's presence and care for the boy. I'd become so irritable, she'd taken to walking on eggshells while still hoping for a breakthrough.

We sat on the couch on an early Friday evening, while the kids played outside in the last light of the day. A tired heaviness hung on her face. She had tossed and turned the night before, and I was sure I knew why. She was concerned over what was no longer just gathering gray over me but now a darkened sky which might send a storm ripping through our lives any day.

The weight of her concerns had driven her to start seeing a therapist, and earlier this day, she'd had her third therapy session.

"How'd it go?" I asked.

"It was good, honey. I think it helps. She's a great counselor."

"That's good." We sat in silence, neither of us knowing how to broach what needed to be spoken. "Krynnie, I know you probably talked about me and about us. If you feel like you can share, I'm here to listen."

I saw her face deciding how transparent to be and eyes that searched for words. Then she relayed her conversation to me in a way that seemed as if she spoke to her therapist still. As if she were sitting here in our living room.

"Well, I told her, 'I'm worried about him. He has this deep capacity to love. He's such a wonderful man and he cares so deeply for others. It's just…I'm worried he's somehow gotten weighed down and can't climb out from under whatever it is. I've watched him slipping farther and farther away from me, and it's even more surprising to see how he plays with the kids less and less. He's always loved our kids and he's been the most amazing father. I think he wants to give them what his dad didn't give to him. But now…"

She trailed off into quiet tears and held her hand to her mouth with a tissue. I squirmed in my seat. I wanted to argue. To push back and deny. But I knew it was true. Still, there was context, wasn't there? I was working to earn a living for the family after all, and I deserved a break, didn't I? I felt her gaze searching me for clues. Did she dare share more, or would I grow defensive?

I put a hand on her knee. "It's okay. Please keep sharing. I know it's not easy."

"Well, first, so you know, she told me it's obvious you love me and the kids. I told her so many of the good things about you. I don't want you to think we were teaming up against you."

What was she about to say that she needed to tell me that? This might not be so good.

"She wonders if you're fighting your own past. Like maybe something is coming to the surface. Something you aren't comfortable with. Benji, she had an interesting point."

Though I didn't want to hear more, I knew Krynn needed me. I had to ask, "What's that?"

"She said, when she sees people go through times like what you're going through, they can go one of two ways. Either run away and hide, or lean in and find out what's under the surface."

It was precisely what I'd been fighting and why Rafael was now kept at a safe distance. I didn't like where this was going.

"The people who dig down deep sometimes can find places that need healing." Her eyes were full of tears and love. "Benji, I'm here for you and I love you, but I can't fix it for you. You're holding on to so much. I watch you. There's something inside that you aren't talking about. I wish you could just let go more. I see you with the kids. There are these moments when something else comes out. Moments when you're a fun-loving, tender-hearted, caring, joyful man. Actually, it's a boy, really. When you let yourself play and be creative and spontaneous, the gray is gone and you're like a boy."

Though I felt my face scowling and my body recoiling, it didn't deter her. She leaned in close and held my gaze. "You don't even realize what it does to us all when you let that boy out. We all love it so much."

What would it feel like to be light and fun and full of joy? To play with her and the kids and move beyond all that weighed me down. It hurt to hear I wasn't the man they craved. I wasn't the hero or the knight in shining armor.

"I get it, Krynn. I just can't be everything everyone wishes. Sorry."

"Benji, I..."

"What?"

She sighed, gently rubbed my back, and walked to the front door. "I'll be right back, sweetie. I just need a moment of fresh air and want to give you a minute. I know that was a lot to take in."

She'd managed to be gentle, but I knew if she was stepping away, she was avoiding a fight. Probably for the best. Too many of those lately, and the kids might come in any minute.

Through the living room window I watched her stroll to the end of our driveway. A man walked down the street with two large dogs, one white and one orange. Was he stopping to talk to her? He held an outstretched arm with one finger pointing out and seemed to stare at it.

What was he looking at? Curiosity was eating at me, and I went out to our porch quietly enough I wasn't noticed, and now eavesdropped.

"Mind if I ask why you're looking at your finger?" Krynn asked.

"Look closely," the man said, still focusing on the finger.

Krynn stepped closer. "What a beautiful butterfly."

From a distance I could just make out its wings slowly moving back and forth.

"It looks so peaceful, doesn't it?" the man said. "This one has been learning to fly only today. It's moving its wings to grow stronger. It hasn't gained its full strength yet."

I watched Krynn appear entranced by the rhythmic sway of the wings. Did she think like me? Did she wonder how strong she would have to be to fly?

"Over the past few days, if you'd seen inside its cocoon, it would have looked miserable," the man said. "It was squeezed in on all sides, fighting against walls that held it captive. Yet it was the pushing, the striving against the cocoon that gave it the strength it needed once it emerged. They're one of life's great dichotomies, butterflies. Without strength and fight, they could never fly, and yet, look at its wings."

She studied it as did I. Though I remained at a distance, I could make out bits of beautiful colors and patterns on the wings, which continued to sway steadily like a metronome. What beautiful music was this great composer leading?

"What do you see?" he asked her.

"They're silky. They look so soft."

"Yes. The butterfly has to be strong, but without these fragile wings to catch the air, all their strength would be wasted. It's the gentle wings that amplify the strength of the butterfly."

It flapped its wings and flittered into the air twenty feet above them before flying away toward a garden down the street.

I watched until the butterfly disappeared from view. The man had quietly moved along and was a block away now. *Who was he?*

Before Krynn could spy me, I slipped back inside and resolved to be gentle with her the rest of the evening, even offering to tuck all three children in for her at bedtime. I finished saying good night to each, and watched Krynn doing the same.

"Do you think I could go see the mountains Benjamin talks about? They sound fun," Rafael asked her.

Though I couldn't see her face, I knew from the movement of her body and the sound of her voice that the invitation had moved her. "Yes, of course, sweetie. Thank you for asking me."

"Can it just be us? Could I have some time with you?"

"Well, Raf, I wouldn't want Lucas and Abigail to—"

"It's okay, Mom. Maybe we can play with Grandma," Abigail said excitedly.

"Sure, I'll ask her."

Later as we lay in bed, she asked, "Benji, do you want to come with us? I know Raf would love it if you would come."

"Sorry, babe, but with an empty house, it'll be too good an opportunity to catch up on work to pass up."

She rolled over while I searched for words to reach out. Anything to make things better and find closeness. But none would come before my eyes grew weary and we both fell asleep. I was living up to the patterns she had seen growing—hiding from hurt and disappointment behind walls of silence.

Early the next morning, Krynn shuffled to the kitchen where I sat with Rafael. She looked like it had been a long night. She wrinkled her face. "What are you doing up, Raf?"

"I found him waiting here," I answered.

He'd sat quietly at the kitchen table just waiting for someone in the house to join him. He'd been so excited for their hike together, he woke up early and snuck downstairs without waking Lucas or Abigail.

He got up from the table and gave her a hug. "Thanks for taking me hiking. Do you think I can stay at your house longer? I like it here."

She looked at me and must have been happy to see me smiling, though I doubt it affected her answer. "You will *always* be welcome in this house, Rafael." She gave him a kiss on the head and stuffed their hiking snacks in a small pack. "You sure you can't come, Benji?"

"Sorry, babe. Just making a trade. If I get work done today, I'm all yours the rest of the weekend."

"Okay, but we'll miss you." She took Rafael's hand and they headed for the car.

As the door closed, he called out, "Don't work too hard, Benjamin."

Don't work too hard? What did that mean? And where would a little boy pick up that phrase? I went back to the bedroom to grab my laptop and peered out the upstairs window to the driveway where Krynn was waiting for Rafael to buckle his seat belt.

It would be nice to go with them. To forget about work for a day and hike in more of my favorite woods. They were going to a place with sweeping views, clear running snowmelt creeks, and alpine lakes. "Not today," I sighed.

The car started.

If you're ever going to reach out to her, what are you waiting for? She loves you! I found myself sprinting down the steps. I jerked my jacket off the coat rack, which toppled over, then ran out to the driveway. Krynn must've seen me running toward them in her rearview mirror. She stopped the car suddenly.

I threw open the passenger door.

"What's wrong? What happened?" Krynn asked.

Half laughing, half trying to catch my breath, I puffed out, "Can I...come...with you guys today?"

Krynn's mouth hung agape while her brow wrinkled in confusion. She looked like I'd spoken another language.

Rafael grinned so widely, his cheeks puffed out showing a bit of baby fat he hadn't yet grown out of. "Can he?" he asked Krynn.

"What about the kids, Benji? My mom isn't here yet."

"She'll be here in five minutes. Will you two wait with me?"

Krynn looked at me and grabbed my hand, squeezing it gently. "We would *love* that!" she said, looking into my eyes.

Rafael nodded in approval.

After her mother arrived, we got hot drinks at our favorite local coffee shop, then started our drive. Krynn kept glancing at me in the passenger seat and then at Rafael behind her in the mirror. She was grinning.

"What's got you so happy?" I asked.

I hadn't realized Raf and I had both cupped our drinks with two hands, holding them to our noses, absorbing the smells and the warmth wafting up toward us. She had watched us and saw us each taking in a deep breath, smelling the aromas before us. "Just happy is all. I love you, Benji. I love you, Raf."

"Love you too," we both answered in unison.

The sun was just rising over the foothills we were driving up. The sky lit up with peach, rose, and orange colors even a master painter couldn't match. I looked at the skies and at Krynn. She looked even more beautiful than the sunrise. To pass the time, I started playing a guessing game with Rafael.

"Benjamin?" Raf interjected at one point and, as had become normal, answered his own beckon before I could. "Thanks for playing with me again. I really like when you play with me."

With the air still cool and crisp this morning in the mountains, we began our hike. Pine trees surrounding us reminded me of the smell at the cabin where I'd leaped from the rock. I stopped on the trail to pull in as much of the fresh scents as I could and spied Rafael doing the same.

Krynn gazed at us again.

"What?" I asked with a smile.

"Nothing, baby. Just happy."

I knew her well enough to know many of her thoughts by now. I knew she had watched the morning sun shine on my face as I pulled in the mountain pine air and that she could see a softening of my countenance. Her face showed more hope than it had in some time. I'd been an outdoorsman in the past, often going on hikes and backpacking trips. Over the past several years I'd done less and less of that. I knew that, for her, seeing my face register something that looked like rejuvenation, kindled hope for me, herself, Lucas, Abigail, and even Raf. She knew better than to assume this one moment meant I had no more troubles ahead, but it was a moment she'd needed.

I pressed again, "Why so happy today?"

"I see something other than gray over you today. I'm thankful for that." She was surprisingly direct, though her voice was so cheery it was easily received.

"I love it here. I'll never get over that smell. It reminds me of your cabin, Raf. Something about that sweet pine reminds me how I felt when I jumped off the rock. Remember warming in the sun with the sound of the river flowing by?"

"Yeah. It's one of my favorite places. That and the jetty where I would go with my grandma."

"Oooh, yeah! When the ocean air is fresh, and you can watch the sun set and the waves roll. That's really amazing!" I could hear my own voice sounding childlike.

Krynn giggled. "You two are cute."

For the next three hours, the three of us hiked up to a ridge with expansive views of the valley below and no fewer than six snow-capped mountain tops all around us. Here on the ridge we were above the tree line. We could see for miles nearly 360 degrees around us.

The last part of the hike was across rock and boulder fields with barely any vegetation to speak of. It was a harsh landscape, not nearly as nice as the first part of our hike along creeks edged with grass and flowers. I grew pensive during the rock crossing, and Krynn must have sensed it.

"You okay, honey?" she asked.

"Yeah, I'm okay." I knew she knew better, but it served for now.

As we crossed the field of jagged rocks, I thought about all Rafael had been through and how, before I'd allowed hurt and anger to lead my decisions, I'd felt so much love and affection for the boy. I was returning to the places in my heart where I cared for him, and I wasn't sure that felt safe.

We reached a viewpoint where we stopped for a gourmet chocolate bar Krynn had packed. After a few minutes enjoying the views, I gave her a hug and a kiss. "Shall we?" I said, suggesting it was time to hike back to the car.

"Sure, let's go."

"Shall we?" Rafael repeated, then answered himself enthusiastically, "We shall!"

We all laughed and began picking our way across the rocks again. As he did at the cabin, Rafael hopped from rock to rock with bounding grace and skill. I watched in admiration of the little sprite before me, and losing focus on my own footing for a moment, stepped on a loose rock, falling down to avoid twisting my ankle. As I fell, I scraped my knee on a large rock, tearing open my pants and leaving the knee bloodied.

"Are you okay?" Krynn asked, hurrying to me.

Rafael leaped his way to me. "Are you okay, Benjamin? That looks like it hurts."

I grunted and stood up to check myself. "Well, it hurt, but yeah, I'm okay. I can still walk."

I looked again at the ripped pants and bloody knee with dirt in it and blood dripping down my shin and grew angry at myself. "Dang it!" I said loudly enough to make Krynn and Rafael a little uncomfortable. "That was so dumb!"

The wind shifted, and all three of us quieted. None of us knew what was happening, but we had a premonition. It was a feeling something special and beautiful was surrounding us.

From between two rocks beneath us, a butterfly flapped its wings and flew among us. Then a second appeared and a third. More and more butterflies emerged. Some came from the rocks below, some through the air from somewhere beyond us. Hundreds of the little winged creatures glided softly around and over us, their wings catching the rays of the afternoon sun and the rising warmth from the rocks. Their grace offered respite from fear, doubt, and concern.

The breeze blew softly on my skin, and I felt the electricity again. The familiar voice spoke in my head, *In the hard and sharp places, my gentle love is with you.*

Krynn seemed lost in her own thoughts, and her face and arms were covered in goose bumps. She looked serene.

"Benjamin?" Rafael said.

I looked at the boy. Oddly, I didn't feel like pushing him away. The peace I felt in this place seemed to have distanced my hurts and frustrations. How wonderful it was to feel only care for him and joy that he was near. "Yeah, Raf?"

"Can I look at your knee?"

An odd request, but what could it hurt? "Sure, go ahead."

He came closer and looked at my knee, then up at me. A butterfly landed on his shoulder. "Can I touch your knee?"

It was messy. He shouldn't be touching it. So why was I giving him permission? "Okay, Raf, but be careful please." What was happening?

Krynn recoiled and scowled at me, surely wondering why I would let the boy touch the bloody mess.

Before she could object, Rafael reached forward and touched a finger to the wound.

I stopped breathing and leaned toward my wounded knee as I witnessed it repair itself and watched the blood disappear. The hole in my pants was the only remaining sign I had fallen. Otherwise my leg looked uninjured and clean.

I looked at Krynn with wide eyes, both amazed and terrified. Was I having a psychotic episode? Surely this would be the final confirmation all was not well. I waited for Krynn to confirm I was losing my sanity. It was all that was left. She would confirm it, and I would need to be in an institution long enough to recover.

If I could recover. This was it. I'd been traveling across time and space in dreams I considered completely real, now a time traveling child had invited himself into my home, and apparently could heal injuries with his touch. I searched her face, but she only stared at my knee.

Without a word, she touched the knee with her own hand, which she checked and saw was clean. Then she rubbed her eyes and touched it again.

She saw what I saw?

We both looked at Rafael. "Raf, I'm...I'm almost afraid to ask," I stammered. "What...what just happened?"

"I'm not sure." His innocent face confirmed he was telling the truth. "The man told me—"

"Wait. Do you mean the man who has been helping you? The one I've met too?"

"Yeah. He's the one who brought me here, to your home, I mean. He told me I'm supposed to help you. He said you forgot some stuff and I could help you remember. He said there would be a few times I could fix some things for you. He said I have the heart of a healer. I don't really know what he meant, but when I saw your knee, I wanted to see if I could fix it."

What was I hearing? It was unbelievable! But then, nothing in the past few months of my life had been all that believable anyway. Why not pile on more? If I was losing it, I may as well make it fantastical. "Okay, Raf, I'll bite." I ran my hands through my hair.

Krynn couldn't make sense of it either. She'd confessed to me how it was unbelievable and magical the boy had shown up, and hard to understand why she felt like he was like a best friend for her from the moment she'd met him. It seemed she'd chosen to enjoy his presence rather than question it. I watched her now realizing how preposterous this was.

And had he said he could fix some "things." Plural? "What else are you here to fix?"

He looked unsure, as if he wasn't certain he was supposed to tell me. Then he looked at Krynn and I understood. *He's here to fix my relationship with her.*

"I can help your family," he answered. "I can help you."

He looked at us both. He carried authority and conviction, and I was taken aback. Then I felt a wind like I'd not felt before. As it picked up, I almost feared the boy, which shocked me. Only this wasn't quite fear, was it? It didn't feel as negative as that. There seemed to be a sacred power flowing through him, capturing every ounce of my senses, to the point I couldn't look away from him or think of anything else in the universe.

His eyes grew wide and lit up, and the hair on his head all stood up as he spoke. I yielded to the power before me and submitted to listening and receiving what would be said—not *to* me, but what would be spoken *over* me.

"The man told me a story about a man who faded like you've started to."

My neck grew taut, and I turned slightly but couldn't turn away. My breathing became shallow and my heart raced in my chest. I looked down to see my hand going translucent and stuffed it in my pocket before Krynn could see.

"He lost his passion and his love for others. He started to think of only himself and lost his connection to people. He lost his taste for anything lovely or wonderful. Soon nothing could please him or give him joy. Even water stopped helping him, and he began to dry up. He withered and faded so badly, he'd become nothing but a pile of dry bones."

I marveled how the boy could use such words. He didn't sound his age at all. It was like some other power was speaking through him. Tears started streaming from my eyes. Though I wanted him to stop, I was under some power preventing me from halting what was happening. I couldn't stop these words, which were like fingers pressing on my heart.

"The man's family and friends cried over him and had to move on with their lives. Then one day, a powerful stranger visited the pile of bones. The stranger had love for all people in his heart and felt sad the man had been reduced to nothing more than dry bones. The man had powerful magic and commanded the bones to stand up into their shape like a skeleton. The bones obeyed and stood, but were nothing more than bones still. The man then spoke to them, 'So you know I'm the joy you were missing and so you'll choose to help others, I will not only cause you to stand, but I'll give you back the life you lost. I will reclaim and regenerate what was lost by you and give you much more.'"

If only I could run away! If only I could stop the boy! The pain in my knee had been far preferable to the bursting heart I felt inside.

"The man blew out his breath over the bones, and they became covered with muscles and skin. The dead pile of bones had now been transformed back into the man who had withered away, and he looked even healthier than before. He was alive and went back to his family. For the rest of his life, the revived man loved everyone he met, even strangers, and helped many people. He formed a special, close friendship with the stranger who helped him with many more things, and they spoke together often."

I knew why it hurt so deeply. I was withering and would lose everything I loved. I was breaking things. I was breaking Krynn, breaking my children, breaking myself, and I didn't know how to fix it. I felt like giving up. My head dropped, and I stared at the ground. "I can't do it. I don't know how," I whispered.

"It's okay. I know you don't know how," a voice answered.

The man who'd called himself The Good Father now stood before me. I looked at Krynn and Rafael to see if they could see him too.

"They feel me here, but they don't see me right now. Rafael has grown close to me. He's a good friend and he knows when I'm close. Krynn has known me since she was a little girl, and she understands more than she lets on. She cares for you deeply."

The man's piercing look into my eyes made me feel my chest had been peeled back, exposing my very spirit. I knew he could see every part of my heart. Every last thought, feeling, and action I'd ever had was laid bare in front of us. Everything I had worked so hard to keep and to hide for myself was out in the open. It should have been devastating. But this wasn't devastation. This was...relief? "I have nothing left to hide from you," I said. "You know it all. You see it and..." I stopped.

"You're so close. It's okay. You can say it." His gentle encouragement soothed the raging chaos within.

Tears streamed freely down my face. Krynn and Raf appeared

frozen in time. I was in a warm, safe bubble that I might never want to leave.

"Leap. Let go," the man said.

It was the first time I saw the face and heard the voice at the same time, and the first time I accepted who the man was. He was The Good Father. He would never leave. Never hurt. Never fail. Never break a promise. Never betray or yell or attack. He wouldn't miss games or recitals. Wouldn't spare any effort to help, to heal, to build up, to encourage. He would never give up hope. Never quit. He would always love.

I finally allowed myself to say what I felt. "You know everything about me and yet you love me. Why? Why me?"

Uttering those words triggered an epiphany. I realized I didn't even love myself. I finally had words for what Rafael felt. If his own father hadn't loved him enough to stay, maybe he wasn't worth love. Maybe he was faulty. It was what I had been feeling too, and only now did I finally know it.

"Benjamin, my hand will *always* reach out for you. All you have to do is take it."

I stared at the ground and kept my hands to my side, though what I wanted most was to reach out to the man's extended hand. "I...I...I need your help."

At the word *help*, the man spoke with a voice that shook me to the core. "Come alive!" he bellowed and blew his breath at me.

Even the ground seemed to tremble. A hurricane swirled over and around me. It seemed it might carry me away, but it filled me instead. Parts of me long dead and decayed were being repaired and returned. Joys, hopes, and dreams I'd killed off flooded into my heart. A victorious smile broke widely across my face—one that could not be hidden.

Krynn and Rafael awoke and saw me smiling wide. She told me my skin nearly glowed brighter than the sunlight beaming on me. I had the same sensation I'd had when I'd leaped from the rock—a feeling of lightness, like everything that hurt me was gone in this moment. I knew this didn't mean it was gone forever—that today was like the beginning of something new being built, and not a final work. It felt amazing.

I looked at the two dear people near me and felt compassion for them. Not pity, but a visceral, heart-wrenching care. A feeling that could drive one to sacrifice their life for another.

I wrapped my arms around Krynn, who held herself close to me and nuzzled her head on my chest. Then I looked at Rafael, whose innocent and lonely eyes broke my heart. I released Krynn and knelt on one knee in front of him. "I love you, Raf. I love you, and you can stay with us."

Krynn couldn't believe what she was hearing. She'd been dreading the day when I would demand the boy had to leave. She was so sure it would happen that she'd prepared herself for a knock-down, drag-out fight about it, and wondered what further damage to our marriage might come of it.

Raf's entire face smiled and he threw himself into my arms. I stood up and twirled him around.

After being set down, he asked Krynn, "Can I hold your hand for the rest of the hike?"

"Strong and soft," Krynn whispered to me, though I wasn't sure what she meant. "This boy is special."

I knew she had the same feeling I had when I first met Rafael. The will to do everything in her power to protect this boy.

"I'd like holding your hand, Rafael," she said, wiping a tear from the sweetness of the boy's request.

I led them out the rest of the hike, turning to smile at them now and then. Rafael held Krynn's hand the whole time and she loved it. It was the most beautiful and the happiest she'd looked for as long as I could remember.

When we arrived home, I was feeling a little mischievous. After Krynn's mother left, I disappeared into the garage for a few minutes, then snuck into the backyard and called for the family to join me. When they reached the edge of the patio where the grass began, I pulled a can of silly string from behind my back and sprayed Krynn straight in the face, then sprayed it all over each of the three kids. All of them stood in shock, wondering who this crazed man in front of them was. I tossed four more cans at their feet and ran away, giggling and yelling, "You're it!"

Krynn was the first to understand the game. She grabbed the can closest to her feet and chased after me, yelling to the children, "Everyone get him!"

Rafael grabbed a can and doused Abigail and Lucas with string, then ran around the yard, screaming, "Can't catch me!"

For the next three minutes all was chaos, streams of shooting string, and laughter. The neighbors must have wondered at the commotion over the fence. By the end, all five of us lay in the grass panting, giggling, and surveying an absolute mess all around.

"C'mon, everyone, it's time for bed," I said. "I'll tuck you in tonight."

The kids gave the typical, "Aww, Dada, can we go to bed later?" response.

I put Rafael on my back and carried Lucas and Abigail in

my arms to the house, then set all three down. "Time for bed, little puppies."

All three climbed into their beds in their shared bunk room before I came to tuck them in. In a refrain familiar to them, I began, "Who's your dad?"

"You are," Lucas and Abigail answered.

"And who loves you?" I asked

"You do," they answered.

"Who's my son and daughter?"

"I am," they each answered.

"And who do I love?"

"Me!" they both said enthusiastically.

I moved to Rafael's bedside and put a gentle hand on his shoulder. "And I love you too, buddy."

CHAPTER TWENTY-THREE

Scott stood on a rocky beach at the southern tip of far northwestern Vancouver Island. Heavy fog had settled in over the small bay and the forest whose trees encroached on the beach. The mist shrouding all around him was so thick, he could barely see the vessel he'd chartered to bring him this far.

The man who'd ferried him out gave one final parting, "Be careful in there. This is wild land, ruled by the wolves, the bears, and the weather. It's unforgiving."

"Unforgiving. Got it," Scott said.

The ferryman had tried to talk Scott out of what he thought was some sort of outdoor excursion, at least four times on the sailing to this point. Scott knew the man couldn't comprehend how focused he was, and didn't care to explain. He'd placated him for as long as he needed to get where he wanted to be, and now could finally be rid of the man and his advice.

As Scott watched the boat slip into the fog and disappear from view, a shiver of fear ran through him. What would it be like to disappear into the mist, never to return? The fog felt neither compassion nor pity. It continued to roll in from the sea unabated. He looked at the forest. It appeared to be raging against the mist, with neither one giving in to the other.

For its part, the density of this rainforest, where it rained nearly three of every four days, rivaled any jungle. Ahead of him, Scott could see only impediments to progress. It would be an incredibly challenging journey he was about to undertake. The darkness of the canopy and the thickness of its underbrush might swallow him if he dared enter. His next steps would put him on a final path that only ended one of three ways. This would be his last effort before disappearing, he would successfully find the talisman and return victorious, or the forest—more jungle than forest, really—would swallow him and never release him.

It was overwhelming. He stood gazing at the immovable object taunting him. A shape slinked in the mist just at the edge of the forest. It stopped and looked at Scott, then disappeared into the thickness of the woods. By its stealthy movements, its size, and what little of its shape could be made out, it was a wolf.

He remembered the stranger who had told him not to follow the wolves on the night he'd found the map that had brought him here. If he'd listened to him, he'd never have made it this far. Anger swelled. He'd made so many trade-offs, ended so many relationships, and experienced so many hurts just to get this far. That anyone—*anyone*—could get in his way disgusted and enraged him. It was enough to propel him forward.

It was time to announce his arrival to the woods and any nearby creatures. No sense seeking stealth in a forest covered by branches, leaves, and other debris he'd be walking over. "You and me, wolf—we're gonna keep out of each other's way," he declared. "Don't try to stop me or you'll find out just how determined I am. On the other hand, if you want to show me the way, well, I know you know the secrets of this place."

He picked up his pack of supplies and headed into the forest. His belly burned with fire fueling him forward.

As the day progressed, the forest's efforts to fight against him only increased his will. With a machete in hand, he spent the day fighting back the brush attempting to block his path. When he wasn't fighting the plants and debris—and sometimes when he was—he was climbing nearly impossibly steep hillsides and grabbing at roots, branches, and the underbrush itself for purchase. The mist turned to heavy rain, and all was wet and slick.

While he climbed a steep hill, his hand slipped off the wet undergrowth he held, and he was sent sliding twenty feet back down, bruising his hip and an elbow.

He cursed and sat for a moment, attempting to regain the energy to find a way up the hill. Rain dripped down his face as his mind wandered back to Los Angeles. It must be warm and dry there. He remembered how encouraging it felt to be given a new lead that was much more tangible than any he'd had in his years of searching. He picked himself up and gently touched his bruised hip.

"Nothing stops me. Nothing," he said, and attempted the climb again.

It had been a grueling eight hours of bushwhacking, and he'd barely made it more than three miles, since he'd had to backtrack multiple times when the terrain became treacherous . He clung tenuously on the side of the steep, rain-soaked hill.

Thunder clapped loudly overhead, startling him.

He screamed against the wind now throwing branches to the ground around him. "If it's a battle of wills, forest, you've met your match. You hear me? You'll have to kill me or disappear me, otherwise you better get used to me! *I'm. Not. Quitting*!"

He finally reached the top of the hill, which seemed more like a mountain to his tired body. He doubted he'd sleep much tonight as he settled in under several trees he hoped would act as lightning rods if necessary. There was no use trying to climb down the other side of the hill in the dark. It was too treacherous.

A wolf howled, and was answered by another and then two more.

Soaked to the bone, Scott began to shiver. He reached into his pack for an emergency blanket. In the long waking hours of the night, the thunder, the swaying trees, and the wolves gave him steady reminders he wasn't safe. To distract himself, he attempted to let his mind wander again. A bolt of lightning flashed overhead, bringing him back from daydreams about a tropical island. He shifted his weight off his bruised hip, adjusted the blanket, and tried to find a comfortable position.

His eyes opened, and he was surprised to have fallen asleep at the top of the hill. The brief respite from the storm had only served to give him fitful dreams of saying goodbye to Aila and Rafael, and of wolves surrounding him.

Thankfully, he found the storm appeared to have passed. Thick gray clouds still lingered and blocked much of the dawn's light.

The mist shrouded the valley below him, and were those wolf prints near where he'd slept?

They looked fresh. He looked at the tracks for a moment and noticed they left the hilltop in the direction he would be heading. "Guess we're going to the same place, pal."

Then his heart skipped a beat and his breath caught in his chest. Not just one, but two wolves. One set of prints was larger than the other, with one set missing a toenail on one of the right paws. *Just like Alaska.* A shiver ran down his spine. Was he more afraid or excited that these could be the wolves he'd seen before? But that wasn't possible, was it?

But what if...?

It might be a good omen if these were the wolves who'd been there when he found the clue that led him so close to his lifelong obsession. "Maybe they're leading me there. They *want* me to find it."

A breeze blew over the top of the hill as Scott was about to begin the new day's hike. A sliver appeared in the clouds, and the sun broke through where Scott stood. This was odd. Such strong déjà vu. He recalled the day he'd sat on the ridge over Blueberry Lake and had an unusual conversation.

"I wonder," the strange man had said. "I wonder if that will work? You might find the treasure you're after. Me, I've found people seem happiest when they've stopped searching for things 'out there.' Life's funny that way, isn't it? Sometimes when we find what we want, we find we don't want it, and sometimes when we give away what we want, we find it, and realize we can't lose it."

That old busybody was a little cracked. He shook his head and took a step forward.

The sun pried the clouds a little farther apart, and the breeze blew stronger—except it didn't move the trees. But why could he feel it if they showed no signs of its presence?

"Scott," a voice behind him said with authority.

He stopped.

"Scott, the last time you saw me, you may remember I told you about hunting for treasure. There's always more to find. It's not likely to satisfy, and what's more, you may end up as prey. There's a better way though.'"

Scott closed his eyes and pursed his lips. How could the presence of the man make him feel so good and so upset at the same time? "Yeah, I remember," he said, turning to face him.

He stiffened his back as he prepared for whatever the man had for him this time. He was sure the man would try to dissuade him from going forward, and he'd come too far. There was no stopping now.

"People's destinations in life are often a matter of the paths they choose to walk...or not walk," the man went on. "The person who walks on rocky paths often twists an ankle or stubs a toe. And those who follow their own paths sometimes don't know where those paths lead."

"You're speaking in riddles again," Scott said with no small amount of frustration in his voice.

"You're a man who's chosen his path. With focus and determination, you have never veered from it. I'm here to tell you something about your path." The man sounded caring, as always, but Scott sensed some urgency that he hadn't noticed in previous exchanges.

"I'm a man who believes everyone has to find their own path,"

Scott told him. "People who say there's one path are full of it. There are a lot of ways people can get to good places, and I say to each his own."

"The one who walks a dangerous path in a dense forest on their way to a dangerous place may miss what the bird who flies above the forest knows."

Scott shook his head and scoffed. "Riddles."

"Scott, I have a trade to offer you that I will make plain and not mask."

"About time for some clarity. I'm too tired and cold for games."

The man looked at him with compassion, which only annoyed him since it meant all his attempts at cynicism were being ignored and met with kindness. "Scott, you're on a path that leads to emptiness and hurt. I know you believe it will deliver what you need—what you seek—but what if I told you I have what you seek? What if I told you, if you give me the walls you hold around your heart, I can give you peace and hope in return. For hurt, I can give you joy. For hardness I can give you gentleness. I can show you the path that leads to love and which will heal both you and Rafael. All you have to do is trust me and be vulnerable with me. I will protect you and never hurt you, I promise. Choose the path of love, not of walls and hurt."

It was an intriguing offer. He wanted to discount everything the man said, but he knew it was genuine and he sensed some sort of power about him. Maybe he could deliver on the promise. He wanted to accept the trade.

The hardness around his heart melted slightly. He closed his eyes and couldn't help but see his father floating away before never being seen again. His determination steeled. *No.* He shook his head. "I choose me," he said with a cold calmness belying the hot fire inside. In fact the rage was good. It would propel him forward. "My father didn't choose me. I deserve this. I...choose... *me*." He picked up his pack and walked away.

The man sighed sadly, then called after him, "The wolves have prepared it all for you. The boat is there. The island waits for you. I won't stop you, though I wish with all my heart I could."

Scott began to turn around, but forced his face forward and walked away. His mind was made up and nothing could stop him. His foot stepped directly on the footprint of a wolf with a missing nail as he began the treacherous descent down the mountain toward the northwest edge of the island.

That night—now his second in the forest—he once again shielded himself from the rain, the wind, and the wolves, and attempted to keep his mind off Rafael. His love for his son would only slow him down. Even Rafael might have to be put outside his walls for a time, at least until he found the talisman or the island.

He guessed it was sometime near eleven when the wolves started howling near him again.

CHAPTER TWENTY-FOUR

Rafael lay awake in the bottom of a bunk bed with Lucas above and Abigail in the other bed nearby. The three of them had played with Benjamin in the yard until they were exhausted from running, being tickled, and trying to wrestle him to the ground. They'd had a wonderful evening capped off with hot chocolate and extra helpings of homemade whipped cream Krynn made.

The kids had talked and giggled in bed until Benjamin finally came in for one last hug and a gentle reminder that these little ones needed sleep. Rafael clutched Benji closely. He'd been so happy in Benjamin's home with Lucas and Abigail. So why couldn't he stop thinking about Dad? Fatigue finally coaxed him to close his eyes.

He didn't know how he knew or why he knew, but he was absolutely certain—Dad was in the present time and on Vancouver

Island. It had hit him the moment he'd closed his eyes. He knew it was true without question. But what should he do about it?

"He's leaving, Benji," Rafael whispered. "He's leaving and I know where he is."

He lay thinking, scared and lonely. He desperately wanted to stop his dad from leaving. Wanted to convince him to stay and to give more twirling-through-the-air hugs. What if seeing him could heal Dad the way it had been helping Benjamin? What did the man mean, he had the heart of a healer? Could he convince his dad to stay and to be whole?

He was wracked with doubt. How could he, a seven-year-old boy, undertake a journey to a place he'd never been? What if he didn't make it to Dad in time or, worse yet, what if he reached Dad and he still left? There would be no coming back from that. It felt like it could end him. He was frozen in fear.

Then something changed. A new feeling grew. Something fierce and strong. Resolve swelled within him. It was time to leave childhood behind. It was time to grow up and not let things like fear stop him. He would bury the childish things and focus singularly on what was required of him.

"Benji," he whispered in the night. "Little boys can't go on big journeys. I'm too scared and too little. I have to be hard now. If I'm soft, I'll stay here, scared. I have to stop him. You're soft and cuddly and fun, Benji. You're a friend for little boys. I can't be a little boy anymore. I have to go. Make friends with Lucas, okay? He'll be a good friend. I have to be hard now. Goodbye, Benji."

He stood, gave Benji a big, squeezing hug, then tucked the stuffed dog into the bed he had just gotten up from and tiptoed to the door.

A voice broke the silence in the room. "Whatcha doing, Raf?" Lucas asked.

Rafael came back to the side of the bunk so he could whisper. Abigail's heavy breathing told him she still slept.

"I have to go, Lucas. My dad isn't too far away. I think it's maybe a six- or seven-hour bus ride. I don't know how I know, but he's at a place called Vancouver Island. All the way at the top part of it. I have to go find him. Can you take care of Benji for me? You can have him now. He's a special friend and so are you. I want you to have him." He passed the dog up to Lucas, who hugged it.

"Why aren't you keeping him? Maybe he can go with you."

"Not this time. I can't do kid stuff if I want to be brave. I have to be hard now. Please take care of Benji for me and let him take care of you too."

"Okay. I'll take care of him. But I wish you weren't leaving."

"Me too, Lucas. You and I have a lot of fun together. I think your dad will be okay now. Keep telling him to play, okay? And please don't tell him I left until tomorrow. I don't want to make him sad, and I can't have him stop me."

"Okay, Raf. I won't. Are you sure you have to go though? It seems scary."

"I have to try to stop my dad from disappearing. I think I might be able to help him. Maybe he'll stay and we can all fix the disappearing. Maybe the man who calls himself The Good Father can help him too." He leaned in even closer. "Want to know a secret, Lucas? I think I might know how to fly. I can't tell you how yet, 'cause I'm not sure I'm right, but I think I might have figured it out."

"Wow, Raf. Will you teach me some day?"

Rafael looked at the floor. In truth, he wasn't sure he really knew how to fly. He had an idea that had begun forming, but he wasn't sure it was true yet. "If I do figure it out, you and I will fly together. And Abigail too. And I'll teach your dad. It would be super fun!"

He smiled at Lucas and put his hand up toward the top bunk. Lucas took his hand and squeezed it gently. "I love you, Lucas," he said before tiptoeing quietly out of the room.

Lucas lay in quiet shock until he whispered to the room Rafael had left, "I love you too."

Rafael reached the stairs and took one last look at Benjamin's bedroom door. How good would it feel to crawl into the covers and be safe and warm with Benjamin and Krynn. He shook his head. He couldn't be a kid now.

Several hours later, he was staring absently out a bus window into the night. He had ducked just behind a woman walking on, appearing to be her son and felt clever for having pulled off the ruse.

Aside from the occasional headlight coming in the opposite direction, he mostly saw empty darkness. Without the ability to watch the landscape, he felt disoriented, not seeing whether the bus was making forward progress or where he was at all. Hopefully he'd gotten on the right bus.

He'd boarded at eleven p.m. and it was now nearing one a.m. The soft glow of floor lights and the humming drone of the bus lulled him to sleep. He relented to fatigue, closing his eyes and leaning his head against the hard, cold window. It made him wish he had his little stuffed dog, who was both his trusted companion and a soft pillow.

Lucas would take good care of him.

After some time, he slipped into a fitful sleep, dreaming of wolves and stormy seas and of the feeling of Scott's hand on his shoulder.

※

A NEW MORNING HAD dawned. Steam carried the aromas of a freshly brewed cup of coffee to my nose as I enjoyed a lazy Saturday morning. Abigail sat nearby watching television.

"Mama! Mama! Where are you?!" Lucas shouted through the house.

The sound of fear in his voice startled me and I jumped from the table. He nearly ran by me in the hallway when I reached out an arm to gently pull him close.

"Whoa, whoa! What's wrong, buddy? Can I help you? Wait, what's in your hand?"

Benji's detached leg was in one of Lucas's hands and the injured stuffed dog in the other. What had happened? "Oh, no! Rafael is going to be heartbroken," I couldn't help but exclaim. "That little dog means the world to him! Raf! Raf! I'd better go help him." I turned to head upstairs.

"He's gone, Dada," Lucas said sheepishly.

He was mistaken or was playing at something. "Now is not the time for hide-and-seek or other games, son. Raf! Come on out, buddy!"

"No, Dada. He's really gone. He left during the night."

Why would Lucas say such a thing? It couldn't possibly be true. How and why would Rafael leave?

I searched Lucas's face for signs of a game or a lie. He looked pale and afraid. Maybe his older sister could explain better. "Abigail, have *you* seen Rafael this morning?" I asked.

She looked afraid to answer. "I think Lucas is right, Dada. I don't think Rafael is here anymore. His bed was empty when I got up and I haven't seen him."

They had to be wrong. I would reason with them and get to the bottom of it. "He couldn't have gone anywhere. He takes Benji everywhere. He doesn't ever leave that dog behind."

I looked again at the leg separated from the body and felt sick to my stomach. Why did I care so deeply for a little stuffed animal, and where were all these extreme emotions coming from these days?

On cue, Lucas nervously explained, "He gave Benji to me, Dada. He said he had to be hard and couldn't be a little boy anymore. He said his dad is not too far away and he has to chase him to help him. He seemed different, Dada. Not as fun or as happy."

Terror pressed on my shoulders and chest. I could barely breathe. I dropped onto a bench in the entryway, where we'd been talking.

"Vancouver Island," Lucas said. "He's gone to Vancouver Island. He said it was at the top of the island."

Shock silenced me. The world shrunk to just me, and I lost the filter from my thoughts to my mouth. "He thinks he can find the talisman or help Scott not disappear. He'll never make it. He won't survive. The wolves or the forest or the weather will get him."

Lucas's and Abigail's alarmed faces stared at me. Seeing their father look terrified and speak of Rafael not surviving had been unsettling.

Lucas tried to snap me out of it. "He said he might know how to fly, Dada. Maybe he and his dada will be okay."

The injured dog still hung from Lucas's hand. Rafael had given Benji up and was out chasing after Scott, alone. The sight of the ripped-apart dog disturbed me to my depths. "Lucas, how did Benji get ripped so badly?"

He grimaced. "I'm sorry, Dada. I'm sorry," he said with pleading eyes and no pause for breath. "I didn't mean it. I wanted to twirl him through the air and pretend we were flying."

"You did *what*!?"

His whole body shrank. He looked little and powerless. I knew I should stop.

"How *could* you?! That boy deserves help! He deserves protection! He deserves to stay a little boy, and here you go ripping up his last connection to childhood and joy? How *could* you, Lucas? What an *awful* and *thoughtless* thing you've done! You should have been more careful! Benji is not a toy! For goodness' sake, *grow up*, Lucas!"

What was spewing out of me? Where did this all come from? I stormed out to the back yard to cool off before I said worse things. There, I dropped into a patio chair and put my head in my hands. *Idiot. What an idiot.* I knew better. I knew not to open my heart to the kid and the man. Now I'd lost him. This is exactly why I didn't want the kid around in the first place. *He'll never survive and I'm not sure Scott will either.*

Head still in my hands, I sighed. Lucas hadn't deserved such a harsh response. I was so scared for Rafael, so sad about Benji, and so raw from my own recent experiences that it had all just come boiling out of me. He didn't deserve all that.

I squeezed my eyes shut in agony, and my mind raced through all the moments I'd shared with Rafael. There was the day I'd seen him when I sat on a boulder and felt the shivers down my spine, seeing both Rafael and The Good Father for the first time. Then the second time I saw him, when we had played on the hill with the cars. A thought began taking hold as I remembered walking in creeks barefoot with pants rolled up, jumping from rocks, chasing kids on the beach, playing with silly string, sharing hugs, feeling laughter, shedding tears, experiencing heartache, joy, and pain, and having deep conversations.

I admitted something to myself. *All my best memories from the past few months—maybe my best memories for years—have come while, or just after, I was with that little boy.* Whether it was playing with him, remembering the joys of childhood, or enjoying time with my wife and children, every moment had seemed connected with Rafael recently.

I had decided to allow him to stay in our home out of pity and for the boy's good, but now I realized a profound truth. The boy himself was something good in my life. Now what would happen if the gray overwhelmed him too?

A hand set down on my shoulder, shaking me from my thoughts. "What do we do?" Krynn asked through tears.

There was only one answer. But what would she say? I put my hand on hers and looked into her eyes. "I have to find him, Krynnie. Is that okay with you? I mean, is it okay that I need to leave right away, just as you and I have been reconnecting? You and the kids...I...I love you all so much. Krynnie, I'm worried about him, and I have this unexplainable worry about myself. If he doesn't make it, I...I don't know what that will do to me."

Krynn moved around in front of me and held my head. Her eyes blazed with fierce love. "You do whatever needs to be done, and you go save that boy." Though she was crying, I could see that if she were able to save the boy, she would have already left.

We were interrupted by Lucas, who had been eavesdropping at the patio door. He spoke with a pitiable voice. "Here, Dada, I fixed him. Please don't be mad. I'm sorry. I put all my stuffed friends in a bag for the next time Mama gives stuff to Goodwill. I don't need that stuff anymore. I'll be big now, Dada. I'll be tough like Rafael and like you. Please don't be mad at me or leave me like your dad did." With sweet eyes and a sad face, he held out Benji, who now had his leg held on by black duct tape Lucas must have found in the garage.

I carried many deeply held wounds, but none had ever hurt so badly as this. My heart burned with anguish and regret, and I thought about the time the stranger had spoken to me at the beach. I was now sure he also was The Good Father.

What was it he'd said to me when he'd talked so much about footprints? *It takes care to set them just right. Care and thought.*

I'd been careless and I knew it. I had not only wounded Lucas, giving him a wound like many I carried, but I'd also left the wrong footprint, which Lucas was now following. I was passing hurt forward. Hurt that had existed through so many generations, it was as though my DNA had adapted and it was born-in. Was I hard wired to continue the hurt?

I needed help and hoped The Good Father could hear my silent prayer: *I know you're real, and I know you have good things for me and for my family. I know you're a healer. Can you please heal me and heal Lucas? Can you rewire me?*

I closed my eyes and felt comforted in a way I hadn't known since before my own father had left, and I knew what I needed to do. I got down on one knee to look eye to eye with Lucas. "Lucas, I was wrong. I was *so* wrong. Lucas, I have some hurts and *I'm* the one who needs to grow, buddy." Tears poured from my eyes. "You are beautiful, son."

Fear and doubt melted from his face when he heard the word "son."

"My anger was like darkness that tries to cover light. Lucas, never give in to the darkness. Shine your light. Light will *always* be stronger than darkness. So be a little boy. Smile. Laugh. Be silly. Be loud. Play like a puppy, jump in creeks, and hug your sister and your Mama...and me."

I gently pushed the stuffed dog back to his chest and wrapped my arms around the little boy's frame. Krynn watched him close his eyes and grin as he rested his head on my shoulder—his father's shoulder—as he soaked in love that protected, built, and healed.

I set him back a step and motioned Abigail over to us. With a hand on each of their shoulders, I looked in their eyes. "My lovely children. Please know this: I'm not perfect, but I will *always* love you and I will work on being better. None of my mistakes are your fault, and you don't deserve to be hurt. Know that I love you and you never have to blame yourself for my mistakes, okay?"

They were too young to fully comprehend what was being spoken over them, but I saw they each understood the feeling perfectly. They were being given a new kind of protection. It was not a hard shell being put around them, rather it was a warm and comforting presence. They'd never heard their father talk like this before.

I became serious. "Guys,"—I looked at them and at Krynn—"I have to chase after Raf. I have to see if I can help him. I'm not sure he can do what he's doing without my help. I know it'll be sad for me to leave for a few days, but I have to go. Stay here and take care of Mama, okay? And you take care of Benji, Lucas. He misses Rafael too."

I hugged each of them, then readied myself to find the little boy.

⁓

WHEN RAFAEL HAD ARRIVED in the city of Vancouver on the mainland, he couldn't believe his luck at hearing two men talk about taking a float plane out to the tip of Vancouver Island, and had snuck into the back of their car and then onto the plane, hiding among some gear and coats. It seemed impossible they hadn't noticed him, but then, since he'd had the magic to summon Benjamin across time, he assumed he might now be using magic to hide himself. It wasn't worth much time thinking on it. He was consumed with finding Dad.

The men landed the plane by a small inlet on the southern side of the most northern section of the island. They dropped an inflatable raft into the water and climbed into it to fish, after anchoring the plane. When they looked like they were far enough away to be out of earshot, Rafael grabbed a life vest from the plane and buckled it around himself. He couldn't quite get it on correctly and grabbed a second one to hold onto.

He attempted to climb carefully out of the plane's cabin. He planned to step onto the pontoons, but his little legs couldn't quite reach on their own. He dangled from the cabin by his arms. He wasn't strong enough to pull himself back up. There was no use now. He'd have to let go and plunge into the water below.

As he let go to drop down, one of the straps from the vest he'd buckled on wedged itself under a piece of metal bolted down to hold the seat in place. The strap pinched into a tiny space where the seat's frame bent up at the floor and held Rafael suspended in the air above the frigid Pacific waters. He struggled to shake loose, but it was no good. He dangled, spinning in the air awkwardly, and had slipped most of the way out of the life vest, which now forced his two arms upward and nearly covered his face.

What could he do now? Though panic surged, he couldn't just quit. He had no choice. He dropped the extra life vest to the water below, in between the two pontoons. Wriggling his little frame, he worked on sinking lower in the vest in an attempt to drop from it entirely, but the closer he got to extricating himself from the dangling life preserver, the more it forced his arms up and the more they bore the entire weight of his body. Searing waves of pain shot through him, making him feel faint.

Why am I here? Why did I do this? He groaned, summoning the energy to make one final push. He kicked his legs and twisted his hips and torso as violently as he could. With a sudden slip, he dropped into the bone-chillingly cold water.

Mama had taken him to many swim lessons, and Dad had played with him often enough in rivers and the ocean, so he was a much more competent swimmer than the average seven-year-old, and was more competent than many children much older than him. He kicked as powerfully as he could with his legs, bursting through the surface with a great gasp from the shocking cold. His chest constricted, and he found it nearly impossible to take full breaths.

In spite of his skill and experience with swimming, he looked at the shore and knew he wasn't strong enough to swim through the rolling waves all the way to safety. It was too far, and his shoulders still caused him to wince in pain from larger movements.

He treaded water to scan for the extra life vest, only to see the current had now taken it thirty feet away from him, and farther away from the shore. He hung one arm over a pontoon. He could attempt to climb back up into the plane, but it would be no good with his short legs. Going back wasn't an option even if he was able. He was ready to die trying to reach his dad if it came to it. He could swim for it, but he feared he might drown before he could cover the distance.

The only choice was to swim for the vest. He let go of the pontoon and did as much as he could to focus on the form he'd learned in lessons at the pool and from Dad. Sidestroking so he could breathe and rest as much as possible, he made his way toward the flotation device that was now his only hope.

The cold water didn't bother him as much now. He didn't realize this meant he was becoming numb to it. The first steps toward hypothermia had started their course and he felt fatigue growing. His shoulders burned and his lungs couldn't take in as much air as he wanted due to the cold water. His face dipped under the sea and he swallowed saltwater.

He kicked his legs hard and brought his head back above the surface, spitting up the salt water and dry heaving. He almost vomited what little food was in his nearly empty stomach and gagged several more times. He panted for breath. If his head dipped below the surface again, he wouldn't be able to come back up. For a moment at least, he could attempt to ignore the throbbing in his shoulders. He threw the last reserves of his strength into a freestyle kick toward the life vest. After a few strokes, his body screamed for air, but he wouldn't have the strength to surface. If he opened his mouth, nothing but saltwater would fill it and it would be the end. Something had gone wrong. He must have missed his target or was too tired and wouldn't make it. Then, by some miracle, his hand slapped the top of the floating orange life preserver.

He'd made it.

He held onto the vest tightly and started the long swim out of the sea. When he finally reached shore, he had to rest on his hands and knees to steady himself and catch his breath. He shivered and his teeth chattered from the cold. Turning his back to the icy ocean, he looked at the entrance to the forest. It was dark and foreboding, even by the light of day.

A clap of thunder over his head seemed to be an announcement from the island, telling him to go back. Raindrops landed on his head, and the trees lurched in gusts of wind. Maybe he should quit after all. How could he survive the dark jungle in front of him when just reaching the shore had already nearly killed him?

Dad was somewhere in those wet, menacing woods. "No!" he yelled. "Hard, Benji. I told you. It's time to be hard." He marched forward until the jungle swallowed him.

The forest canopy hung high over him, blocking out much of the sky and reminding him how small he was. In spite of the thick covering, the rain and wind still managed to find their way in.

Large drops of cold water dripped off the trees, finding his head, neck, and shoulders while fir needles and branches fell around him. At least the act of walking and fighting his way through the underbrush was warming him up a little.

∼∼

I DISEMBARKED FROM A boat I'd chartered to take me near to the tip of Vancouver Island and stood on the shore next to an abandoned life preserver. Maybe it had fallen off a boat and washed ashore.

The vessel's captain tried talking me out of entering the woods. "Storm's brewing," he said. "Like I told the other guy a little over a day ago, be careful and watch for the wolves, the bears, and the weather. This forest is unforgiving. A mistake could cost you your life."

The other guy. He must have meant Scott. "I understand," I answered. "It's just something I have to do. I'm chasing a treasure as important to me as my life."

"Not sure any treasure could be worth that."

"Let's just say I found a treasure worth pursuing," I told him, and the man let it go.

I watched as the boat motored off and could faintly be seen through the rain being driven in sideways by the strong winds. I walked to the edge of the woods and searched the ground, hardly believing my good luck. A child's footprints! "He was here!"

I bent to examine where the footprints led and saw they headed into the thick forest in a northwest direction. Then my blood ran cold. *Oh no. Not them too.* Circling some of Rafael's footprints and then following them, were a wolf's footprints. It looked like the wolf was missing a nail on one of its paws.

"Please help him!" I hadn't prayed much before, but now it was coming out without me thinking about it. "He needs you. Please watch over him."

Seeing the wolf prints made me sick to my stomach. Paranoia took hold, and every sound of raindrops, wind, and swaying trees sounded like a wolf in my imagination. Visions of the large wolf with the scar on its hip overpowered me. I couldn't stop picturing both Rafael and myself being attacked. Fear crept through my veins, first laying its icy grip on my heart and then moving throughout my body. My eyes grew wide and I instinctually hunched over. I wanted to be anywhere else, but how could I abandon Rafael to his fate? Still, I didn't know how to break fear's hold on my feet—to shake them loose and move forward.

I barely found the courage to utter one word and it came out in a wheezing, weak sound. "Help."

I heard a loud *whoosh*, followed by another and another.

Now what could that be? I dreaded what I would see but had to know. At the edge of the shore, a magnificent crane took off from a large boulder. It climbed in the violent winds, looking so graceful it seemed it ignored them entirely, like it was untouched by them. The crane flew over my head, then climbed above the canopy and traveled in a northwest direction.

The Good Father had asked for my trust, just before a crane stood guard on the bridge in front of the wolf with the scar until the wolf relented and left.

It couldn't be the same one, could it?

Whether it was a coincidence, an omen, or something more,

it emboldened me. Taking a deep breath, I headed into the rain forest in pursuit of Rafael, following the direction of the crane.

I hope there aren't wolves watching me.

∼

AFTER A FULL DAY of immense effort, Rafael had managed to get to the top of a hill where he could see above some of the trees. His clothes had ripped in several places and what was left of them seemed more a combination of dirt, water, and blood than clothing. Every part of his body ached and his stomach rumbled as loud as the intermittent thunder—as if he needed a reminder that he hadn't eaten much food since leaving the house.

By the dying light of the sun—what little of it came through the thick storm clouds above—he could see it seemed he was only about two miles from an area where the forest didn't seem to absorb the light as much, though he couldn't be certain how far it was he was looking. He hoped the area that looked lighter would be the northwestern tip of the island that his premonition had told him to aim for.

Pausing his movement to look at the path ahead meant he'd now have to regain momentum. He sighed heavily, searching for his last reserves of energy. He might be able to make it to the island's tip, but the ordeal cemented a thought: he would need his dad to carry him from there or he would never make it out. He'd gone as far as he could.

He'd barely survived the swimming disaster, then he'd undertaken a trek through harsh lands; climbed on, over, and around slick rocks; pushed through thick underbrush; and battled cutting branches and brambles. He hadn't eaten in a day. He had twisted ankles, aching shoulders, bruised legs and arms, cuts and scratches all over, and ripped clothes.

The rain had been pouring hard all day, soaking everything in sight. In his fatigued state he didn't judge his first step well, and as he stepped onto the northward slope of the hill to go down to the land below, he slipped.

His body landed on the side of the hill and went sliding, careening, and bumping its way down the slope, before finally stopping at the side of a swollen creek. He was splayed out in dirt and water. Pain reverberated through every fiber of his being. It was a miracle he hadn't broken anything, but multiple cuts, scratches, and bruises from the slide had been added to the rest of the day's injuries.

Everything hurt. His body was a memorial—a shrine to each fall, unseen bramble, cold raindrop, and gust of wind. He lay crying at the edge of the stream, which, after receiving so many raindrops for hours on end, made no acknowledgment of the tears he added to it. It didn't notice and didn't care.

He tried to get up on his hands and knees. Every movement throbbed and felt raw. He was more automaton than little boy. His mind had separated itself from the pain. He was a living contradiction. Both numb and wracked with pain. Both able to march step by step and nearly reaching his end. The brain forcing the body onward and the two in constant debate. The only way the brain was now winning was to mask the heart, lest any feelings risk derailing the effort required. Here in this forest, with what was now a raging storm, any softness would be crushed. Rafael's mind dedicated itself only to his will and determination. He shut off his feelings. It was a requirement for survival.

Still on his hands and knees, head hanging, he watched little streams of water drip from his hair to the ground. "Hard," he said, standing.

He wobbled on his feet, then steadied himself and walked forward.

A large branch the size of a small tree fell not far from him, splintering on a boulder. In the distance he heard a wolf howl, then, shortly after, another answered.

⁓⁓

At the sound of howling wolves, I picked up my pace and fought more boldly against the brush. I hoped Rafael was close, but if he was, that would mean the wolves were near him too.

"Help," I said again into the darkness of the storm and the night taking hold of the forest.

CHAPTER TWENTY-FIVE

Rafael finally reached the point where the rainforest gave way to the sands and the sea. Exhausted, bruised, and cut up, he staggered as he stepped across the border where the thick jungle met the beach.

The storm was nearly a gale now. Lightning blazed and thunder cracked overhead. Raindrops as large as small pebbles drove hard onto his hair and face, dripping over his eyebrows so rapidly he was forced to squint. Rivulets ran down his cheeks and over his mouth, open from fatigue. He scanned the beach, illuminated every few moments when bolts of electricity splintered across the sky. The waves heaved. All was violence around him. There was no respite. He'd come so far and could see nothing other than rage. He began to cry.

"Rafael! What are you *doing* here?" a voice screamed over the noise of the storm.

Did he dare to hope it could be Dad? Through sheets of rain and the alternating of darkness and blinding light, he couldn't make out the figure walking toward him. The man approaching him held his arm up, shielding himself from the storm. It appeared the man was semitransparent.

Beyond the figure approaching with visible pain in his steps, there was a small boat. It rested on the sand, just past the stopping point of the waves that appeared to be trying to overtake the jungle itself, only stopped by the stubbornness of the land before them.

Another flash of lightning revealed the figure. It was Dad, only it almost wasn't. He was now a mere illusion of himself. A wraith, barely able to solidly contact the earth enough to push into each step. He moved painstakingly slowly.

Rafael sprang forward. Despite his injuries and extreme exhaustion, he ran toward the hunched figure with abandon, his arms spread wide. He ran as wildly as the storm itself. There was no thought, only the desire to leap into Dad's arms. If he could reach Dad, he could speak words of healing into his ear, call him to be whole and ask him to stay. Maybe it wasn't too late.

Scott watched Rafael running, and time slowed. A bolt of lightning reached fingers in every direction across the night sky. Rafael was nearly frozen in place. Each raindrop could be seen as it slowly sank toward the soaked ground.

As the world barely moved in slow motion, a vision flashed in his mind. He and Rafael held hands, lying in thick grasses with a sweet breeze blowing overhead. An eagle circled majestically above. A few feet away a crane stood in the reeds watching them. Then a voice echoed in his head. It was the stranger speaking in the conversation they'd had on the ridge in Alaska.

See that eagle? She's hunting treasure for her children. Such a practical demonstration of her care. And yet, I can't help but think, she is most real to them when she is there, in the nest with them.

It would be amazing to lie in warm grasses and be together. He stiffened himself with pained effort to stand tall, spreading his own arms to meet Rafael's. Maybe he could will himself to be real enough to pick up the little boy and twirl him through the air. What if he could twirl him enough to lift them both above and away from the storm?

For a breath, time stopped. The wind abated and the lightning bolt halted its creep across the sky. Rafael remained paused in mid-stride, with arms wide. The raindrops hung in suspended animation. A breeze blew across Scott's face and a shiver reached into his soul. Then he blinked and time moved forward. Rafael reached his last step before Scott and leaped into the air toward the open arms. As he did, Scott had another vision, and the world paused again.

He was alone on a tropical island. The sun shone and he worked at building a cabin. A protective, mostly see-through energy shield covered the island. Nothing could get in to take him away and make him disappear. He was alone, but he was real—if not to Rafael, then at least to himself. A little garden next to the cabin was full of lush produce, and palm trees swayed above. He held a socket wrench in his left hand to tighten a bolt, securing a deck to the cabin. In his right hand was a 5/16ths socket.

He returned his attention from the vision. Rafael hung in the air in front of him, with a panicked face. Was it panic though? He looked different than Scott remembered him. No, this didn't quite look like panic. It was desperate resolve.

Why did it remind him of the wildflowers in Alaska? With great strength and tenacity, they grew in harsh conditions, fighting for survival. They knew only forward effort, straining to the sun, even from underneath the snow and rock. Despite their dogged grit and harsh surroundings, they were fragrant, lovely, and fragile.

Rafael looked like a wildflower. In the middle of this storm, doing everything it could to break him, he would only move forward. He would never quit until he was broken.

Scott's body slumped. He didn't feel that kind of strength. He looked at Rafael, then at the boat and beyond, into the motionless sea that still sat frozen. Somewhere out there was a secret place. A place he could secure himself against the disappearing and hide away from the emptiness.

He *had* to find it.

He had failed to learn how to fly and would disappear soon if he didn't reach it. It would hurt Rafael deeply, but he didn't know another way. Only one of those two visions seemed possible.

Pain ripped through his chest and stomach, and a painful lump gripped his throat. The world felt darker, and numbness took hold of him. He knew what he must do, and, as if to acknowledge he'd reached a decision, time resumed.

Rafael passed through Scott's open arms and body, landing hard in the sand, barely catching himself. He looked up, his face a mix of sand and horror. His eyes searched Scott, now seeing nearly straight through him. The pouring rain made its effort to rinse the boy's face clean. Only a little sand in his eyebrows and the corner of his mouth remained.

Scott lowered his arms and hung his head. No memory of breezes remained in his mind. He now only knew emptiness.

~

Rafael studied his dad, who looked rail thin. Somehow barely more than skin and bones. Frailty hung over his father's frame, shrouded in fear. It couldn't be hidden. He realized his father was afraid. Afraid he'd lost his way and couldn't find home. Afraid he'd broken everything. Afraid he didn't know what to do, how to fix it, and whether he could go forward.

"I'm sorry, Raf." Dad stared off in the direction of the dingy as the rain and wind still raged. "I have to go. I can't stay here with you. I have to go. I'm sorry. I'm so sorry."

"Don't...don't go," Rafael whispered. He couldn't seem to gather his voice. He searched inside and couldn't find the ability to speak above the storm. Inside him was a scream, but it was trapped and wouldn't come out. His whisper couldn't be heard above the crashing waves, the rain on the forest canopy, the roaring thunder, and the whipping winds.

Dad reached out a hand to rub Rafael's head. For a moment Rafael could feel the warmth of his hand. He closed his eyes and remembered hiking together and stopping to eat peanut butter sandwiches, getting a little on his cheeks. Tears washed more sand from his eyes, and his shoulders shook from sobbing.

Dad's hand wavered again. He could no longer feel Rafael's

head. He pulled his hand back, staring at it with pained brokenness. He couldn't find more words. He was so far gone, he couldn't even hug Rafael. He made the American Sign Language sign for "I love you."

Rafael's trembling hand mirrored the sign back.

Dad slowly, painfully moved toward the little rowboat.

Rafael lost all the blood from his face. Acid filled his stomach. He couldn't move. Couldn't speak. Couldn't think. He just watched. A nightmare was unfolding before him, and he was powerless to stop it.

Dad picked up the oars and placed them in the boat. He waited until a wave came up high enough to put a couple inches of water under it, then willed his hands to be real enough to pull it farther into the water.

With the waves making the little boat roll from side to side, he managed to climb in. He grabbed the two oars and began rowing, then reached the biggest part of the surf and crested a wave just before it broke, floating down the other side past the breakers.

Rafael was standing now, squinting through the driving rain, to see Dad between the rolling waves. He held onto the ability to see his father—what little of him could be seen—as long as he could. So long as he could be seen, he remained.

Through the waves and rain, he could now just barely see the boat and the nearly see-through man rowing it. Lightning flashed once more, blinding him for a moment. When his eyes adjusted, he searched the sea.

Gone.

The rowboat couldn't be found.

His eyes settled on a little rock next to his foot. He bent and picked it up, thinking of how he'd told Benjamin that he would throw rocks into the river to let go of hurt and sadness. How the act let him forgive those who hurt him. He looked at the rock, then looked at the raging sea again.

No one was here. No Dad to call him son. No Benjamin to call him friend or comfort him. No Mama to offer an arm for a pillow. No Mariel to offer strength. No Krynn to laugh with. No Lucas and Abigail to play with. He was alone in the storm.

It was hopeless. His hand opened, and the rock slipped to the ground. Maybe he could reach out the empty hand in the direction of the last spot he'd seen Dad. But what was the point? He dropped to his knees.

The tide had risen and lapped up to where it barely touched his knees, sunken into the sand. Soon one of the waves of chaos might come and overtake him. If so, he would be swept out into the madness of the storm.

What would it be like to finally quit? To accept the harshness of the thrashing sea rather than to chase after the breeze. He pictured being home and putting away the racecars and the trucks. Life seemed too serious for those. He would grow up now. He felt himself harden. The shell that had been developing around his heart thickened.

Joy no longer mattered, only survival. He forgot what the sun felt like on his skin or what it was like to wander with two big dogs or to act like a puppy with Lucas and Abigail. He forgot about flying and goose bumps.

He would accept the gray and just keep moving forward. He would build a life where he didn't need anyone, and no one could disappear from him. Maybe even find an island he could live on alone.

Starving and broken, he slumped face forward into the sand. A wave came up just high enough to paint itself against the top of his head. Any minute one might come far enough to sweep him away. He had almost slipped into unconsciousness when a voice filled his mind as though fully audible. "Raf, one more thing. Keep dreaming of flying."

On the edge of unconsciousness, he wasn't sure if the voice was a memory or if he'd heard it just now. "I can't," he slurred, his mouth partly in the sand. "I can't try to fly any more. He's gone."

"I'm sorry," the voice said.

Was the voice in his head or was it real? Whatever it was, he was sure the voice understood him in the places where words couldn't go. Whoever it was hurt as badly as he did. Maybe worse.

"You can't fly with him, but you can fly with me."

He blinked his eyes barely open. Through the blur of tears and rain, he couldn't be sure of what he saw. Something was flying through the storm toward him. It emanated its own light, warding away the darkness that couldn't touch it.

A crane slowly, blurrily came into view. The rain veered around and away from the bird, and its wings flapped with power and grace. Near it, the waves themselves were calm. A shiver ran down his spine.

He closed his eyes and lay unconscious in the oncoming tide.

CHAPTER TWENTY-SIX

I stand at the edge of the woods and the beach and try to squint away the blinding storm. All that has happened has brought me to this forsaken, inhospitable shore. I'm spent and desperately afraid of what I might see when I step out of the woods onto the shore.

Please let him be alive.

In a last attempt to cling to hope, I replay the moment I met Rafael, then step forward. I shield my face from the rain attacking me and scan for any sign of life. Down the beach at the water's edge, something seems to be glowing.

Glowing? Could it be Scott with a lantern of some sort? If he were here, he could be convinced to help me find Rafael. But the storm is blinding, and my eyes could be playing tricks on me.

If I yell out Scott's name and it's not him, the disappointment would be crushing. "Hey! Hey! Over here!" I wave my arms.

The light grows brighter but doesn't move.

My pulse races. *Who or what is that?* I run toward it. "Hey! Help me! Please! I need help!"

Why aren't they answering? The storm is raging and loud, but surely they've heard me by now.

Is it really a good idea to keep running toward whomever holds the light? Whoever it is, the fact they're out here in this storm means there might be something wrong with them. *It has to be Scott. No one could be foolish enough to be out here. Except me.*

When I get near to the light, it disappears.

I jerk to a stop at the sudden disappearance of the one and only hopeful thing in this God-forsaken storm. My eyes take a moment to adjust to the restored darkness. Rain pelts my face, and I protect my eyes again, gritting my teeth against the wind.

Is that a boy? Horror overcomes me.

I'm standing no more than five feet from a prone, unconscious boy whose head is being lapped at by the ocean. "Rafael!" I shriek. "Rafael! No!"

I run to him. Kneeling in the rain-soaked sand, I scoop his limp body into my arms, weeping over it. I'm confronted with my worst fears.

I haven't gotten to him in time. The little boy is dead, and I will never recover. How can I ever feel joy or hope again? I hold him to my chest with body-shaking cries.

For a moment the wind lets up. It's been furious for so long that the silence replacing its deafening sounds now feels foreign. Did I just hear a breath? I can hardly believe it. I move my ear to his lips, feeling the warmth of his breath. It's faint, but it's the sweetest thing I've known my entire time on the island. It's literally a breath of hope.

It's enough to give me the strength to keep pushing forward. I've arranged for the boat to return in two days' time. *Why couldn't I have had him meet me here?* If only I'd known I was going to cross to the north shore. I'll have to cross the island again to the spot where we landed. I look at the forest and wince at the thought of covering that harrowing ground again, this time with a limp boy to carry. But I'm willing to push forward until I have no more of my own breath to give.

"Let's go, Raf." I shift him onto my shoulders and stand, careful not to jostle him. The wind gusts, declaring its return, and pushes me so hard I nearly fall over. Bent over, braced against the near-hurricane-level winds, I head for the dark jungle. I can only hope the wolves have given up their pursuit in this awful storm. If not, hopefully the rain and debris will mask our scent.

As I reach the spot where the trees and sand meet, I see Scott's and Rafael's footprints meeting and Scott's going back toward the waves. I know what the footprints mean.

He's disappeared.

It'll be no use standing in the gale and wishing him back. We can't waste time here. I carry Raf into the woods.

The moment we enter the dark canopy, the blood curdling howl of a wolf comes from down the beach. With the trees creaking, branches crashing, rain pounding, and wind wailing, I can't be sure just how far away it is, but I know it's too close. Away in the trees, another howl answers. This one is farther and yet also too close.

"They're coming for us," I tell Rafael, who hears nothing.

My sole purpose in the world at this moment is to deliver Rafael to safety. There is nothing I can do about the wolves. All I can do is move forward.

As difficult as it's been to get to Rafael, returning across the island seems far worse. Now that I'm carrying him, I can only spare one hand at a time to brace myself or grab for support when I need to climb. Sometimes I can't even do that and am forced to wobble on my feet, stumbling this way and that trying not to fall or to drop him. Branches and other debris constantly crash around me, and I can't stop shivering from the cold biting at my bones. My clothes are useless, having been soaked by the constant downpour. I may as well be naked.

Several hours of stilted effort pass, and I haven't traveled nearly far enough in that time. My shoulders burn. I briefly try shifting the boy's weight and carrying him in front of me, but it doesn't do. It's not long before my biceps scream from the weight, forcing me to put my shoulders back to work.

A new fear emerges. *What if I lose my way in the dark and the storm? I can't see the landmarks to ensure I'm keeping true to our course.* My lungs, legs and shoulders beg me to stop. My stomach rumbles and my head feels faint from hunger. "I have to stop and try again in the morning, Raf. We'll go again the second I can see."

I'm about to set him down when I hear the wolves howling in succession. First behind me, then to my left, then my right.

Three of them now?

My heart sinks. The wolves might never let me pause to rest. No matter how much my body is shutting down, it's move forward or be caught in the night. "We'll just have to risk it, buddy." If only there were stars to guide me, but the storm has veiled them too.

For three more hours I fight with everything I have. I wrestle fatigue, hunger, rocks, roots, and falling branches to continue moving. One step at a time, I pick my feet up and move them forward. My mind does everything it can to separate itself from the body and force muscle, bone, and sinew forward.

By now, I'd have dropped to the ground in exhaustion if not for the constant, terrorizing sound of the wolves. Their group has grown to four, by the sounds of them. Every few minutes they engage in a torturous call and answer seemingly designed as psychological warfare meant to dispirit me and force me to quit.

I feel like my strength might fail any moment, and I try distracting myself with the memory of Rafael, Lucas, and Abigail playing in my sunlit backyard. I haven't seen the sun since that backyard meal. Sunlight is a foreign concept in this perpetually cloud-covered land.

The brief distraction from my pain and fatigue helps me plod onward, but it also means I don't see a hole in my path. Raf and I crumble in a heap into a hole three feet deep and long enough to fit two full grown men, which has been created by a downed tree's roots pulling up dirt with them. Lying on my back, I blink my eyes against the dripping rain from the gigantic tree above us. I hurriedly check Rafael and see he's still breathing.

Wracked in pain, I'm not sure I can get myself up, much less pick up Rafael and carry him out of this hole.

I'm spent.

Sleep sounds agonizingly, maddeningly tempting. I don't have the strength or the will left to move. There's no choice. I must rest, even if just for a few minutes. I can close my eyes just for a minute and try again shortly.

At least this spot offers the smallest bit of protection from the elements, if not from the wolves. My decision is made. We'll pause here until I can regain the resolve and energy to move again. We'll rest in this little hovel.

"Let's just hope the wolves get disoriented in the storm."

I place Rafael's head against my chest and close my eyes.

CHAPTER TWENTY-SEVEN

"It's nice to see you again, Rafael."

His eyes closed, Rafael curled his lips into a smile. That voice! So warm and comforting. Something feels different. There's a sense of peace so profound it's erased any memory of the storm. In fact, it seems this is a place no storm has ever touched.

His eyes open to Grandma Mariel's living room. Sunlight embraces the Santa Barbara Valley and the mountains beyond and fills the room. And what is that smell in the air? It's a reminder of sweet, peaceful days.

"Here's some fresh lemonade," she says, handing him a glass. "I made it myself, from the lemon tree. Several times I've thought it died, but every time I nurse it a little, it comes back. It's very resilient and just needed a little love."

He soaks in the sight of her with a grin on his face. The cup is raised to his lips and the cool mix of sweet and tart quenches his thirst.

Grandma Mariel smiles at him. "It's amazing how something so sour can be so refreshing. All it takes is a little sweetness added to the lemons and they make a wonderful drink."

He takes another sip, then looks around the room. Confusion settles on his face. Why can't he remember anything before the living room and the lemonade? "How did I get here?"

"I think you picked a place you felt safe and happy."

"Picked?" He scowls.

"Think about it a moment, Raf. I think you know where you are. You chose somewhere safe, warm, and happy."

Safe and warm. There are places unlike this, aren't there? Places of chaos and cold. The floodgate opens. The storm! Dad leaving. Memories with Benjamin. The crane. Yes, that's right, the crane. Had he really seen it? The way the storm and the waves calmed around it was surreal. And the voice telling him to keep dreaming of flying. Had he really heard that?

"Is this a dream?" he asks. "Or am I dead?"

Whoa. His own words surprise him. But then, it is unexplainable. How had he come from a place so forbidding to a place so wonderful and not remembered anything between?

"That's tricky," she answers. "Neither and both."

He just stares at her blankly. What does that mean?

She stands, rubs a gentle hand on his back and takes his glass to get more lemonade. "Here you go." Her sweet touch on his shoulder feels so good.

Though the lemonade is cool to his lips, it warms his heart. He wonders if he could stay and never go back to the storm. Just enjoy the couch, the view, the smells, and the safety of being high above the ocean on a ridge no wave can ever reach. "Can I stay here if I want? I mean, like, stay forever?"

"In a way, yes. You could choose that. You can hide here and not have to feel the storm."

That would be fantastic! But something in her tone feels like there's a catch.

"But if you choose to stay here, you won't be able to go back. You won't have to feel the storm anymore, that's true, but you'll also miss so much. You'll miss hugs from loved ones, and laughter. You'll miss loving another so much you would change your life for them and the feeling of holding your own baby someday. You'll miss sadness, but you'll miss joy and deep hope also."

The boy remembers where he'd just come from. In that place, he's tired. Not just in his body, but in his spirit. This might be a trade he'd be willing to make.

"In order to stay here, you have to hide your heart away. You can't share it with others. It would, in a way, be like a part of you dying and being buried here. You can hide and be safe. You can have the lemonade and be here where there is no storm. Understand, Raf, you would disappear from your world, and I fear so would Benjamin shortly after."

Benjamin. Yes, Rafael is tired, but maybe he has a little left to fight for Benjamin. Maybe even help him fly. But here there is peace. Why go back? Not just Benjamin though. What about Lucas and Abigail? Deep love fills his heart. No, even still, he should stay here. He's being pulled apart. It's all so much, he wants to cry, but something about this place holds him back. Crying might break the peace of this place. A peace he's desperate to preserve.

"Rafael, I have something I want to show you." She takes his hand, and in that moment he feels safe and cared for. That confirms it. Of course he'll stay.

Together they walk to her bedroom, where she lets go of his hand and opens a small chest on top of her dresser. It's high enough that he can't see what's inside.

"Rafael, you don't know my whole story. When I was twelve, I had to leave my home. Those were hard times in this country, and my parents didn't have enough money to support us children. My father was hurting inside and began to hurt all of us too. I went and lived at a boarding house where I did small jobs to pay for my room and board.

"I was like you, then. I couldn't take it anymore and wanted to get away from my pain. One day, as I was cleaning out a room from someone who had passed away, I discovered this chest. I didn't think much of it and put it in my room with my things.

"Over time I came to realize the chest had some kind of magic, but I wasn't sure how it worked. One day, I met a kind stranger."

She'd met a kind stranger? Could it be the same man helping him?

"He explained it to me. It was a chest I could put my heart in. It would be protected, and I could stop feeling the pain. Then he gave me the same warning I just gave you. I could be done with the pain, but I would lose so much. He offered to help me, said there was a better way and that he had the power to heal my hurts, but that I couldn't hide. I was too afraid of the pain and decided not to try his way."

She reaches into the chest and pulls out a picture.

"I thought the chest hid your heart," Rafael says.

"In a way, it does, Rafael. This is a picture of me as a little girl. It represents the vulnerable parts of who I am and memories I wanted to forget. I put it in this chest, and the magic of the chest killed many memories and feelings I had. I decided to become someone very hard. I gave up vulnerability and childhood and traded them for strength." She sets the picture on the dresser and picks up a small statue sitting on the other side of the chest.

This is something new. It's a statuette of a young boy reaching up to a grandmotherly figure with arms wide for a hug and the grandmother answering his arms with her own. The sight brings a smile to his face. "What is that?" he asks.

"I'm making a new trade, Raf. The stranger came back recently and offered me a new choice. It was right before you came to stay with me, and now I know what I want." She slides the chest over and puts the statue and the picture on display where the chest used to sit. "This statue represents you and me, Rafael." A tear rolls down her cheek and a thin smile curves her lips. This is a new smile he's never seen from her. A smile that's borne of her insides and not just her face.

"I love you," she says as she reaches to hug him. Words she hasn't uttered in many years.

A powerful wind, stronger than either of them has ever known, rushes through the room. Amazingly, it doesn't stir any of the things in the room. He might be blown away, and yet he feels safe. Grandma Mariel's posture straightens and her complexion lightens. She's glowing.

"I love you too," he says back.

They hug, both of them feeling filled inside.

"Raf, I can't tell you what to do. Only you can make that choice.

The chest is yours now, and you can put your heart in it."

"Check your pocket." She points.

His pocket? There couldn't be anything but sand in there. But he wouldn't disobey her in this happy moment. Dutifully reaching into the pocket, he finds two pictures. Where have they come from?

He knows these pictures. The first is of himself at four. He was lying in lush grass taller than himself, all matted down where he rested. Arms folded up behind his head, backpack still on under him. He was so happy that he had no mind to take his pack off before lying down. Happy, and a little lazy maybe. Peanut butter smeared on his cheeks and a little on his chest, signaling he was full. That and his bloated belly. Baby fat he still carried shined bright in the warm early summer sunlight, and his chubby cheeks wore an oversized grin. The boy in the photograph was happy and looked without a care. He was a boy on a hike with his dad and he was full of heart.

The second picture was taken about two years after the first. A moment he hasn't forgotten. It was cold and gray out. He had on a brown wool stocking cap, a hand-me-down jacket, and old jeans that weren't quite the right size. The boy in this picture held a soccer ball that he'd received on this Christmas Day. He'd come to the nearby park to kick the ball around with Dad, who stood next to him with an arm around him, and both were smiling. Not the full, careless peanut butter smile of a confident young boy. There was something behind the eyes. A kind of knowing. A sense of innocence seemed missing from this smile.

Rafael studies the pictures, especially the second. That was the day he had sat silently in an old green Chevy Nova that their church had bought for them, as Mama drove him home from Eugene to Corvallis. It was on that Christmas Day he said goodbye to Dad, who was moving away. That boy knew a kind of hurt the boy in the first picture didn't yet understand.

Rafael looks in the mirror. The boy from the second picture is the boy looking back at him today. That boy didn't smile as much as the boy lying in the grass. It's uncomfortable feeling what's behind those eyes, and it doesn't belong in this place of rest.

He turns from the mirror. All he has to do is place both pictures in the chest and close it. Why not go a step farther too? He can toss the chest in the ocean. He'd walk to the end of the jetty where he and Grandma Mariel had so many wonderful walks together. He could throw it in the ocean with the pictures in it, watch it sink, and be with her drinking sweet, refreshing lemonade forever.

But what would happen to Lucas, Abigail and Krynn? They've come so far but aren't yet whole. His heart longs for them to be complete and full of joy. "Grandma, Mariel. Why did you say Benjamin might disappear if I stay here?"

"Rafael, I can't explain it yet. There are things only you and Benjamin can discover for yourselves. But let me say it this way. Benjamin needs you. Without you, I'm sure he'll never fly. He'll forget the breezes and fade into the gray. He may even disappear, just like your dad's father and your dad did. Then..." She stops and looks like her face is in anguish.

"Then what?" He has to know.

"Then Lucas may disappear someday too." She looks away, seeming to consider if she's able to continue. "Rafael, the stranger explained it to me, and I think I understand the disappearing now. It's been passed from generation to generation for ages now. It's more sickness than curse, though it will continue forever until someone is able to finally break the curse. If Benjamin can't fly, Lucas will suffer the same fate. The curse runs in their family line as well."

Rafael thinks of the day he and Benjamin played at the river near the cabin. Benjamin grinned so widely as he flew off the rock to the river below. That was a smile like the boy in the first picture. A deep happiness and joy Benjamin's face couldn't hide. *Benjamin needs more of those moments. And he has to teach Lucas and Abigail to smile like that.*

"Raf." Grandma Mariel breaks his thoughts. "The stranger came here recently and gave me a message for you. He said, 'Keep dreaming of flying.' I've thought about it, and I think you're supposed to help Benjamin fly and help him teach Lucas and Abigail too. I think you and Benjamin can break the curse, but only if you choose not to make the trade. Only if you go back and accept both the hurt and the joy. If you don't run and hide."

She sighs. "Don't you see? It's the running away that's the curse itself! Someone has to stay. Stay for themselves, but even more, stay for others. I think I've realized, the disappearing is a choice. It's hard to accept. It's more pain than one should have to bear, but I've accepted it's true. Generation after generation in this family have chosen to disappear rather than stay."

She's covered in sadness as she stares out her window toward the sea. Rafael knows her thoughts, because they're his too. Is his dad already gone forever, like his father before him and his father before that?

"Rafael, the stranger is a special man. He's like a father to those who hurt. He said he could heal you, the same way he offered me so long ago."

Rafael looks at the pictures. "I don't want to leave you. I'd miss you."

She takes his free hand in hers. "I love you."

He closes his eyes and lets the words wash over him.

When he opens his eyes he steps toward the chest. No matter how much he might love Benjamin, Krynn, Abigail, and Lucas, the thought of waking up in the middle of that storm and seeing the empty sea, with no Dad in it, is too much to bear. He'll have to deal with the heaviness of knowing Benjamin might disappear like Dad. He'll even accept that Lucas might suffer the same fate.

This stings most. Yet still, he simply can't stomach the pain in his own life and can't go back. What needs to be done must be done, then he can forget. He reaches up to put the pictures in the chest. He's about to drop them when something in the mirror catches his eye.

In it, there are six figures. A quick double take in the bedroom confirms he and Grandma Mariel are the only ones here, but sure enough, there are six people in the mirror. There he is in the mirror with the kind stranger behind him. And there's Lucas and Abigail to his left, and Krynn and Benjamin to his right. All of them face his mirror-self and hug him in one big group hug.

Lucas then turns and stares at the real Rafael in the room. Lucas's face is so sweet and innocent, it's triggering powerful protection instincts in Rafael. Maybe he should rethink his choice. Maybe he would accept pain for Lucas's sake. Again he pushes it away.

Then Lucas, Abigail, and Krynn are suddenly gone from the mirror, leaving Rafael, Benjamin, and the stranger who turns and looks at mirror-Rafael and at Benjamin. The stranger holds out his hands as an invitation to them.

The two in the mirror hesitate, then a darkness—a swirling cloud like the color of a coal train's smoke—grows over them. It's menacing and awful—a thick, billowy mass that can't be seen through. Rafael watches in horror as they try to shield themselves and hide from it, but it's growing too fast. The cloud coils all around them and grips their hearts with fear, despair, and depression. Terrified, he wants to look away from the mirror. The mere sight of the darkness sparks panic and depression in him as it has to the two in the mirror. Yet he can't force himself to turn away.

He gasps as the darkness begins seeping from the mirror, spilling into the room. It drifts over the dresser and onto the floor. Rafael watches with a sinking feeling as it reaches his feet. He should run! But fear has frozen his feet to the floor. The darkness starts to wrap around his legs like chains. This can't be happening!

In the mirror he sees a wolf behind him. When he turns, it's actually in the room with him and he can barely breathe. It has a large scar on one of its hips. He's beside himself from both the smoke and the wolf, but still can't move.

The wolf snarls and takes a step toward him.

The man! Why hasn't he asked him to help yet? Then something unexplainable happens. The swirling, menacing cloud passes from the mirror-Rafael and Benjamin onto the stranger, and the stranger becomes overcome with grief. He weeps with a sadness that Rafael didn't know existed.

The poor stranger seems he'll be overtaken by the crushing

weight of the madness enveloping him. Darkness hovers around him and enters into him. He bends under the weight of it. The darkness has become so thick, the stranger can no longer be seen.

What do I do? He's gone!

The wolf creeps closer to Rafael and Benjamin in the mirror and toward Rafael outside the mirror. It's now within striking distance of all three when an explosion of blinding light emanates from inside the storm and the dark cloud disappears.

Rafael shields his eyes and squints to keep watching.

The stranger reemerges and is dazzlingly bright.

Not gone!

The light reaches the wolf in the mirror, who howls and disintegrates before their eyes.

Rafael notices his mirror-self and Benjamin—who also shine brightly now—look at rest and happy. The stranger turns from the mirror-Rafael and Benjamin to the real Rafael and puts his hands out, inviting him forward in the same way this intense scene began.

Rafael looks at his feet and sees the darkness still hovers like mist in an eerie swamp. The wolf in the room is snarling, looking ready to pounce at any moment. For a moment, he pulls the pictures back from the chest.

He looks at Dad in the picture from Christmas Day. "You didn't know how to fly. You knew that and you knew you could never teach me." His eyes tear up, looking from the picture of one of his happiest days to the one of his deepest sadness. He falls to his knees, still looking at Dad, tears pouring from his eyes. "I forgive you," he says into the haunted eyes of the man from that Christmas morning. "It's not your fault. I forgive you."

With those three words, the wind returns. Light blazes around Rafael and the darkness is blown away. He lifts into the air and can see nothing but light for a moment, then when he can see the room again, the wolf has disappeared.

Grandma Mariel watches in amazement.

Then he gently returns to the floor, takes a breath, and places each picture at the feet of the statuette with the picture of little Grandma Mariel. "I have to go back," he says.

"I know. Raf?"

"Yes?"

"I love you."

"I love you too."

She takes him by the hand and leads him back to the couch where she places a quilt on him that she has hand stitched. He lays down to fall asleep warm and secure. Just before he closes his eyes for the last time, he sees the lemonade on the coffee table near him. It really is sweet in a way that doesn't seem to leave any bitterness on the tongue and only refreshes. Then he falls asleep smiling and thinking of Grandma Mariel.

CHAPTER TWENTY-EIGHT

A large drop of cold water falls from a tree directly into the back of my open mouth, choking me, and I wake up shivering. I've slipped in and out of consciousness throughout the night. I'm bleary-eyed, suffering from lack of sleep and extreme hunger.

Where am I? Why am I not in my bed? Where's Krynn?

Denial hangs over me, and I entertain a fantasy. I'm not dying in the forest with a lost little boy being chased by wolves and risking hypothermia. This isn't real. I allow my eyes to close again.

In the darkness behind my eyelids there are no wolves, no lightning storms, no hurt little boy, just darkness. A strange thought finds a foothold in a tiny corner of my mind. *If I stop caring, I can disappear like Scott. I can release my emotional tether to Rafael and...*

A chilling and terror inducing voice, not my own, rings in my mind. "Go ahead. Think it." It's a voice I haven't heard before.

Coldness chills my heart in this dream state far more than the real air bringing my body nearer to hypothermia. The voice has stirred uncomfortable ideas.

If I didn't care about anyone... It's too hurtful. I won't allow it to finish.

"Go on," the voice prods. "You won't have to hurt anymore."

I'm unaware I'm nearly gone in the real world. My heart rate and breathing have slowed. A puff of steam rises from my mouth with my fading breath. I'm on the precipice of passing into complete unconsciousness. In this dream place, I'm not sure it matters anymore. I tried my best, didn't I? I fought and I lost. It can't be done. I can't save myself, much less anyone else. Can't fly or teach anyone else to fly. Can't save Rafael. Can't bring back Scott.

What I can do is to embrace the cold and the storm. To lean in. To allow the sweet peace of the cold to calm and numb me.

"That's it," the voice calls. "A little cold to numb the pain, and then no more cold."

My head lolls from one side to the other. If my eyes were open, I would see my hand appear transparent. I'm beginning to disappear. In the world behind my eyelids, I see I'm passing through some sort of tunnel. All around me is darkness, save for a small bit of light glowing behind me. Ahead of me, at the end of the tunnel, stands a lone wolf. It's strangely tall, with thick fur, and looks perfectly formed except for one six-inch scar on his hip. This is the one I'd followed when Krynn was hurt so badly.

The two of us stare at each other. The wolf nods at me and proceeds away out the other end of the tunnel. Maybe there'll be something there I need. Something to offer respite from cold and pain. I'm not sure what, but I want to search for it.

I begin to walk through the dark tunnel. My stomach is nearly retching at the idea of being near the wolf again.

I need whatever it is that can help me forget my pain. I'll just be more careful this time.

Each step comes slowly, but each one also feels easier than the last. As I proceed, fog fills the tunnel behind me. It becomes darker and more menacing, the farther I get in.

In the real world, my heart rate is dangerously low from hypothermia and, in addition to my hand, the rest of me is rapidly becoming more and more transparent. I'm now almost totally gone.

Another voice cuts through the darkness of the tunnel. "I can't see your footsteps anymore, Dada."

Through the haze of my hypothermic mind, and the fog all around me in the tunnel, I don't immediately process whose voice it was I just heard. I take another step forward.

A new vision appears. I'm now in a living room and a haze hangs around me as in a dream where the details aren't filled in. Darkness surrounds the room and hangs in the air. In front of me is a little boy whose face shines in contrast to the dark room. His smile is sweet and full of innocence, joy, and adoration.

Something moves in the deepest part of my heart, which stings yet calls to me. I know what the look means, feel what the boy feels, without any words needed to explain.

It's the look of one seeking for an answer. A gazing into a father's eyes, searching for a place where needs are understood and provided for. A reaching for a place where safety can be found. A hopeful belief that these needs will be answered with loving and strong arms and the knowledge that, if answered, the little boy can become a complete man, equipped to love and to be loved. A man who would never disappear.

I hate what I'm feeling but can't look away. Pain and love are at war within.

"Dada? I can't see your footsteps. I'm not sure where to walk."

That's Lucas's voice!

I'm shaken from the living room vision and I look back behind me in the tunnel, but can't see anything but dark, swirling cloud. Dread overcomes me.

Did the wolf hear Lucas? My knees want to buckle beneath me. I can't think. I don't know if I can find the way out of this place. I'm not sure how to get to the voice. *Trapped in here!*

The ground begins to rumble. Slowly it builds, then grows into violent shaking, until the whole tunnel is in massive tremors all around. I wobble this way and that.

It's going to cave in on me!

What's more, the wolf has reappeared and is rushing toward me with bared teeth. I can't stand straight, much less run with the earth shaking under my feet. It's now almost reached me and jumps toward me with a raging snarl, ready to snap its teeth around me.

With a jerk, I'm awake and no longer in the tunnel, but conscious again in this hole in the earth.

"Dada! Dada! Wake up!" Lucas shakes me vigorously. Rafael still lays motionless beside me.

"Lucas!" I shriek. "What on earth are you doing here? This is no place for you! It's not safe! What have you done? What have you done? Why are you here? Oh no! Oh no! Oh no!" I bury my head in my hands, muttering, "No. No, no, no, no. Please no!" I can't hide the fear gripping me.

Desperately desiring my approval, and shaken by my fear, Lucas appears to be searching his mind for the words to fix everything. "You weren't breathing, Dada! I just wanted you to wake up! You weren't breathing! It scared me. I just wanted you here. I wanted you to be here with me. Please, Dada. Please don't go!"

"Son," I say. The word reverberates not just with Lucas, but within myself. It's such a powerful word, both Lucas and I feel it through our whole bodies. "Son, come here." Still feeling too weak to stand, I put my arms out.

Lucas throws himself into my arms, burying his face in my chest, and I wrap my arms around him.

"I'm here," I say, holding him. "I'm here. I'm here."

Lucas cries into my chest, but my shirt is so wet from rain, I don't notice the difference.

"Shhh. Shhh. It's okay. It's okay, son."

I look at Rafael, still curled against my side. Here, in this little pit, with the storm still swirling all around us, we are a pitiable group. Two little boys—one unconscious, one weeping—and a man too weak to move.

With Rafael at my side and Lucas on my chest, at least there is some shared warmth.

This is the first I've been warm since I stepped foot on this island. It's some comfort, though the moment is fleeting.

I stroke Lucas's hair to soothe him. *I can't let him die out here! Even if I die trying, these little boys are getting home!*

I picture Krynn and Abigail sitting on the couch, sharing a

blanket with the boys. It's a vision I'll need to cling to if I'm to summon the resources to move.

I'm not making it, but whatever happens, I will get these boys to safety and to that couch.

My will is solidified within me and resolve has taken hold. I will never go back to that tunnel again.

"Lucas, stand up, okay?" I say.

Lucas dutifully obeys.

The fallen tree has ripped away from a root coming out of the ground above me. "Let me put one arm on you and I'll put my other arm on this root." Slowly, painfully, with a lot of grunting, I make it to my feet. I'm lightheaded from hunger, hypothermia, and exhaustion and nearly faint.

Lucas pulls out a little bag. "I have this beef jerky I saved."

My stomach has been empty almost two days, while I've climbed, slipped, carried, grabbed, and shivered away my energy stores. Lucas's offer brings tears to my eyes. "Your kindness and generosity amaze me, buddy. You're a wonderful boy." I pat him on the head.

He beams and hands me the bag.

I eat a piece of jerky and give the rest back to him. "You keep it, son. You'll need it."

I don't have the heart to tell him I assume the one piece I took may be enough to help me hike the two boys a few miles, but the rest will have to be for Lucas to survive the rest of the trip on his own. I hope a few pieces will be for Rafael too, but I fear he might not wake up and there's no way Lucas can carry him.

"I'm proud of you, Lucas." I sigh. The path ahead is daunting. "I wish you were home safe. This is no place for a little boy. But

I want you to know, I'm so impressed with you. You're so brave and so smart. But most of all, so kind. You really are a wonderful boy, and I'm glad I'm your dad."

Lucas looks as though he's forgotten the storm. Judging by his face, there is no lightning. No thunder. No whipping winds or sideways rain. Just joy, pride, and hope.

"Dada?"

"Yeah, buddy?"

"I really liked playing with you at the beach. I liked jumping in your footprints."

"I liked when you did that too, buddy."

"And I liked when you chased me and grabbed me, and we played in the ocean."

"Me too, buddy."

"Dada?"

"Yeah, buddy?"

"Is Rafael going to be okay? Is he going to wake up?" Lucas looks worried.

What do I tell him?

I allow myself a moment to imagine Rafael is only asleep and not comatose, teetering on the edge of death. The only way I can will myself to keep going is to hold onto hope—a hope I don't understand. I hope The Good Father will never let these two boys die such untimely deaths, though I'm sure I won't survive the day.

If I can get The Good Father to help the boys, at least they'll be okay. I sigh again. None of my thoughts make sense. I haven't seen The Good Father for days. So why is there hope?

"Dada?"

Lucas! He's been waiting for an answer. So what do I tell him? Just hand him a piece of your own hope. "Lucas, We're going to do everything we can to get you and Rafael to safety and get him the help he needs."

Summoning the last fumes of strength, I reach down for Rafael's limp body. Wrapping my arms around him, I pull his frame back up over my shoulders in a fireman's carry. Lucas looks at me with awe. I'm unaware that this act of sacrificial kindness—giving my last energy for the helpless boy—is shaping Lucas in unseen ways. Watching his father give his strength away for one who can't return it is making him strong. It's a moment that may reverberate to future generations, if only he survives the ordeal.

"We'd better keep moving as much as we can. Follow me," I say, without realizing I've told him to do the one thing he wants most—to follow me.

A crackling bolt of lightning bursts through the air, momentarily lighting up the storm all around us, allowing me to see how awful our predicament is. The bolt touches down, snapping a tree in two, not far ahead of us. The tree falls with a roaring crash, shaking the ground all the way to our feet and lighting with flames.

Thankfully everything here is soaking wet, or a fire would be blocking our escape.

I stumble forward, nearly falling every two or three steps. The overgrown forest, the wet ground, the rocks, and the roots are all conspiring against any escape effort, fighting to stall forward progress until the wolves can find their prey.

My foot slips on a wet rock. As I fall, I contort my body and shift Rafael's to shield him from injury. As I strike the ground, pain sears through a nerve at my shoulder blade and runs down my arm. Rafael slips from my grip, but thankfully I've positioned him to land on my chest and he rolls off onto the wet ground without any new injuries. I'm not so lucky, having used my body as his crash pad. Pain screams through my shoulder and down my arm.

Through gritted teeth I let out garbled sounds. It won't do, yelling curses and scaring Lucas. "Help me stand again, Lucas. I need your help."

Together, we clumsily get me standing again. I reach down for Rafael one more time, and it's as if the lightning is now in my arm. I recoil before even lifting him an inch, yelling in pain and frightening Lucas. I breathe as much of the pain out my nose as I can. "It's no good. My right arm is dislocated. I can't pick him up unless I get it back in."

Lucas stares at me in terror.

He'll never be strong enough to push the arm back in. I don't know how much longer I can go, but I have to keep trying until I'm dead.

It isn't even a morbid thought at this point. It's just an accepted outcome of what will happen soon. I'm not afraid of it or even focused on it.

But I'm not quitting until it happens, so let's do this.

I press the hand at the end of my injured arm against a nearby tree trunk and prepare to lean my weight against it. "Look away, Lucas. And plug your ears." I stare down my arm braced against the tree, and try to find the courage to throw myself toward it.

Why can't I just do this! Come on, man! Get it done!

A wolf howls, and another answers. *They can't be much more than a quarter mile away.*

It's the motivation I need. Desperation and panic remove all indecision. I stiffen the arm, rock back away from the tree to get momentum, and throw all my weight forward, flexing the arm as hard as I can against the tree.

With a painful yell, I fall to the ground, clutching the wounded arm with my other hand.

By the look on his face, my pained cry scares Lucas more than the howls calling out around us.

I reach down to pick up Rafael once more and groan in agony. The weight of the boy pulls at the arm, sending waves of nausea-inducing pain throughout my body. Dripping from sweat and the down-pouring rain, I manage to get him back on my shoulders.

Okay. Step one. Now move!

I walk forward to the sound of the wolves' call and answer. I've barely taken ten steps when I trip on a root, spilling Rafael forward into the dirt. Instinctively, as I crash toward the earth below me, I put out my hands to catch myself, re-dislocating my arm. I roll onto my back, grip the injured arm, and close my eyes both to wince in pain and utter a stream of curses Lucas will never hear.

A panicked Lucas stands over me. "Get up, Dada! Come on! You have to get up!"

Another bolt of lightning pierces the sky, illuminating our surroundings. For the first time, I see we're in some sort of clearing. The tree I'd leaned on was one of the last in a ring around a circular opening, roughly two hundred fifty feet in diameter.

It's too cruel. I've found the first clearing I've seen this whole hellish time on the island, only now I'm too injured to move through it.

Lucas urges us forward again. "Dada! Let's go!"

I'm going to have to tell him I can't move. "Lucas..."

Then, as I'm lying on my back with the rain pelting my face, I hear a voice I thought I'd never hear again.

"Are you okay, Benjamin?"

Rafael!

I turn over onto my good arm and twist my neck to see Rafael's figure lying just beyond me. Had I really just heard him? "Raf? Is that you, buddy?"

"Yeah, I'm back. I came back."

"Came back? From where?"

"I'll explain later."

"Raf, I'm so glad you're awake! I have to be honest with you, buddy, things aren't looking great. I've hurt my arm, and I think I just twisted my leg pretty badly too. Buddy, I don't know if I can go any farther. I think you and Lucas may have to go on without me."

"Benjamin, *we* are going to make it *together*." There's authority in his voice that I haven't heard from him before. "You, me, and Lucas. Don't quit. We're almost there. It's almost done. Keep fighting. You've almost made it!"

I smile wryly. *This kid just has no give in him when he wants something. That's what I'm counting on to give him a fighting chance to get out of here with Lucas.* "Listen to me, Raf, I'm serious. I have a hurt leg. I'm getting hypothermic. I'm weak from eating nothing more than one piece of jerky for days and from carrying you. I have a dislocated arm. Raf, those wolves. They're coming. I can't move fast enough, but I can slow them down. I'll distract them. Make them focus on me. You run. You run and don't look back, and you take Lucas with you. I'm not making it out of here, boys. But *you* are."

Neither boy looks like he is going to obey. The wolves howl, now near the edge of the clearing.

"Go! Get out of here!" I command them.

Rafael, still weak himself, gets up on his hands and knees with difficulty, only to wobble and fall onto the ground again, this time rolling beside me. "Benjamin, I don't think I can get up without help," he says feebly.

Lucas watches in dread, not knowing how to help either of us.

The sky lights up with another crackling bolt, and we see the silhouettes of a large group of wolves spreading out around the clearing. Another bolt reaches its awful fingers down from the sky, enflaming a second tree. It acts as a torchlight for the horror scene unfolding around us. One wolf, larger than all the others, moves toward the center of the clearing where I'm lying next to Rafael and a cowering Lucas.

There is nothing left in me. I can't even weep. The wolves all slowly shrink their circle around us behind the lead of the largest one, which is close enough now, I can see it has a scar on its hip.

These damned wolves.

Raging hatred for the creatures grips my heart and gives me the adrenaline to get up on my knees between the boys and the wolf. It's the last act of defiance I can muster.

"You'll have to attack me first!" So filled with hatred and rage, I can't remember anything other than the storm and the wolf.

Did he just look at me with approval? What? It's as though my hatred and bitterness are what he desires.

I'm shivering violently from on-setting hypothermia, every shiver making me involuntarily flex, sending pain through my arm. I close my eyes against the pain, and hear a voice—the same one from the tunnel—calling me to let the cold take me.

"Not this time." I clench my fists. This *will* be my end, but it will not be an end of surrendering to the cold and to disappearing. I will meet my end in sacrifice for these two boys who have my heart. I'm going to reach forward until I'm broken and ended. I won't ever quit, whether someone is there to reach back or not.

The wolves close in their ring tighter.

"Boys, when the wolves come, I'll do what I can to distract them. When I do, you two have to run away together. Keep going. Don't stop. Don't look back. Lucas, you have to help Raf. Help him stand up and go as fast as you can together."

"They've surrounded us, Benjamin," Rafael says. "There's nowhere for us to run."

The boy is right. This is it. If only there were actually some way to fly, but it's no good. Flying has only ever been a dream that could never have been real enough to overcome the disappearing or the wolves. Those are real. I hunch over the boys and hold them under me. I can no longer imagine a way to save them, but I will at least comfort them to my dying breath. I imagine myself becoming a hard shell around them to keep the wolves at bay.

To my astonishment, Rafael rises.

"Raf, I didn't think you could stand! What are you doing?"

He wobbles and looks like he might fall again, then rights himself, spreading his feet wide to stay upright. He stares up to the top of the trees. "Benjamin, I understand now. We have to be strong. Not hard. Strong. There's a difference. Hard things sink down, like the rocks. But strong isn't enough. We have to be soft."

Is he lighting up?

He changes before our eyes. His face grows stout, and his clothes begin to emanate light. Mud, dirt, and blood fall from him, leaving him looking perfectly untouched.

He looks at Lucas. "I figured it out, Lucas. I know how to fly. We have to be strong *and* soft. We can't give up. We can't make hard shells. We have to love with fierce love. A love that always hopes. Always trusts. Always gives. Always keeps going. Even when it hurts. We have to reach for the light even when everything around us pushes back. We have to be strong like wildflowers." He gazes upward and puts out his hand, reaching toward nothing. A hand reaching in hope to be held in return with only nothingness on the other end.

I watch startled and bewildered as Rafael begins lifting into the air and a blinding light surrounds him. The wolves quicken their pace and are now less than a hundred feet away. Rafael hovers just above us, and he sounds kind and commanding. "Just reach, Benjamin. Let go of the shell, be soft and strong. Reach even though it hurts."

I shake my head. "I can't even stand, Raf! I'm too weak. And how can I reach? My shoulder is dislocated. I couldn't put my arm up even if I wanted to. I don't know how to be strong and soft. I can't do it!"

The wolves break into a run toward us.

I shrink in panic.

A whipping wind suddenly swirls around us, sending shivers up and down my spine.

Lucas stands, screaming. "Please, Dada! The wolves! They're

coming! What do we do?"

"Reach out, Benjamin!" Rafael pleads. "Let go!"

The Good Father! Every time I've felt the breezes, The Good Father has had something to do with it. "Why aren't you here? Where *are* you?" I yell to the treetops. "I need you!"

The large wolf with the scar hunches down into one final stride, preparing to leap at me, while the thinner one does the same toward Lucas.

Above the din of the snarling wolves and the rushing winds filling my soul, I hear the whispering voice. "Reach. Let go."

"Dada!" Lucas yells, putting his arms up to shield him from the wolf leaping in midair toward him.

I put my head down, and reach out my dislocated arm with blinding pain. Against all the nerves screaming at me to leave the arm down, I keep it up, my other hand instinctively grabbing Lucas's hand. Holding him with one hand, I reach the other toward the empty unknown.

In an instant, my arm returns to full strength. All the pain leaves my body. I'm not hungry, tired, or hurting. A strong, warm, loving hand grabs onto mine, and I shoot up into the air. The two wolves bite at our feet, missing them by inches.

As we rise up to the tops of the trees, I see The Good Father is with us, holding Rafael's and my hands. The four of us rise above the clearing and stop in the air, all shining brightly, but The Good Father's light is most brilliant.

With a bellowing voice, he commands the wolves below, "They are mine! Be gone!"

They whimper and whine as they scatter this way and that, confused and scared. In a moment they're gone.

"I'm here, Benjamin," The Good Father says gently.

Hearing his voice fills all of us with deep peace.

"I've always been near to you. You only needed to reach for me. The curse was never meant to punish. It was meant to teach. You can't fly, but I can fly for you if you will just hold my hand."

My heart overflows with so much joy, peace, and gratitude. I'm overwhelmed, but manage to say thank you.

"I love all three of you," The Good Father says.

We can't help but smile, and I think I'll never fight back a smile again. It feels too good now. My heart feels joy and my face wants to match it.

"Let's go to a happier place," The Good Father says, and in the time it takes to blink an eye, we find ourselves on the jetty where Rafael once spent happy evenings with Mariel.

The warm sun surrounds us on a beautiful early evening in Santa Barbara. We're wearing new, clean clothes and see no signs of injury on any of us.

An older woman stands at the end of the jetty.

"Grandma Mariel!" Raf exclaims as he runs to her.

CHAPTER TWENTY-NINE

I stand at the end of the jetty and watch where the ocean meets the sky.

Is Scott out there?

"Can he ever come back?" I ask with a depth of sadness only the ocean knows.

The Good Father's eyes carry hope. "I won't ever quit trying. Don't you give up hope either." He winks and gives me a hug. It's the hug I've wanted since I was little. Dead places hidden deep in my soul sprout new life as healing tears release harsh memories.

The Good Father beams at Rafael and Lucas, who stand side by side. "I'm so pleased with each of you. You're going to be happy together."

They grin at him with the smiles of boys receiving the praise their hearts want most.

"You are sons to me."

The two appear to grow bigger and their eyes shine brighter. No gray can be seen on either of them.

Cinnamon and Sheba, who have been standing nearby, declare they're done waiting for Rafael's attention by barking happy sounds. Rafael immediately goes to them, and they cover him with kisses.

Aila stands near the jetty wall, close to Mariel holding her heart, and smiles at Rafael, who is now rolling on the ground with the two big dogs.

"Job well done," The Good Father tells her. "You're like a rose that has shed its thorns, and many will one day thank you."

Her face shows a twinge of bashfulness, and she tries to deflect. "I'm not sure I've done anything, really."

"You've given Rafael love you never received, even from your own parents, and created a future for him that you weren't given. Your love and sacrifice will echo for generations."

She can't help but smile, though she still looks a little embarrassed. Rafael sneaks under her arm and snuggles up to her, and the two of them share a loving look that fills us all, before he steps back to stand near her.

There seems to be an extra gleam in The Good Father's eyes when he looks at Rafael. "There's a very soft spot in my heart for you," he says as he gives the boy a hug that promises unending security. "I will always be here for you. Always. Even to the end of everything."

I don't know why I feel it in me when he speaks to Rafael. Truth spoken over him has chased away doubts and replaced them with confidence. But for me or for him? Or for both of us?

Rafael walks to the jetty wall where Mariel still stands staring out across the ocean. The setting sun glows orange on her rosy cheeks, making her look every bit the angel he's told me she is. Without a word, she clasps his hand into her own.

My heart might leave my chest. I can barely take this. *They've both found love and hope.*

"I love you," she says to him, then returns her gaze to the horizon.

"I love you too."

He closes his eyes and raises his other arm, embracing the breeze, the sun, and the ocean mist. It seems the two of them might be carried high into the air where they can soar and look down on the earth below, glowing in the sunset. "I wish I could stay with you," he finally says.

She wishes with all her heart to say yes. I can see it in her eyes. Then she looks at me. A smile forms on her lips.

I'm crying, but these are not the tears of a wounded heart. These are tears of one awakening to a new life. The tears of old ways being washed away by sun and angels and salt spray. *What's happening to me?*

"You'll be with me again someday, Raf," she says, but keeps staring into my eyes. Her eyes are filled with such care. Why do I feel like a child around her? If only I could spend hours just being near her. "Right now, I think it's best if you stay and help these two." She waves toward me and Lucas.

Stay? He can stay? I was sure he would leave to be with her. "You mean, he can come with us?" I don't yet believe it can be true, for fear of the pain I would feel if I dared hope, only to see it dashed.

With eyes possessing unspoken understanding, she passes

Rafael's hand to mine. "He'll need your help, Raf. He's doing better, but he needs your help for a while. Will you do that for him? You can leave with me, but if you do, he might not learn as well as he could."

"Learn what?"

"How to fly."

Rafael looks from her to me, then down at our clasped hands. A small smile appears as he takes in the sight of my large, gentle hand wrapped around his small one. Feeling our inexplicable connection, I sense his thoughts. He loves me and knows this is where he belongs, though he'll miss Mariel with an aching.

Lucas holds my other hand and looks up at me with admiration and joy. "Dada, can we do something fun today?"

I look at Rafael. "What do you think? Can you stay and play with us?"

He lets go of my hand and gives Mariel a hug.

Of course he's leaving. How could he not stay with her? The world seems it will end. Heartache is crashing toward me.

Rafael looks up at her, then back to me again. She gives him a smiling nod, and he steps away from her arms toward me. "Maybe we could fly together?" he asks.

My world changes. The sun comes out from behind a passing cloud and shines on my face. The gleaming brightness is only outdone by my smile, which I have no interest in fighting back. Childlike enthusiasm courses through my veins in ways I haven't felt for years. Goose bumps cover my arms and face and spike the hairs on the back of my neck. "Yes, let's be birds!"

Mariel smiles approvingly.

"A big bird like you needs a rider," Rafael says. "You should make Lucas the rider!"

I whirl around, swoop up Lucas, and put him on my back. Spreading both arms out wide, I close my eyes and prepare to fly.

I run and twirl as my son holds tightly to my back and a wave crashes on the jetty, sending spray over us. Safe and secure, Lucas erupts in gleeful sounds.

Rafael, Lucas, and I all giggle while we run here and there around the end of the jetty as waves splash over the wall around us.

The Good Father laughs and puts his hand on Mariel's shoulder as she lays her head on his. "Mariel is a beautiful name," he says. "It means bitter, but it's a sweet and beautiful name."

"I wish Scott were here to see this, but I do feel happy," she sighs, watching us play. "I'm so glad Raf and Benjamin found each other. You know, the thing is, I don't feel bitter. Not anymore."

He squeezes her shoulder.

She looks lighter. Sadness drops off her. My nose catches a hint of the sweet fragrance of fresh roses, lemon trees, and pleasant candles.

"No, not bitter," she says. "My heart and my spirit are sweet now. Thank you for bringing Rafael and Benjamin home, and thank you for giving me your hope in place of my hurts. I have peace."

As we play, I spy Krynn a ways back on the jetty. She stands smiling at us, and the warmth of her face draws us to her. We fly to her and Abigail, who laughs at our infectious joy. *How I love that little girl.* Her smile magnifies the joy that is filling me.

Krynn looks beautiful in the sunset glow with the breeze in her hair. It will take a lifetime to express how much her undying loyalty and unreasonable love for me have changed my life.

"I feel like we all need ice cream, don't we?" Krynn suggests, to shouts of approval from the children.

"Can we have lemonade too?" Rafael asks.

Krynn smiles at him. Besides when she looks at our children, I've never seen such pure love in her eyes. She would move mountains for him. "Of course!" she replies.

I put Lucas down on the ground and hug Abigail, then kneel to hug Lucas, who puts his arms around my neck.

"Are you going to be here now? With us?" Lucas asks.

Here. It's not a place he's asking about. It's the presence of love, attention, and affection. It's the nurturing these little birds need.

"Yes. I'm going to teach you and Abigail to fly! I'm going to be here. Always. I won't be disappearing. I love you. Love never disappears, buddy. Love always remains." One by one, I look into the three children's eyes to show them I mean it.

"And I'll be here too!" Rafael says.

Krynn kisses them each on their heads, then I move to her and she gives me a kiss. "Whoa," I say. "Now *there's* electricity." She gives me a playful hit on the shoulder, and her eyes tell me she felt it too.

"I never told you how much Rafael reminds me of you, and vice versa," she tells me.

I reach into my pocket and pull out a picture. "This is a picture of my dad and me on the day I said goodbye to him. It was Christmas Day. The next day, he and my step-family moved away to another state. I've kept it hidden and was going to get rid of it."

She looks at the picture of me, my dad, and my soccer ball.

"Krynn, I want to tell you something hard to explain."

"Anything, babe. You can tell me."

I move us away from the kids, letting them watch the waves just out of earshot. "Krynnie, I don't know how to explain it, so bear with me a minute. I don't know why this has been happening now after all these years. It's just...I basically didn't like myself. Little me, I mean. The more I thought about my childhood and tried to figure out what it meant to me, the more I had to come to grips with the fact that it's like there's a little me in here." I place my hand on my heart as tears roll off my face.

"I *really* wanted him to go away—this boy inside me. Because when he reminded me of his hurts, he started making them mine, and that made me so angry. I don't have time for hurts, and I just want to go forward, not backward, you know? I wanted to drive him far, far away from me. So I got serious and life just sort of turned gray. I think I was killing a part of me over the years, and you had to experience the gray that overtook me."

Krynn's face is awash in shock. I've always been open with her, and we've been married many years, but even she has never known these depths before. She watches my countenance changing as I become softer and stronger, and somehow this isn't a contradiction but a kind of harmony.

"But I know now, Krynn. That little boy deserves to be heard. He deserves to be loved and to play and laugh and hope and do crazy things. I guess I'm saying I'm done trying to bury him or chase him away. And I'm done pretending there aren't hurts, but I also know there is healing for the hurt too. You and the kids get to see that part of me from now on. I'm sorry it took me this long."

I look down at the picture again. "I think I'll keep this. My dad loved me in the ways he knew how. It's not his fault." Then, fighting to speak past tears, I tell the man in the picture, "It's not your fault."

Krynn hugs me tightly.

"There's one more thing," I say, stepping back. "I've had all these memories flooding in. Some are sad, but there are also so many good ones. Sweet memories of people who loved me. Krynn, I've realized I was never alone. And it's almost like this cloud of people is behind me helping me keep going. All the memories of people who took me into their homes, gave me rides, gave us food when my mom needed help, coached me in sports, taught me in school, and corrected me when I made bad choices. All these people. They loved me. They bought me pajamas and a backpack and helped me buy my mom Christmas gifts."

I look back up the jetty. "And I've been remembering the way special people like my mother and my grandmother fought for me. Their love was deeper than I can ever understand. Both of them came from such hard places and yet loved me so much. I know not everyone believes in God, Krynnie, but I have to say, I think these people were being God to me. Like he used them to take care of me. They probably think they did little things, but to little me I now see those little things were *big* love. And it's a gift now to remember it all. I know now, I was always loved by a Good Father who saw me, provided for me, and was *for* me. I know now, I'm loved and my path is to love others, starting with you and the kids and going from there."

"Benji, I...I don't even know what to say," she says through tears and takes my hand. "Something is different in you. Something new and something really, really good."

We both look at the ocean one more time, and a fresh breeze wipes away our tears as the kids come to our sides.

A young couple sitting nearby on a bench has been watching us. "It's usually so busy here at this time," the man says. "Strange there have only been those four here."

"Right, just that one family. You think there'd be more people on a nice night like this," the woman answers, putting her hand in his. "Wasn't that sweet the way that boy and his dad were having fun running around? Those four seem happy."

"Yeah, they do. I'd love to play with my kids that way some day and be like him." Then he points in front of them. "Look!"

A beautiful crane flies between the setting sun and the ocean below.

"I didn't think those even lived around here," she says. "It's so graceful and beautiful!"

I watch the crane fly by, and it gives me an idea. "Will you fly with me, family?"

With Lucas on my back again, I take Krynn's and Abigail's hands. We laugh and each spread our arms wide and pretend to fly together. We laugh as we run, without a soul around other than the couple on the bench.

The waves splash far behind us at the end of the empty jetty, where no one stands. We fly all the way to the beginning of the jetty, Lucas laughing as he rides my back and Abigail giggling, holding my hand. Here, alone in our own world, in the embracing glow of an orange sunset, we four are beautiful and rare. We move with such grace that we cut through time as though in slow motion.

The sight is soul changing.

THE END

ACKNOWLEDGEMENTS

To The Good Father. Thank you for always seeing me and for always walking with me. I have never been alone.

To my wife, Sarah. There aren't words. Thank you for grace, fierce love, laughter, and for a plastic spider ring and a visit to the church of Elvis. My life has been on the best path ever since.

To my children, Ethan, Abigail, and Matthew. You have my heart. I am so proud of you. These arms will always be ready with hugs for you.

To Mom. Your heroism is known only by a select few, none more than me. You left behind a broken world and gave me one full of hugs. May you be blessed beyond understanding.

To Dad. I love you and I know you love me. Thank you for love of the outdoors, introducing me to sports, and for countless jumps in lakes and creeks.

To Myrna. You have always seen and loved the little boy and for that I'm grateful.

Miss you Grandma Mariel. Thank you for two of my favorite places. The Cabin and your back porch at night. Tell Grandpa Leo thanks for the M&M's and for a huge hand that held a little one.

To my village... First, to Joel and Charmaine. Thank you for my pajamas, for a model of a man being strong and gentle, and for your warmth. To the Rodecaps. Thank you for cinnamon sugar pancakes and the spot by the heater. To both Bittner families. Thank you for coaching, teaching, leading and hosting me. To the Houghtons, Klinkners, Dobeks, Larsons and so many more. Thank you for rides, warm houses, friends, food, a backpack, and countless ways you provided for me.

To coach Mariman (RIP.) Thank you for teaching me to believe in myself. To Miss Flora, thank you for telling me to shut off the inner critic.

To every editor and artist who contributed your help and professionalism, thank you. Christy and Kendall, your expertise was invaluable.

To you dear reader, apologies these thanks grew long. So many more thanks could still be written, and I hope it serves to remind you, especially for vulnerable children, it will take many hands and hearts to lift from hurt to love. I also hope you see little things are the big things to little hearts and, finally, that you yourself deserve to be whole. It bears repeating. You are worthy. You matter. You are seen.
—*Eric*

AUTHOR BIOGRAPHY

Eric Thompson grew up in tiny Philomath, Oregon, and now lives in the greater Portland area. Raised by a single, immigrant mother without a college degree, he was impacted by her grit and generosity, as well as the care and hospitality of their church community.

He saw the love of Christ in action as people from his church provided clothes, food, a car, and much more. From the time he was young, seeing people open homes and take time to teach, correct, coach, and include him came to shape his world view and his character. This is why he believes a gift as small as pajamas can alter the course of history, and why people can tell the ones who believe in Jesus by watching for who acts like him.

Though he came from humble roots, Eric found success in life. He earned an undergraduate degree in psychology and two masters degrees in business, and spent twenty-one years working for Nike. His time at Nike afforded him the opportunity to see the world, sending him off continent over forty times.

What matters to him is paying forward the love he received. He has volunteered with Big Brothers/Big Sisters as a "big" for three years, coached over twenty-five seasons of youth sports, volunteered in church Sunday school and youth groups, served on the board of three combined churches, and assisted in other forms in his community.

In spite of his success and beautiful family—wife Sarah and their three amazing children—Eric came to realize he carried scars from childhood as a result of his father moving to another state. Through personal exploration and professional counseling, he learned about the powerful effects of parental absenteeism. He is now dedicating his "second career" to sharing a message of healing and hope for people with similar wounds, and to calling and equipping parents to engage in the lives of their children.

A FINAL NOTE

Dear reader, it would be invaluable to hear from you. Would you please consider sharing a review wherever you like to purchase and/or read books? I'd also love if you would please visit me to connect or share feedback at: https://www.erictauthor.com/

Thanks, and looking forward to hearing from you.

—*Eric*

Made in United States
Troutdale, OR
06/26/2023